A *WESTERN* NOVEL

TRAIL'S
END

By WILLIAM MacLEOD RAINE
Author of "Famous Sheriffs and
Western Outlaws," "Guns of the
Frontier," "Oh, You Tex," "Sons
of the Saddle," etc.

WILDSIDE PRESS

TRAIL'S END

List of *Exciting* Chapters—

Trail's End

COLLIE PUP AT HEEL, Jim Silcott wandered into the Grub
Stake looking for a game. It was early, and there were no
customers yet. Back of the roulette wheel stood Kroelling,
piles of chips and silver dollars in orderly array within
reach. Soon he would be busy, but just now he was at
leisure and enjoying a cigar. He nodded at Jim, giving the
wheel an idle whirl. A professional gambler, he had lived
in tolerable peace because he minded his own business
strictly. For a moment now he stepped out of character.

"Some of the Hat T boys in town today," he said casually. "Drinking some. Jud Prentiss one of them."

Jim understood that underneath Kroelling's indifferent manner lay a warning. Probably there had been
threats made.

His eyes narrowed slightly. "I'll make a note of it in the
paper," he drawled. "They've been working right hard at
the roundup and are entitled to a holiday, I reckon."

"Sure are, Red." Kroelling brushed the ash from his
cigar. The cold eyes of the man were blank. He had said
all he meant to say, and did not intend to violate neu-
trality further.

Silcott pointed to a corner of the room back of the poker
table and said, "Down, Pixie!" The collie looked at him
appealingly, then moved reluctantly to the place indicated
and lay down. Jim dealt cards for solitaire. In a half an
hour at most the boys would gather for draw. Having put
the Powder Horn *Sentinel* to bed for the week, Jim expected to sit in for a long session. He did not worry much

about Prentiss and his riders. When Russell Mosely moved it was usually under cover.

Only one of the aces showed in the first game. Jim riffled the cards and started to deal again. On the sidewalk outside the Grub Stake he heard the tramp of many boots. They turned in through the swing doors. Five of the men were Hat T riders. The sixth was Jesse Lamprey.

Jud Prentiss had his thick, hairy arm hooked under that of Lamprey. Jesse's feet moved reluctantly, dragging the floor. He was not here to get a drink but because he could not help himself. Any other company would have suited him better. His gaze jerked nervously round the room, looking for help he did not expect to find. It came to rest on Silcott. Jim read in the tortured face stark fear. The man's Day of Judgment had caught up with him.

The irruption of men bellied up to the bar. Prentiss said, "On me. Set 'em up, Walt."

The man in the white apron put six whisky glasses and a bottle on top of the bar. Prentiss pushed the bottle toward Lamprey. "Help yourself, Jess."

Unsteadily the victim reached for a glass and poured a drink. Some of the liquor spilled.

A long, lank man with heavy-lidded eyes laughed. "You shaking for the drinks, Jess," he jeered.

"I didn't sleep last night, Sneve," Lamprey answered, his voice thick. "Fact is, I'm not well. I reckon maybe I better not drink."

"Never heard you refuse one before," Prentiss commented. "Maybe you'd rather not drink with us."

"Nothing to that, Jud. Nothing a-tall." Hastily Lamprey picked up his glass again. "Long life, boys."   \

"When good friends meet unexpected they ought to celebrate, oughtn't they, Jess?" Prentiss asked, sly mirth in his ugly, flat-featured face.

Again Sneve laughed cruelly. "That's right, Jess. A fellow never can tell what drink will be his last, so he oughtn't to lose out on one."

The startled eyes of the unwilling guest slid to the slate-gray ones of the long man. He tried to laugh, and the sound of it broke in his throat.

"We can't all live to be Methuselahs," Prentiss said, and his glance took in the man playing solitaire at the poker table. "If we did it would clutter up the world a heap. We got to think of other fellows' pleasure and comfort, Jess."

Silcott understood that the quarrel they were fastening on Lamprey was a cut-and-dried rehearsed one. It was meant not only to punish him but to intimidate the editor. With Jess disposed of, Jim would be next in line. If he started to leave he would be stopped. He was to sit there while Lamprey took his medicine, so getting a foretaste of what was in store for himself.

For Lamprey he cared nothing. The man boasted too much and performed too little. He was a handsome, shallow bluff without character or stamina. Jim sized him up as certainly fool and probably knave. By the grapevine route word had reached Silcott that the fellow had tried to play both ends against the middle in the land-grants feud. It would be like him to do something of that kind, for his conceit would lead him to believe he could outwit those whom he was double-crossing.

Silcott accepted the code of the West that every man must fight his own battles. An outsider kept clear and minded his own business. It was like a private game of poker, in which a stranger did not take chips. But this difficulty moving to a head did not quite come under that category. It was being staged at the Grub Stake because the Hat T hands had found out Jim was there.

What he would do Jim did not know. It would depend on how the play came up and how far it was to go. Jud and his men were likely obeying orders from Russell Mosely. He had probably told his foreman not to go too far. If the old fox wanted him and Lamprey destroyed he would not arrange a public killing that had no appearance of a duel. But men like these warriors of the Hat T outfit were undisciplined devils who might go through to a finish regardless of orders. Jim did not intend to lift a finger for Lamprey, but on his own account he might decide to intervene so that the entire attention of these ruffians would not be concentrated on him alone later. He was carrying a forty-five, which would be of very little use in a gunfight with the odds five to one against him. For if guns started to smoke he could not depend on Lamprey. That young man would be trying a bolt for a door or window.

The editor's mind ran over all the possibilities of the situation because life on the frontier had taught him wariness. He had seen more than one man killed because of carelessness. These men were unfriendly to him, and they had been drinking. It was an explosive combination. None the less he was of opinion that Prentiss intended the disciplining of Lamprey to run only to a thrashing. The foreman of the Hat T was a notorious fist fighter and bully. He enjoyed beating up men unable to put up an adequate defense.

A fat, bald little man with a high color made his contribution. "Jess is all for a short life and a merry one," he said, and te-heed at his own wit. "Ain't he just been to Santa Fé for a blow-out?"

"That's right, Pete," Prentiss agreed. "Did you see the elephant plenty, Jess?"

Lamprey swallowed a lump in his throat. "I wasn't there but one day, boys. Went to see a fellow about selling some beef stuff."

"A fellow can get around quite a bit in a day," Prentiss said, almost in a murmur, his chill, light-blue eyes fixed on the man they were giving the third degree. "Didn't happen to bump into D. L. Stratton, Esquire, I reckon?"

Tiny sweat beads stood out on the forehead of the harassed man. His eyes darted from one to another and his mouth twitched. A sickness ran through him. He was trapped. Mosely had spies at Santa Fé, just as he had at home. One of them must have seen him slipping into the law office of Stratton, who represented the claimants under the Armijo land grant.

"You've got me wrong, boys," Lamprey said, after a pause. "I wouldn't lift a hand against the Hat T claim. You know that."

The big hairy man beside him grinned maliciously. "Did someone mention the Hat T claim? You must have been seeing D. L. on private business, I reckon."

"About a loan," Lamprey said hoarsely.

"Naturally you'd figure on Stratton, who is lined up with the enemies of Hat T, being glad to help one of its friends," Prentiss told him, with dripping sarcasm.

A boy, not over eighteen, pushed through the swing doors hurriedly. He walked to the bar and stood beside Lamprey. The lad was the younger brother of Jesse.

Prentiss frowned at the white-faced boy whose entrance had disarranged his plans. With the point of his cigar he indicated a sign, *No Drinks Will be Served to Minors.*

"Run along, kid," he snapped. "You got no business here."

"I'm staying," the boy answered.

"We're talkin' business. You ain't wanted."

Though the youngster was manifestly afraid, he stood his ground. "I'll go when Jess does," he said flatly.

The big man slammed his fist on the bar so hard the glasses jumped. "Goddlemighty, don't talk back to me!" he roared. "You'll go now, *muy pronto.*"

Out of the corner of his thin-lipped mouth Sneve

dropped a warning. "Beat it, Phil. You got no chips in this game."

Young Lamprey was under pressure. He knew he was no match for one of these rough, hard-bitten punchers, far less all of them. And back of all his churning thoughts was fear, a paralyzing dread of what was to come. But there was courage in him. His feet clung to the place where they were planted. He shook his head.

The fat little man, Pete Yeager, spoke to Jesse Lamprey. "If you don't want a cutter bent over the kid's head, tell him to get the hell outa here."

From a throat dry as a limekiln the older brother mumbled, "Better go, Phil." He added, with a thin, unhappy smile, "We're having a little powwow."

"You bet we are," Prentiss jibed, forgetting for the moment the younger brother. "When you got back from Santa Fé you hotfooted it up Tincup Creek. Why?"

The worried eyes of Jesse shifted. "I was looking for some strays that got off their range."

"See Bar Overstreet?"

The answer seemed to be dragged out of Lamprey. "Come to think of it, I did yell a 'Howdy' at him."

"You and him had yore heads together half an hour."

"Just swapping windies. But I don't reckon it was more than a few minutes."

"See Allison?"

Again there was the reluctant, dragging answer. "I might have, but—"

"Make up yore mind. Did you or didn't you?"

"I—bumped into him."

"Been bumping into a lot of our enemies lately, haven't you?"

A denial of the implication burst from the lips of the accused man. "It's not the way you think, Jud. I'll go see Russ Mosely. I'll tell him—"

"You'll tell him nothing," interrupted Prentiss harshly. "Russ don't want to see you. He's got yore number, you damned double-crossing coyote."

"I swear—"

The big gunman rode him down. "You know what happens to coyotes when they're trapped," he said brutally. "Their hides are hung on a fence to dry."

Sneve murmured something in the ear of Prentiss, who swung round on the younger Lamprey.

"That's right. I told you to get outa here, kid."

"Jess and I both," the boy said stubbornly, and added quickly as the heavy-set, bowlegged cowboy moved toward him, "I'm not armed."

Prentiss doubled his great fist and measured the distance. Before he could lash out with it a voice from the poker table stopped him.

"Do your instructions cover beating up the kid too, Jud?" Silcott asked quietly.

The bully stared at him, for the moment flung off his stride. "What's that?" he snarled.

"You heard me," Jim said evenly. Not a lean muscle of his light body moved. Only the deep-blue eyes were quick with life.

"You declaring yoreself in?" the Hat T foreman asked roughly.

"Do I have to declare myself, Jud?" the newspaper man asked with cool scorn. "Isn't my name already on the Mosely black list? One scrub editor to be rubbed out when it can be done safely without witnesses."

"Hell! You're not so damned important. Who cares how many witnesses see you cash in?"

It was a rhetorical question, but Silcott answered it literally. "Why, Russ Mosely for one. Nice secret murders for the Hat T may be okay with Russ. All in the way of business, of course. I wouldn't know about that. But Russ doesn't crave publicity, except when he is making a Fourth of July oration or a contribution to the church. You ought to know your boss better, Jud. He's no hell-roaring wolf, but a respectable, mealy-mouthed hypocrite who doesn't advertise his strong-arm stuff except when it's necessary to set an example. Get the results neatly, is his motto."

The foreman glared at Silcott angrily. There was a cool insolence about the youth that set him apart. Nobody else within fifty miles would dare to speak so of Russell Mosely in public. "You'll talk yourself into a wooden box one of these days soon," Prentiss warned savagely.

"Like Rogers did."

The audacity of the challenge choked for a moment the words in the big man's throat. For Carl Rogers had been editor of the Powder Horn *Sentinel* before Silcott, and he had been shot down from ambush one night as he was leaving the office. The editor had been leading the fight for the settlers who had bought under the Armijo land-grant claim, just as his successor was doing now. Nobody knew positively who had fired the shot, but Prentiss and two of his men had been seen riding out of town a few minutes later.

The stormy eyes of the foreman clashed with the steady, hard ones of this redheaded editor who walked into peril and through it with a jauntiness that was amazing. Jud had a wide reputation as a dangerous man. It was part of the stock in trade with which he ruled the wild, reckless employees of the Hat T. At the drop of the first hostile word he was ready to fight. Most men sidestepped him when he was enraged. It was known he had killed two men, and there were whispered rumors out of his obscure past that spoke of others. But Jim Silcott had always showed a cheerful unconcern at his choler that moved him as a red rag does a bull. Prentiss himself did not know why he had not trampled down the fellow's impudence. More than once he had been on the verge of an explosion, but some deep-hidden caution had restrained him. This puzzled and irritated Jud, for he was not afraid of any man alive. Yet for some reason he had always postponed the showdown that had to come.

"By God, if you claim I had anything to do with Rogers's death—"

Prentiss did not finish the sentence. His blazing eyes, the dark rage purpling his face, were more potent than any words.

"Any claims I make will be in the *Sentinel,* subscription price one dollar a year," Jim answered, his voice low, almost gentle.

"Don't put my name in that paper ever, unless you want to be in trouble up to yore hocks," the foreman ordered.

"Mayn't I even say that the editor had a pleasant chat with Mr. Jud Prentiss of the Hat T, who was in town with some of his riders Thursday?" Jim asked with light effrontery.

The ranch boss turned to his men with a gesture of strangled fury. "Let's get outa here before I bump off this fool," he growled.

From Sneve's thin lips a question dropped. "Why not now, Jud, since he's asking for it?"

"No, not now," Prentiss blurted out.

His fingers fastened on the quirt suspended from his wrist. He caught Jesse Lamprey by the coat collar. The whip whistled through the air and wound itself round the legs of its victim. Lamprey let out a shriek of pain. Again and again the lash fell. Phil tried to help his brother, but Sneve's strong arms held him back. At last Prentiss flung the sobbing man to the floor. His strong bowlegged stride carried him through the swing doors to the street.

Sneve looked at the editor, his upper lip lifted in a sneer. "Some of the same for you next time, Mr. Editor," he promised.

"Painful, if true," Silcott said lightly.

The Hat T men stamped out of the Grub Stake.

The editor looked down on the whimpering man who was writhing on the floor. "Better get him home, Phil," he said, trying not to show the contempt he felt. "Soda in vinegar will take some of the pain out of the wheals."

He whistled to Pixie, and man and dog walked out of the gambling-house. Silcott had changed his mind. He did not want to play poker just now.

Chapter Two: BLANCO WAKES TO LIFE

ANNE LEFT THE TRAIN at Beaver Creek and stepped into a world where she felt that anything was possible. The air was like wine. Due to some trick of the atmosphere the sawtoothed mountains in the distance looked transparent. A desert of sage stretched away from the railroad tracks, through which ran a brown ribbon of road straight as a gunbarrel.

Beaver Creek had one short street running parallel to the tracks, and back of this a straggle of unpainted frame houses. The business street appeared to be mostly saloons with false fronts and pretentious names. One ramshackle building called itself the Palace and another the Fifth Avenue.

A man in a fringed leather shirt which hung outside his trousers carried her bags to the stage. He told her that he was Hank Brown, the driver.

She looked dubiously at the coach, its body swung on two leather thoroughbraces which were attached to a standard at each end. "Is it safe?" she asked.

"Lady, it's like riding in a baby carriage," he promised.

"The leather swing will plumb rock you to sleep."

There were three other passengers. One was a Chinese with a queue and a blouse over flapping trousers. The other two appeared to be cowboys, somewhat dusty and unkempt and a good deal the worse for two much tanglefoot from the Palace. They went into an immediate huddle over a bottle.

The four horses went off at a plunging gallop and the Concord coach rocked wildly. Hank let them run the superfluous energy out of themselves. Through the shining sage Anne caught a glimpse of a file of antelope silhouetted against a hilltop. After an hour or more the dusty road climbed out of the flats to ridges covered with pines. It dropped down again to the beds of streams fringed with cottonwoods, into which the horses splashed till the water was far above the hubs of the wheels.

They came into foothills bristling with chaparral, from which Anne could look back at a bend in the road on a desert that appeared to be dry, lifeless, and torrid. Dust eddies were whirling in spirals across its surface.

Before they reached Blanco the sun had sunk behind the peaks and left a lake of imperial purple in the crotch.

Hank brought his horses into town on the run and dragged them to a halt before the stage station. Standing on the wooden sidewalk, Anne looked curiously up and down the wide main street. She had seen a dozen like it from the train. The pattern of the towns of the high plains seemed to be set—dusty streets lined with false-front frame buildings. There was no attempt at beauty of design, no effort to soften the garish rawness. The arrival of the stage had stirred the place from its somnolence, but as Anne took in the indolent loungers clinging to the saloon entrances it occurred to her that nothing less than an earthquake could rouse these Rip Van Winkles to active life.

She changed her mind very suddenly. For in an instant Blanco had wakened from sleepy peace to violent conflict. The bark of a pistol started it. A bullet flung up a spurt of dust back of a man who was crossing the street. Either the bullet or the jerk of the man's head when he stopped sent the wide hat skimming into the dust. The man stooped, reclaimed the hat, and put it back on his red head, then ran lightly for the shelter of a doorway. By this time he was the target for several guns. To Anne, watching him with suspended breath, it seemed he did not hurry. Would he never reach shelter? She expected to see him stumble and fall, but apparently he was not hit. His revolver was out now, and she saw smoke from its barrel as he moved.

The loungers had vanished swiftly into the saloons. Both of the cowboys who had arrived with her had dived for the cover of the Concord coach. The Chinese laundryman was racing up the street, his flat feet going klop-klop on the board walk. One of the stage horses was plunging and Hank was clinging to the bridle. Anne stood in her tracks only because she was too astounded to fly. Her motor muscles refused to function.

She saw two of the attackers in doors, another at a street corner. They were shouting advice to one another, voices high with excitement. The intended victim had reached the deep doorway of an adobe building. Here he made his stand.

The lean man at the street corner gave an exultant yell. "We've got him, boys!" he cried. "Come on."

He started forward, with long, ungainly strides, a street light flinging an elongated shadow in front of him. The crash of guns still sounded. The tall gunman stopped, to steady his aim. Before the sound of his revolver had died away an answer rang out from the adobe building. He swayed on his feet, staggered forward a step or two, and as his knees buckled under him plunged to the ground.

The redheaded man disappeared from the doorway into the house, but none of those who had been firing at him moved from cover. A warning against undue haste lay huddled in the dust.

"Someone go see if Sneve is dead," a voice called from the shadows. "You go, Hank."

"I can't leave this horse," the stage-driver shouted back.

"Well, someone else go. Silcott has lit out. He won't hurt you."

"If you're so sure of that why don't you go look at Sneve yoreself, Jud?" one of the cowboys back of the stage wanted to know.

"Hell, I'll take a chance," Pete Yeager said. "Jim Silcott is nobody's fool. He's on his way." The fat little Hat T rider waddled out of the shadows and knelt down beside the prone body. A few moments later he made his report. "Plumb dead. Shot spang through the heart, looks like."

Out of saloons and stores men trickled. They picked up the body and carried it into the Grub Stake. Yeager looked down at the long body lying on a bench.

"He sure was asking for it," Pete said. "Started the rookus tonight and the rest of us came in to back him."

Prentiss looked at him with sour anger. "What you mean, Buck started it? Silcott lay in wait for us and plugged Buck before we could stop him. Sure as I'm a foot high I'll get him for this."

Yeager grinned cynically. So that was to be the story. "I meant that Buck was the first one he began shooting at," he explained.

Chapter Three: RUFE JELKS MOVES OUT

ANNE WALKED INTO THE STAGE OFFICE, her long slim legs a little shaky. She had never before seen anybody die a vio-

lent death, and the shock of it made her feel faint. Abruptly she sat down on a dry-goods box.

The local manager filled a tin dipper with water and
brought it to her. "Sorry you had to see anything so up-
setting, lady," he said.

She took a few sips from the dipper. "I was just thinking how quiet and peaceful the town was when—when
it happened," she told him.

"So it is most of the time," he explained. "We don't
have a killing more than five or six times a year. Of course
the boys kick up their heels some after dark, but they
don't mean a thing. Just high spirits."

"Is—is the man dead?"

"I heard someone say he was."

The girl did not discuss the matter further. "My name
is Anne Eliot. Can you tell me where the hotel is?"

"Pleased to meet you, miss. My name is Hilary Benson."
He scratched his thinning hair to help him cerebrate.
There was no hotel in town. The principal rooming-house
was over the Jumbo saloon, but it was no place for a lady.
All night long an inferno of noise would rise from the
dance hall which would prevent from sleeping a young
woman not used to it. "Ma Russell runs a boarding-house.
Leastways she takes in a few folks. I dunno whether she
is full up or not. I'll take you round there."

"If it isn't too much trouble, Mr. Benson."

He was a gangling, pimply-faced man, with an Adam's
apple that shot up and down without warning. That he
was shy she could see. During the walk to the boarding-
house he was respectful and a little stiff. No doubt he was
filled with curiosity as to what she was doing in Blanco,
but none of it reached the surface.

Anne was agreeably surprised at Mrs. Russell. She was
a good-looking plump woman who radiated health and
friendliness. Though all her rooms were taken she at

once said she would find a place for Anne.

"I'll make Rufe Jelks move over to the Jumbo," she said. And she added, slanting a look at the girl, "Will you be staying long? I mean, will you want the room some time?"

"I'm not quite sure," Anne answered. "I haven't made up my mind. And I don't like to drive another lodger from you."

The landlady made nothing of that. "Rufe is in town only a few days, and he doesn't care where he sleeps. A blanket on the ground would suit him just as well as a bed. But you can't stay at the Jumbo. Some crazy drunk is likely to start shooting up the street in the night."

"They don't always wait for night, do they?" Anne suggested.

"You weren't there when Buck Sneve was killed?" Mrs. Russell said quickly.

"Yes. It was just as the stage got in."

"You poor girl! What a terrible thing to see the minute you arrived. You mustn't think we're all ruffians. Very few of us are."

"I'm glad to hear that. Do you know what it was about?"

"Oh, about the land grants, I suppose. The feeling is bitter because so many people's property is involved. If it is any comfort to you, Buck Sneve was a bad man. He deserved what he got. Red had to kill him to save himself."

"Yes, I saw that." Anne did not know why, but from the first moment she had seen the lift of the red head she had been on his side.

Mrs. Russell led the way upstairs to a bedroom that Anne liked at once. The rag carpet, the chintz curtains, and the big comfortable armchair gave it a homey look. She knew that no other room in Blanco would suit her as well as this one. For one thing, it was immaculately clean.

Yet Anne felt she ought to demur faintly. "Maybe Mr. Jelks won't want to give up the room," she said.

"He will. He's downstairs now." Mrs. Russell called to a man and asked him to send Rufe up.

The lodger who was about to be ousted clumped up the treads, his cowboy boots announcing his progress as he came. He was a black-haired, attractive youth with a wide grin. As soon as he knew why he had been called he offered at once to vacate immediately. Girls as pretty as Anne did not come his way often. Perhaps that added a zest to his eagerness to oblige, though he would have given up the room to any woman who needed it.

"I'll take my war bag out right now and have 'yore grips sent over from the stage office," he told her.

She thanked him, a smile in her soft eyes that reminded Rufe of wood pansies and gave him ideas about his future.

He was back in record time with her bags. The trunk would be over later, he promised. Anne bathed and changed, in time to make a late appearance at the supper table. She was a little dismayed to observe that though the long table was filled the occupants of the chairs were all men. Her arrival made a stir, which the boarders tried to play down, not very successfully. For the outdoor West of the frontier was both very respectful and very shy toward young good-looking strangers of the opposite sex.

Anne sat between Mrs. Russell and Rufe Jelks. She guessed that the black-haired cowboy, who was not nearly as shy as some of the others, had arranged the seating with the landlady. He was apparently a favorite of Ma Russell.

Most of those at the table were brown, boyish cowboys in from the range for a day or two. An exception was the man sitting opposite her, who wore city clothes and had a cold impassive face, almost colorless. Anne caught his name as Kroelling when he was introduced. Probably he was a merchant, since he could not be a cattleman with that complexion.

The girl was aware that her entrance had put a damper on the conversation. They had been talking about the shooting on Main Street. It was the big news of the day and might be the precursor of even more important developments, but out of deference to the young lady they did not want to discuss it in her presence. She had been a witness, and her nerves might be unstrung at what she had seen. Not skilled at making talk and too polite to leave her out of the conversation, they devoted themselves to the business of eating.

Only Kroelling and Rufe Jelks helped Mrs. Russell and Anne carry the talk. The professional gambler asked the newcomer how she liked the town.

"How could she like it when she hadn't been here three minutes before there was gun-trouble right before her eyes?" Mrs. Russell asked severely. "Such goings on ought to be stopped, if we expect decent people to stay here."

"That's right, ma'am—Sure—Y'betcha."

The chorus of approval was unanimous. But the landlady was not deceived as to its value.

"Every last one of you carries a gun all the time," she snapped.

"Not in town, Ma," protested the black-haired puncher whom Anne had dispossessed, with the manner of one who has been most unjustly accused. "I done parked mine at the Tivoli when I blew in. 'Course I got to have one for rattlers outside."

Mrs. Russell looked at him sharply over her glasses. "Rufe Jelks, you're not loading me any. I've known you since you were knee-high to a duck. You and your side partner, Jim Silcott, are a pair of the wildest coots in this territory."

Rufe looked as innocent as a choirboy. "We've reformed, ma'am. Now we've grown up we've put away childish things."

The landlady's grunt was eloquent of doubt.

Talk died down again, except for undertones among the men. Topics that would include Miss Eliot were few. They could not ask her where she came from nor what she was doing in this raw town nor how long she expected to stay, though each of them had these queries in his mind. For the first article in the unwritten book of manners of the old West was that a stranger must not be asked personal questions. Too many residents had come out one jump ahead of the law.

After supper Anne asked Mrs. Russell where the office of the Powder Horn *Sentinel* was. "I'd like to walk down there this evening," she added.

"I'll get someone to show you where it is," the landlady said, and she stepped out to the porch to find an escort. Her eye fell on Rufe Jelks.

"Do you think you can take a young lady down to the office of the *Sentinel* and bring her back safely?" she asked.

His face lit. "Oh, lady, try me."

On the way to the office Anne gathered information. This was a cattle country, though there was a good deal of mining in the hills. The big outfit, she learned, was the Hat T, owned by Russ Mosely, though there were a good many other much smaller ranches but of fair size. It was a fine country for those who like the high plains.

"What is this land-grant feud I hear about?" Anne asked.

"It's a long story which goes back to the old Spanish days when the King of Spain gave great grants of lands, through his governor, to grandees who were supposed to have served the country in war. A grant covering a big part of this district was given to Don José Gandara, who by what I hear was quite a guy. He had money enough to burn a wet mule, and he fed at his different rancheros hundreds of vaqueros and servants every day. Seems Gandara didn't put much stock in this little gift of a million acres, more or less. Those were free and easy days, and a man didn't fool much with recording his deeds and that sort of thing. He just stuck 'em in a box and forgot about it. The story is that Gandara slept on his rights.

"After Mexico had freed itself from Spain, Governor Armijo carved a big chunk of half a million acres or so out of this grant and gave it to another bird named Antonio Aguilar, who peddled bits of it to cattlemen coming into the country. That started a rookus, for a smooth, smiling crook named Russ Moseley had already hopped down to Mexico City and bought out the Gandara heirs for about a dollar and a quarter."

"I read bits of this in stray copies of the *Sentinel* that came to me," Anne said. "It seems the *Sentinel* was on the side of the Armijo grantees."

"Was and is," Jelks answered. "Red Silcott took up the fight where Rogers dropped it when he was killed."

The girl stopped in her tracks and stared at him, dismay in her face. "Killed?" she repeated.

"Yes, miss," he said gently. "Shot down from ambush as he was leaving the office one night."

"I didn't know that," she said in a low voice. "Mr. Silcott wrote that he had died and he would carry on till I let him know what I wanted to do."

Looking into her agitated face, Rufe Jelks knew now who this mysterious stranger was. She was the niece who had inherited the *Sentinel* from her uncle.

The girl continued to look at him, the color drained from her cheeks. "You called him Red Silcott. Was it Mr. Silcott they were shooting at this afternoon?"

"Yes."

"They mean to kill him too, then?"

"That's the notion they have tucked in their nuts." Jelks smiled grimly. "They haven't got away with it yet."

"Who are these murderers?"

"The Hat T Ranch."

"Isn't there any law in this country?"

"Heaps of it, most of it owned by Russ Mosely, the Grand Mogul at the Hat T."

"But I won't have it," she said quickly. "I won't be responsible for a man in my employ getting killed. He'll have to go away—at once."

"Tell that to Red Silcott," he said dryly.

"He can get work somewhere else. It's a big country."

"Red has a ranch here. He won't leave it."

"But he'll have to leave it!" she cried. "He can't stay here and be killed."

"I don't reckon you understand folks in this part of the country, Miss Eliot," the range rider explained. "A straight man can't let himself be driven out, not if he has any nerve. He has to stick around and go through."

"That's silly, when ruffians are waiting around in ambush to kill him," she protested. "It's just a foolish pride."

"Maybe so. But I'm betting you can't get Red to agree with you—not to the extent of making a getaway."

"Why not?" she demanded. "Won't he see reason?"

"If you knew him you'd understand. Red isn't just a country editor, like they have in Indiana and Ohio. He's a cattleman, brought up on this Western frontier. He owns a ranch up on Tincup Creek and didn't start running the *Sentinel* until they got Rogers, when he figured it was kinda up to him."

"Why was it up to him?"

"He was a friend of Carl Rogers," Jelks said simply.

"Is it up to him to get murdered because he was a friend of my uncle?" she asked sharply.

"He doesn't aim to get murdered."

"He very nearly did tonight."

"Yes, but he wasn't expecting that attack. He is now," young Jelks went on, trying to make it clear. "Red is a tough *hombre,* Miss Eliot. He was a grown man when he was seventeen. That is, he could look after himself in a difficulty. I wouldn't say he was exactly a rooster on the peck, but certainly nobody could run on him. He would as soon fight as eat. This is a hard country with quite a few bad men and outlaws in it. This man Prentiss is a killer, but he couldn't make Red back up an inch. We're the same age, twenty-three; and already he has a wide reputation."

"As a brawler?" she asked scornfully.

"No, Miss Eliot. As a man doing his best to make this a decent country for folks to live in. He's going to be a big man some day."

Anne did not argue that. She gave up and started walking.

He liked the way she walked, as though the life in her sang a song in her veins. She was a fine, healthy young animal, and he guessed that her spirit would fulfill the promise of the slim, strong body. There was an unstudied charm about her, an apparently complete indifference to the effect she might produce. Yet she could not help being aware of how much her loveliness must stir the thoughts of men.

"The *Sentinel* office is down here near the edge of town," the young man explained. "I don't reckon Red will be there, seeing he has made up the paper for the week, especially when he knows the Hat T men may be looking for him."

"You mean, they'll keep trying to kill him?" she said, making a question of it.

"They're not exactly pleased at what happened to Sneve," he replied. "Maybe they'll wait to see Russ Mosely before they act. I wouldn't know about that."

The blinds of the office were drawn, but through a chink Jelks thought he saw a glimmer of light in the back room. He gave, not too loudly, the hoot of an owl. After a few seconds he repeated it.

Presently the door opened a few inches.

"It's Rufe, with a young lady to see you," the cowboy said.

They were let in, and the door locked and bolted behind them. Through the darkness they followed the man who had admitted them, to a small room in the rear lighted by a coal-oil lamp. Anne noticed that the window blinds were fitted so closely that nothing could be seen from the outside.

A redheaded young man looked at Anne in astonishment, waiting for an explanation of this irruption. There was a revolver in his hand. He had not thought yet to lay it down.

Chapter Four: JIM MEETS HIS BOSS

WHEN JIM SILCOTT disappeared from the porch of the adobe house he found himself in the home of a hot-tamale vendor known to the public as Fatty. He had no more claim to the cognomen than his wife Maria, who stopped her laundry work to stare at the intruder with big, soft, startled eyes. The shots in the street had not disturbed her, since guns popped frequently whenever cowboys wanted to ventilate their enthusiasm. But a man in her parlor with a smoking revolver in his hand was more alarming.

"*Que quieren?* (What do you want?) ," she gasped.

"Pardon, señora," he explained. "I've been attacked and had to run for shelter. Don't be afraid. I'll just pass out of the back door if you'll allow me. Tell them I'm gone, and they won't hurt you."

"*Si, señor.*" She waddled to the back door to open it for him, the loose flesh threatening at every step to break through the flimsy dress.

Silcott cut across a vacant lot, moving swiftly through the gathering dar! ᵃss. He guessed there would be no immediate pursuit. '1 ᵤₑ ambush set by the Hat T men had failed. By.sheer luck he had escaped the trap and had wounded one of them. Just now they would have to look after Sneve. No doubt they were cursing one another for their failure. Presently, after they had recovered from the repulse, they would consider vengeance. They might first report to Mosely for orders. Or Prentiss might take the matter into his own hands and after some fast drinking range the town in search of him.

At a Chinese restaurant on a side street he had a ham sandwich wrapped up to take with him. Five minutes later he was in the frame building which held the equipment of the Powder Horn *Sentinel*. Pixie greeted him with joyous barks and tail-waggings. He passed the presses and went into the small back room he used as sleeping quarters. Before lighting a lamp he lowered the blinds to prevent being shot through the window.

Jim had friends in town to whom he could have gone, but he did not want to drag any of them into this. A good many in the Powder Horn district were unfriendly to the Hat T, but few of them were prepared to declare themselves publicly. The riders of the Hat T were too ruthless in punishment, and just now Russ Mosely was riding the top wave. He was the local political boss, and his influence extended to state and even national politics. He was so rich, powerful, and shrewd that there were not many who cared to risk a malevolence that might easily ruin them. His only open enemies of importance were the settlers who claimed title under the Armijo grant and

Jim Silcott of the *Sentinel*. The small cattlemen grouped
against him he felt he could handle, but Silcott was as
annoying as a mosquito. Not a week passed without some
article in the *Sentinel* attacking the injustices or the tyr-
anny of the Mosely regime. In time, unless the editor was
stopped, an opposition party would set itself solidly
against him.

Secretly a good many citizens applauded Silcott's audacity, though they predicted the same end for him that
had come to Rogers. But they had very little to say when
the adherents of the big boss were around. Only devil-
may-care rebels like Rufe Jelks, who had nothing to lose
but their lives, defended Jim in season and out.

Silcott ate his sandwich and sat down at his desk to
write. He drew up a will, to be signed later, and he wrote
several letters. One of them was addressed to Miss Anne
Eliot, Massillon, Ohio. He did not intend to be killed if
he could help it, but it seemed best to have his affairs in
order.

Jim was still writing when there came to him the hoot
of an owl. He straightened himself, to listen. It came a
second time. That meant Rufe Jelks, unless it was a decoy.
When they had been wild young cowboys together the
owl hoot repeated had been a signal between them.

He rose, picking up the revolver from the desk where it
lay within reach. Very quietly he moved to the front door
and listened. He heard voices, one that of a woman.
Noiselessly he drew back the bolt and unlocked the door,
opening it a few inches. As soon as he made sure the man
was Jelks he let him and his companion into the building.
After making the door secure again they went back into
the office in the rear.

Jim stared in vast surprise at the young woman with
Jelks. In the dust and disorder of that dingy office she
bloomed like a cactus in the desert. The face was delicate

and sensitive, with the lovely planes that distinguish the less obvious beauty in women. There was a spirit in the poise of the slender, graceful body that suggested a finely tempered blade.

Rufe Jelks said, "Miss Eliot, meet Jim Silcott."

"I'm *Anne* Eliot," she said to the editor.

"My boss." He added reproachfully, "You didn't tell me you were coming."

"No. I wanted to see how things were for myself. So I came without advertising."

"I'm afraid you'll find Blanco a little rough, but I suppose you don't expect to stay long."

That instant she discovered she had made up her mind. "Yes, I'm going to stay and run my paper."

His blue eyes registered complete astonishment. Young women who looked and dressed like this one did not come to the frontier to run papers. In fact, he did not know of a woman editor in the country. The business of a lady was to stay at home and be protected by a good husband or father.

But all Jim said was, "It's your paper, Miss Eliot."

She liked that in him. He was a man, she guessed, of reticences and reservations, not too easily understood. Also, she liked his appearance. Her first glimpse of him had been for only one heart-stilling moment. She had expected him to carry out in his looks the reputation he had earned as a wild and dangerous character. But this young man, lean and graceful, watching her with a cool, steady regard, suggested anything but the rakehelly scamp she had more than half expected to see. He looked gentle, and now that he had put down the gun, as peaceful as old age. It was hard to believe that the strong brown hand that had for a moment held hers firmly had by a twitch of a finger sent a man to death an hour ago.

"I've been looking for you, Jim," Jelks said, a veiled significance in his casual words.

"When did you get to town, Rufe?"

"This evening—after the fireworks." The cowboy gave further information. "Miss Eliot knows about the fight. She was there—just got in on the stage."

"Sorry," Jim said. He turned to Anne. "But anyhow you know now that this town is no place for a young lady."

"It's no place for you," she answered. "Now that you've killed one of their men—"

Silcott looked at the other man quickly. "Is Sneve dead?"

"Yes," his friend replied quietly. "Before they reached him. His own fault."

"They took me by surprise," the editor agreed. "There was nothing else I could do." But his heart was heavy at having snuffed out a life.

"No," Anne said. "But there's something else you can do now to avoid more bloodshed. You can leave this part of the country."

He shook his head slowly, his gaze fixed on her. "I reckon I can't do that."

"Why can't you?"

"Because I live here. This is my home. I'm not going to let Russ Mosely drive me away."

"How many men has Mr. Mosely?" she asked.

"On the Hat T? I don't know. Maybe forty or fifty."

"How many have you?"

"Just now, two on my ranch."

"And you expect to fight forty?"

"Russ isn't calling all his men off the range to wipe out a two-bit editor. That's not the way he works. All I have to do is to be careful and not let myself be drygulched."

"Drygulched?"

"Ambushed."

"I see. As careful as you were today."

Silcott laughed, a fine set of teeth flashing in his brown face. "You've got me there, Miss Eliot. I was some careless. In fact, I wasn't expecting any fireworks today. My notion is that the boys had been tanking up with fortyrod and were acting without orders from the big boss."

"But next time you'll be ready," the girl said tartly. "They'll probably send you word they are coming."

"I'll have to take my chance of that."

"Not that it's any of my business," she added. "Except that I don't want you killed because you wrote against him in my paper. Though I must say you hold life very cheap out here."

"Some people do, but not most of us," Silcott corrected. "The point is that this is a free country, or ought to be. That's what America is supposed to mean." He grinned at her, to make his explanation less pontifical. "You wouldn't want us to renege on Bunker Hill."

Jelks chipped in with a comment. "Red is right, Miss Eliot. A fellow has to play his hand out."

Anne gave a little gesture of surrender. "All right. Please don't think I want to interfere. It's only that—I saw a man killed today."

They had been standing. Jim thought she might be tired after the long journey and the shock of what she had seen. "Won't you sit down?" he said, and indicated a chair. "You might as well get used to the place if you are going to be the editor."

She took the chair, for the first time conscious that she was weary. To rest her head, she drew out the long pins and put her hat on the desk. Silcott thought he had never seen as fine hair. It was crisp and curly, in color a tawny gold shot with copper.

Anne picked up a letter on the desk. "This is for me," she said.

"No, it's just a report on the *Sentinel*," the writer of it said quickly, and stretched out a hand for it. "Now you are here I can tell you just as well."

The girl did not give him the letter. It seemed to her that he was a little too anxious to get it back. "Since it's just a business letter I might as well keep it," she said.

"I'd rather have it," Jim told her.

"But it has my name and address on it," she protested. "It belongs to me."

He differed firmly. "It doesn't belong to you until it has been mailed and reaches you."

"Well, it has reached me."

Anne realized that it was absurd to be arguing about it, but she wanted to read the letter. Her eyes had fallen on another document beside it, partly covered by her hat, on which was written the words, *Last Will of James Silcott.* He had drawn it up tonight, she believed, with the knowledge that death might be very close to him, and in the same hour he had written her this letter.

Yet she knew it did not belong to her but to him. She had no right to read it, since it was probably meant for her only in case he fell a victim to the vengeance of Mosely's ruffians.

Anne gave the letter to him. "I'm sorry I was stuffy about it," she said. "Of course it isn't mine, since you don't want me to have it."

Silcott took the letter and put it in his pocket. He was surprised at the sudden softening in her manner, but more at what he thought he saw in her eyes, the mist of unshed tears.

"I'd better stay with you a few days till you get the hang of running the paper," he said. "I pay a tramp printer ten dollars a week to set type. He's a good man— quick, and doesn't make many mistakes. Sometimes he drinks too much, but never during the busy time of the week."

"I've never worked on a paper," Anne admitted. "I can't run one unless you'll start me right by showing me how. I suppose you think it's unladylike of me to want to earn my living, that I ought to fold my hands and wait for a man."

She flung out the last as a challenge. Neither of the men took it up. The idea of an attractive woman, not more than a year or two out of her teens, editing a newspaper was revolutionary to them both. If she was forced to work, why not be a schoolteacher like other girls? She could do that without losing caste.

Rufe Jelks chuckled. "You won't have to wait for a man long out here, Miss Eliot," he promised. "This is Thursday. You'll not get more than one or two proposals this week, but right soon you can count that day lost whose low descending sun views from some man no earnest offer won."

"That sounds too poetical to be true, Mr. Jelks," Anne said, tilting a smile at him. "You wouldn't fool a poor lone spinster, would you?"

"Lady, it's going to be a stampede," Rufe prophesied. "You don't know what a dearth of lone spinsters there is in this country. But you can depend on me to keep the herd away from you much as I can."

"It will be so nice of you," the girl murmured. "And now if you'll take me back to the boarding-house, please."

Silcott led the way through the front room, but before they reached the door he stopped. A troop of men were coming down the street outside. They could hear the sounds of their voices and of their tramping feet.

Somebody banged on the door and shouted an order. "Come on outa there, Silcott, or we'll burn the damn shack over yore head."

"Who is it?" Jim asked. "And what do you want?"

From those outside came a yell of anger. "We want you,

and we're gonna have you."

Silcott fired a warning shot into the air.

Heavy bodies crashed against the door. A panel gave way.

"I haven't a gun with me, Red," his friend said. "Have you got another in the office?"

"No. Get Miss Eliot out of the back window. I'll hold these fellows back long enough for you to slip out."

"I'm not going," Anne said.

Chapter Five: JUD POSTPONES SETTLEMENT

THE HEAVY VOICE of Jud Prentiss came to those within the building. "Stand aside, boys. I'll pump some lead through this door before we bust it open."

Silcott rushed Anne back of a hand press and swung her round so that his body was between her and the door. Bullets crashed through the wood, sending splinters flying. As if in answer, a revolver cracked back of the building. There was a sound of breaking glass.

"Too late to get away now," Jelks said in a low voice.

"Yes," Silcott agreed. "We must let them know there's a lady here, so that they will let you both out."

Anne said "No," out of a throat dry from fear. "Not unless they let you go too."

The editor ignored that. He called to the foreman, "There's a lady in here, Jud. Will you let her out before you start anything more?"

Jud roared a contemptuous ultimatum. "Come outa there and quit lying, fellow. You're bucked out. We've got you."

"But it's true," the girl cried. "I *am* here. Anne Eliot, the niece of Carl Rogers."

Somebody outside exclaimed, "Cripes, there *is* a woman there!"

Rufe had an inspiration. "And four men beside Red, all set for the show to start as soon as Miss Eliot is out of range."

"Yeah!" a Hat T man jeered. "You can't run a sandy on us. You're there alone, except for yore woman."

"You'll change your mind when we pump lead into you. Rufe Jelks talking, to Pete Yeager in particular. I got yore voice, Pete, now you get mine."

"By jiminy, it is Rufe," Yeager said excitedly.

"Who else is there?" Prentiss snarled.

Jelks answered, in a thin squeaky falsetto, "I'm here—Bar Overstreet, and so is Curt Allison—and Bob Wise."

There was a murmur of consulting council, out of which individual voices leaped now and again.

"We don't believe Bob Wise is there," Prentiss shouted after the huddle.

"I'm here all right, Jud," a low bass retorted. "Don't fool yoreself about that. We're not looking for trouble, but if you are crazy for war you can sure have it."

Jim helped build up the illusion. "Don't be a fool, Jud. Did you think I was so dumb as to be alone after what happened this evening? If you want me, come and get me. We'll drop three or four of you before you're ever set to start."

There was another long whispered argument. Again Prentiss was the spokesman for the group.

"All right," he growled. "It's off for tonight, if you want to hide behind a woman's skirts like a whipped dog, Silcott. As for you birds from Tincup Creek, we're not gonna forget your part in this. You'll be good and sorry before we're through with you."

"We proposed to send the lady out, and that didn't seem to suit you, Jud," the editor mentioned scornfully. "What *do* you want?"

"Come out here and I'll settle yore hash alone, man to

man," the foreman roared. "Right damn now."

"What do you mean alone, Jud? You have a bunch of scalawags with you, the same as you had a couple of hours ago. Like to play your shots safe, don't you, Jud?"

More shots were fired, but not through the door, since there was a woman in the building. The Hat T contingent went back up the street boasting of what they would do to the defenders when they got them in the open. They trailed into the Jumbo and ranged themselves in front of the bar. If Prentiss drank enough, he might persuade himself and his men that he had not lost face.

The first man his eyes fell upon was Bar Overstreet, who was sitting in a poker game with his coat off and a pile of chips in front of him. Prentiss strode to the table and flung out a curse at the Tincup Creek rancher.

"You blasted fool!" he roared. "Not ten minutes ago I told you I'd settle with you when we met—and here you are."

Overstreet was a giant of a man, with not an ounce of fat on his two hundred and twenty pounds. He looked up at the Hat T foreman, a puzzled alarm in his faded blue-gray eyes.

"What's eatin' you, Jud?" he squeaked, in a tiny voice that always surprised as it came from such a bulk. "I ain't seen you for a week."

"What's the use of lying?" Prentiss snapped. "When you know I talked with you down at the *Sentinel* office less than a quarter of an hour ago—not more than five minutes since. By thunder, you must have run all the way to get here so quick."

The Tincup Creek man stared at him in surprise. "Why, Jud, I been sittin' here playin' draw for an hour and a half. Never left my seat. Ask the boys."

"That's right, Jud," a player corroborated; and another: "He sure has. Hotter than mustard, too. Look at his chips."

Prentiss glared at them, and wheeled away abruptly. He had been bluffed out by Silcott, and his anger boiled. He' was a vain man, and it stung his self-assurance to sing small. The worst of it was that his riders knew, and they would laugh about it among themselves, though not before him. Soon the story would spread all over town and to every little ranch in the district.

"It was that Rufe Jelks," said Yeager. "The joke is sure on us. He's the best mimic I ever heard. You know how he sits around campfires taking off the boys so blamed natural you'd think it was them if you didn't see Rufe sitting there."

"If he thinks he can play monkeyshines with me—"

Prentiss stopped, from the sheer inadequacy of language to express his turgid emotions.

The fat bald cowpuncher slid a look of carefully concealed exultation at his foreman. None of the Hat T men liked the overbearing manner of Prentiss. He was a hard, bad-tempered master, but one to be obeyed implicitly.

"Yes, sir, we'll never hear the end of it," Yeager prophesied. "He raises an ace-full with a pair of deuces, and we lay our hand down. It's going to be tough to take, Jud."

Prentiss glowered at his drink. There was no use going down to the *Sentinel* now. The bird would be flown. It would be some slight satisfaction to wreck the place completely, but Mosely would resent that and let him know it. The *Sentinel* did not belong to Silcott, but to a young woman, and it would stir up a lot of feeling if they destroyed her property. Russ was not a man to make enemies wantonly. He would probably be greatly annoyed at what they had already done, for he liked to play his own game and not have the men make any moves without consulting him first.

Though Prentiss felt as vicious as a bear with a sore

paw, there was nothing to be done about it now. All he could do was to go back to the ranch and wait for his revenge.

Chapter Six: SHERIFF LAWSON RECONSIDERS

WHEN ANNE HAD BEEN A LITTLE GIRL she had sat before an open fire and listened to the stories of her uncle, Carl Rogers, back in Ohio on a visit from the country of the high plains where he lived. Her imagination had quick-ened his stories, and in the coals she had seen the whole pageant of the winning of the West. The Indian and the buffalo, the trapper, the pioneer in his covered wagon, the long, dusty cattle trails—they marched before her in pan-orama.

As she grew up, the vision must have lingered in the background of her mind. She liked the quiet life of Mas-sillon, but there were hours when she found it too well kept and trim. The older people were too well satisfied, the young men too conventional. There had been a great adventure once, but it lived only in the fading memories of men and women past middle life. That was when the men kissed wives and sweethearts good-by and shouldered muskets to go to the Civil War.

Because she was attractive and well connected Anne had plenty of eligible admirers. There were pleasant, likable young men among them, but some restless imp of perverseness made her view them with a too critical eye. Moreover, there had been an episode in her life that barred all men from her. So when the news came of her uncle's death and the inheritance of his property in the West, she knew almost at once that she was going out to see that country for herself. If she did not want to stay, there was always Massillon.

And here she was, plunged into the heart of an adventure far more desperate than any she had sought. It was amazing. All her years had been placid, with no more dangerous experience than a fall out of an apple tree which netted a sprained ankle. Yet the very moment of her arrival red tragedy had flashed across her path.

At breakfast Anne's neighbors avoided any reference to the difficulty at the building of the *Sentinel*. Anne knew this must be because they had heard of her part in it. Since she wanted news of the latest developments, she put a question to Rufe Jelks.

"Have you heard anything this morning about the trouble?"

"The Hat T men have left town. Pulled out late last night. I'll bet they didn't enjoy saying their little piece to Russ Mosely."

Nobody laughed at Rufe's jeer. Nobody made any comment whatever. After a pause Kroelling asked Anne if she was not missing the fine fall coloring of the Ohio maples.

She admitted it was lovely, and declined to be deflected from the subject uppermost in her thoughts.

"You think he won't approve of what his men did," she said to Rufe.

The black-haired cowboy laughed, his reckless gaze traveling round the table. These men might think it best to play safe by having nothing to say, but Rufe had his chips in the game and meant to go through.

"He won't like the way they did it," Jelks explained. "Mr. Mosely is our leading citizen. He supports the church, and incidentally his hell-raising riders support the Jumbo, which Russ owns lock, stock, and barrel. That makes it nice, because the wages he pays his hands out of one pocket comes back into another. You'll enjoy meeting him, Miss Eliot. He's as smooth as the nap of one of these stovepipe silk hats they wear in the East."

"Don't you think you've said enough, Rufe?" Mrs. Russell asked, her warning gaze on him.

"I reckon I have," the cowboy said, his wide, friendly grin on the woman at the head of the table. "If I was living in America I could say any doggoned thing I pleased, but here in Roossia with the Czar on his throne up there at the Hat T—"

"You're still talking," Mrs. Russell reproved.

"I've quit now, ma'am. I'm a clam."

"I once knew a man who lived to be a hundred minding his own business," the keeper of the boarding-house mentioned.

"That's right," agreed Rufe, helping himself to hashed browned potatoes. "I was reading his epithet the other day. It said, *No friends, no enemies. Just no-account. Not good enough for heaven, nor bad enough for hell.*"

"Epitaph is the word, Rufe, not epithet," Kroelling corrected.

"Maybe so," Jelks said carelessly. "I don't spend much time in graveyards, so I wouldn't know. I like to be with the live ones."

"Hmp! If you don't want to become acquainted with graveyards you'd better watch your step, boy," Mrs. Russell told him.

As far as Anne could see, the atmosphere round the table was not unfriendly to what the black-haired range rider had said. She had noticed one or two nods of approval. Nobody had taken up the argument against him. The general feeling seemed to be that critical discussion of Russell Mosley was dangerous and therefore to be avoided.

Jim Silcott called for Anne after breakfast to take her down to the office of the *Sentinel*. He wanted to go over the books with her before turning over the plant. Rufe Jelks joined them. He had reclaimed his revolver from the Tivoli and felt a good deal more completely dressed.

"This town is so dad-gummed peaceful today, Red, that a fellow couldn't stir up a dogfight," he said.

"Is that why you're riding herd on us, Rufe?" Silcott inquired with obvious sarcasm. He knew his friend was going along on the off chance of trouble, but that he would be embarrassed to admit it.

"No, sir. I'm chaperooning Miss Eliot. I aim to be a brother to her and protect her from undesirable birds like you."

"That's very kind of you, Mr. Jelks, but I mustn't keep you from more important duties," Anne said.

"I'm footloose for two-three days. No trouble a-tall for me to play watchdog."

The lock of the battered door at the *Sentinel* building was so badly sprung that they could not get in that way. Jim led them round to the rear and got in by a window. He opened the back door for them.

Rufe left the others in the little rear room, and with a hammer and a saw tried to patch up the front entrance. The editor and the owner went over the finances of the *Sentinel* together, a subject of which Anne quickly tired. She flung it aside with a toss of her curly golden head.

"I never did like arithmetic," she explained. "I'm sure your figures are all right. What I want is to have you teach me how to be an editor."

"It will be the blind leading the blind," he replied. "I've been a range rider and a cowman ever since I left school. After Carl Rogers was killed I jumped in to fill a gap, but I don't know anything about running a paper. Billy Putnam takes care of the technical end of it. I couldn't set a stick in a week. All I do is gather news and write it and solicit ads."

"Well, how do you write news?"

"I don't know the right way, but just stick it down as it comes. Like this: 'Miss Anne Eliot, of Massillon, Ohio, niece of Carl Rogers, the late editor of this paper, came to town Thursday evening to look over the situation. Impressed by the bright future of Blanco, she has decided to stay here and turn the *Sentinel* into a first-class live paper. Welcome to the Powder Horn country, Miss Eliot. This territory needs more young ladies like you to rub off its rough edges.' " He smiled at her. "I'm leaving out the flubdub about how beautiful and accomplished you are. The point is to get lots of names into the paper. Folks get a kick out of seeing their names in print. And butter up the paragraph a little if you can."

"Is that all there is to being an editor?"

"No, there's more than that. Part of it out here is to learn to dodge bullets. But you won't need that. Nobody is going to hurt a young lady."

"What about this land-grant feud? Do I have to take sides?"

"No, you can sit on top of the fence and ignore it. That's what a good many editors would do."

"Tell me about the land grants. Is there a right side and a wrong side to it?"

"I think so. You know most of the bare facts, don't you?"

"I know the King of Spain gave a grant to Don José Gandara, and that after Mexico was free from Spain the government through Armijo gave a large part of the Gandara grant to Don Antonio Aguilar. Just offhand I should think the Gandara claimants were in the right, since Don José's title preceded that of Don Antonio. But my uncle was on the other side, and so are you."

"It's a complicated story. The Gandara grant was an agricultural one, but Don José used it only for grazing. He never took up residence on it, though some of his vaqueros probably built huts where they could live while herding cattle."

"Did he have to live on it to make his title good?"

"Yes. The fact is that he had all the land he needed and was not interested in this great tract. After it was given him he did not want it. This is proved by what followed. The governor later carved slices out of the grant and gave them to other settlers, with no protest from Gandara. Later, when Don José succeeded Megares as governor and captain general of the province, he officially endorsed grants out of the tract, not as from him personally but as from the crown. This seems to me conclusive evidence that he had abandoned his claim. His heirs took the same view, for they made no effort to hold any part of the grant. Purchasers did not even consider the Gandara grant as a cloud on the title when they bought from Aguilar's sons. When Russ Mosely went down to Mexico City and got for a song a quitclaim deed from the Gandaras the general opinion was that he was buying a dead horse. But he has gone into court with documents—forged ones, in my opinion—and is pushing to oust those in possession."

"Is the Hat T Ranch on the old grant?"

"Not the original ranch, but a large part of the range is in it."

Rufe Jelks and a heavy-set man with cold, bulbous eyes walked back through the building to the rear room.

Silcott nodded to the man. "Miss Eliot, this is Sheriff Lawson," he said. He added ironically, "I expect the sheriff has come to find out who destroyed your property last night so he can arrest them."

"As a matter of fact I came to investigate the killing of Buck Sneve," he said bluntly.

"I reckon you know the story as well as I do, Lawson," Silcott replied. "Prentiss and a bunch of Hat T men attacked me and in self-defense I was forced to kill Sneve."

"Not quite the way I heard the story, Jim," the sheriff answered.

"How did you hear it, Mr. Lawson?" Anne asked.

The sheriff looked the girl over before he answered. He was surprised at the question. He did not see how she came into the business.

"I heard that Jim here lay in wait for Prentiss and attacked him."

"Well, you'll be glad to know that isn't true," Anne told him. "I was there from the start. They began shooting at Mr. Silcott while he was crossing the street. He ran into the doorway of the old adobe house to escape. They kept firing at him, and the man who was killed called to the others that they had got him and ran forward. It was after this man Sneve—if that was his name—had fired again from the middle of the road that he was hit."

"Where were you standing, Miss Eliot?" the sheriff asked.

"Beside the stagecoach. In front of the office."

"A new experience for you, wasn't it?"

"Yes."

"Considerably scared, I judge."

"That did not keep me from seeing what happened."

"You'd be surprised, miss, how differently folks see the same thing," Lawson said smoothly. "Some who saw this difficulty tell me Silcott started it."

"But he didn't. I'm absolutely sure."

"So were my informants."

"Would they be Jud Prentiss and the Hat T hands?" Rufe asked derisively.

Lawson turned his cold, hard eyes on Jelks. "You in on this, Rufe?"

Jelks addressed his answer to Anne, in a tone lightly contemptuous. "The sheriff is a mite friendly to Russ Mosely, who nominated and elected him. You can't blame a politician for that."

The officer flushed angrily. "That's not true. But I aim to get to the bottom of this thing."

Jim put a hand on the arm of his friend. "I'll do the talking, if you don't mind, Rufe. The sheriff is quite right. You're not in this." To Lawson he said, "That's all I ask, sir. Dig up the facts. The fuss started at the Grub Stake an hour earlier. Prentiss and four of the Hat T riders were running on Jess Lamprey. That was none of my business. But the kid brother of Lamprey came in and tried to get his brother out of the jam. He wouldn't leave without his brother and Jud started to beat him up. I told Jud to let the boy alone. We had words. Jud grabbed Jess and quirted him, then stormed out of the place. Probably they started drinking again and decided to get me."

"That's your story," the sheriff said with chill skepticism.

"The one Russ tells will be different," Jim said evenly. "By the way, what is the one he has cooked up?"

Lawson looked at him, hard hostility in his gaze. "How would I know? I haven't seen Mr. Mosely."

"I expected he would have reached town by this time and would be giving out orders," Jim mentioned.

Resentment flared in the prominent eyes. "That's an insult, Silcott. I don't take orders from him or from anybody else."

"Glad to hear that. When I hear the boys saying you do I'll tell them they must be mistaken."

The officer slammed a fist on the desk. "I've a good mind to arrest you right now."

"At your service, sheriff," Silcott answered.

"Wait a minute." Anne faced Lawson, a flag of angry color in her cheeks. "If you do I'll have a poster printed telling the truth and have it hung up all over town."

The sheriff glared at the girl, letting the import of this sink into his mind. That would not do at all. He would be running for office again in the spring, and he did not want to alienate a large block of voters who might for sentimental reasons resent what would seem to be an attack on the credibility of this very attractive witness. Mosely would want him to go slow if she came into the picture. For the boss of the Hat T was always careful to give a color of righteousness to his overbearing selfishness. At times he rode over public opinion, but never without a lot of words of justification.

"Have you a particular interest in this young man?" Lawson asked, and let his voice drag slightly.

Anne flushed at the implication. "I have an interest in justice, but perhaps you wouldn't understand that," she retorted. "These men were trying to kill Mr. Silcott. If he is arrested I shall make that known widely."

The sheriff changed his tone. "I am only trying to get at the truth, Miss Eliot," he told her. "At the present time I have no intention whatever of arresting Jim. What he said irritated me, as it would have done any honest man. I take it that if there is a coroner's inquest you will be a witness."

"Of course."

"That will be fine." Lawson's unctuous campaign smile included them all. "I'll be saying '*Adios*,' boys. See you later."

He turned and walked out of the building.

"Just the same he had orders to arrest you and meant when he first came in to do it," Rufe said. He added, chuckling, "Miss Eliot, you sure spiked his guns."

"Yes, he backed off as if you were poison ivy," Silcott laughed. "I'm certainly much obliged to you."

"He as good as told me I was telling a story when I said you didn't fire first," Anne said tartly. "I wasn't going to let him back me down."

"He knows who fired first all right," Jelks said. "But when Russ gives orders he jumps."

"You're going to have a nice little visit from Mr. Russell Mosely today, Miss Eliot," predicted Silcott. "He's going to tell you how glad he is you came to our little town, and if there's anything he can do for you to be sure to let him know. You'll get his side of the story. If you want your stay here to be pleasant, it would be better to co-operate with him."

"Why was his ranch foreman bullying the Lampreys?" Anne asked. "Is this Mosely their enemy too?"

Something in the girl's manner cautioned Jim. "He has been friendly with Jess, but Jud Prentiss seemed to think that Jess was turning against the big ranch," he said.

"Maybe Jess has just begun to find him out."

Rufe started to speak, but his friend flashed a warning look.

"That may be it," the editor said.

"Do you know the Lamprey boys well?" Anne asked. "They come from my home town."

The men looked at her in surprise. "All of us know everybody out here," Rufe replied. "The population is small. Are the Lampreys friends of yours?"

She answered in one word. "Yes."

Chapter Seven: A LAW-ABIDING CITIZEN EXPLAINS HIMSELF

WHEN ANNE ELIOT walked into Mrs. Russell's little parlor to meet the owner of the Hat T Ranch she faced a surprise. From what had been told her she had expected to see evidences of evil and malignity written on his face. Instead, her first impression was of a man strong and masterful but friendly. He had a muscular, broad-shouldered body, a well-shaped head covered with thick, wavy brown hair, and a salient jaw that told of a dominant will.

He held out a hand as he introduced himself, but just at the moment the sun was in her eyes and she did not have to see it. Until she knew more about the death of her uncle she did not care to fraternize with those who had been his enemies.

Mosely ignored the rebuff, if it was meant for one. "First, I want to welcome you to Blanco, Miss Eliot," he said with a pleasant smile. "I hope you will like our town and decide to stay here. The cattle country is rough on the outside, but you'll find most of the people fine, upstanding citizens."

"I have already been welcomed by your men, Mr. Mosely," she told him, a little stiffly. "They paid me a visit last night."

He showed surprise. "I didn't know that. Perhaps you will explain."

"Didn't they tell you that they attacked my printing plant, shot through the door and windows, and would have smashed a way in if my friends had not driven them away?"

"I have to apologize for that, Miss Eliot, and of course I'll pay any damages." He went on to explain suavely, "My men were excited because a young ruffian had killed one of their companions, but that does not in the least excuse them. I'm sorry for what they did."

"Then it was not by your orders?"

"My dear young lady," he protested, "I'm a law-abiding man, a good influence in the community, I hope. Not for a moment will I countenance such wild behavior."

"Then I suppose you'll discharge the men who did it," she said promptly.

He was a little taken aback at her swift response. "Of course. If they really were my men and if they can be identified."

"One of them was your foreman, Jud Prentiss."

"You saw and recognized him?" the Hat T man asked.

Anne knew he had her. "I heard his voice."

"You are acquainted with him, then? You have listened to it often enough to be sure it was his?"

"No-o," she admitted reluctantly. "The men with me knew it."

"May I ask who they were?"

The girl shook her head. "I won't give names," she said.

His smile was not quite as friendly. Anne noticed that it was from the lips only. The gray eyes remained cold and flinty.

"Perhaps I can guess, Miss Eliot. Two scoundrels of no character who are enemies of mine."

She had nothing to say. He studied her, feeling for the best way to break down the hostility he felt. Word had reached him that she was young and pretty, but he was not prepared for a beauty so luminous. The rhythm of her long, lithe body stirred a slumbering fire in him.

"You have just arrived here, Miss Eliot, and naturally the first person you met was this young desperado who is running the *Sentinel*. You are a very young lady, and I must warn you that he has a bad reputation. I advise you not to have anything to do with him. He is not fit to be your associate."

"It is good of you to interest yourself in protecting me," she said.

"I see you are prejudiced against me," he went on. "I'm sorry for that, because I want you to have confidence in me. This man Silcott who has been running your uncle's paper—"

"My paper now," she interrupted.

"So I understand. He is no editor, Miss Eliot. The fellow runs a small ranch close to the Hat T. It is known that he rustles our calves, even though we haven't yet caught him at it. He is always in fights and trouble of one kind or another. A turbulent, unruly scamp who maligns better men than himself. No stability in him. A girl is likely to become interested in a dashing reckless vagabond like this scalawag. I think it my duty—"

"—To warn me not to fall in love with him. You are really too kind to me, Mr. Mosely. I don't deserve such solicitation from a stranger."

He laughed ruefully. "All right, Miss Eliot. I give up. Make your own friends and find out later that I am right."

"You can say, 'I told you so' when you find me weeping," she suggested. "Now if you're quite through, Mr. Mosely, I mustn't keep you any longer."

"But I'm not through. I presume you are here to realize on the property left by your uncle. The *Sentinel* is a white elephant on your hands, but in view of the circumstances I am prepared to buy it from you."

"What circumstances?" she asked, her eyes watching him.

"Naturally you don't know anything about country newspapers. A young lady like you has never been soiled by contact with business of any kind. The only way to make even a living out of a paper like the *Sentinel* is for the owner to edit and run it himself. You couldn't hire anybody else to do it without losing money. I give you my word that is true. Well, there is nothing left for you to do but sell it."

"Except run it myself," she said quietly.

He smiled broadly at her jest. "I hadn't thought of that." In his masterful way, he pushed straight on. "I'll not drive a hard bargain with so charming a young lady. You may depend on me to pay a little better than a fair price."

"Out of gallantry?" she asked.

"Not entirely, though that might have some weight too. The Powder Horn country needs a good paper. I am willing to supply that need."

"I think I won't sell it—at least not yet."

"Why not?" he wanted to know. His frosty eyes challenged her decision.

"It's mine. I want to keep it."

"But why?"

"I've told you. I'm going to run the paper."

"You mean get somebody to run it for you."

She stood before him slim and straight, not at all awed by his driving force. "No, I don't mean that. I'm going to edit the paper."

"That's nonsense," he said curtly, annoyed by her obstinacy. "You can't do it."

She resented his arrogant assurance. He might ride over his men at the ranch and bully the townsfolk over whom he had power, but she did not intend to let him dictate to her.

"Can't I?" she replied, her voice carefully indifferent.

"Of course you can't. In the first place, you don't know how. Already you have become entangled with some men no better than outlaws—wild, unscrupulous fellows of no repute. In the second place, a young lady can't mess around with dirty printer's ink and get into the squalid political brawls that every editor must face. Her place is in the home, where she is shielded and protected by the love of a good man from the evils of the world."

There was a poised steeliness in her bearing that showed she was not in the least convinced, "After I'm all splashed with ink and mud you can remember that you warned me, Mr. Mosely."

He was still trying to conceal his anger and not making a very good job of it, for he was a man who usually got what he wanted one way or another. His smile was meant to be indulgent of her folly, but Anne thought it rather bleak.

"I am older than you, Miss Eliot, and more experienced. Believe me, I am speaking for your own good. Young ladies do not edit newspapers. To try to do so would be to soil yourself. You are too young to start life by making a bad mistake." He concluded bluntly, sharply: "I'll give you twice what the *Sentinel* is worth. I'll buy up the rest of your uncle's holdings at a fair valuation."

"No, thank you," she said without the least hesitation. "I don't want twice what the paper is worth. If you want to buy it the price will be a dollar a year." She added maliciously, "If you want to call me an obstinate fool you may go ahead, Mr. Mosely. I'll forgive you. Very likely I am."

He was still not ready to give in. "This isn't a joking matter, Miss Eliot," he said, his grave manner rebuking· her levity. "You don't know what you are undertaking. It is a proud tradition of our country that young ladies do their part by preparing themselves to make happy homes for their future husbands. Their duty is not to mix in the broils of business but by their sweetness and beauty help to make better the lives of the men they love. What you propose is not proper for a young lady."

"And if there isn't going to be any happy home for her to brighten?" Anne asked. "Is she to sit in a boarding-house and embroider samplers?"

"That's too absurd to consider in your case, Miss Eliot," he answered blandly, with a little bow. "I think you are not quite reasonable, and that you know it yourself. If you lowered yourself to do such a thing I am afraid people would not respect you. I am speaking plainly, with no intent to offend."

Anne·was annoyed and felt a perverse delight in irritating him. "I suppose being reasonable is doing what you want me to do," she said sweetly.

"I am older than you," he went on, ignoring her thrust, "and as one who knew your uncle—"

"—And was no doubt a close friend of his," she interrupted tartly.

Undisturbed, he answered, not batting an eye at the thrust, "No, we were not friends, but we respected each other. A young lady cannot safely disregard public opinion, Miss Eliot."

"I'm not greatly concerned about gossip. Sensible people will change their minds when they see that printer's ink will wash off."

He shook his head. "I hope you won't regret this, but if you are really going to manage the paper you ought to get a competent man to assist you, for a few months, at least. I know one at Santa Fé who might be induced to come."

"Mr. Silcott has promised to help me till I get on my feet."

He flushed angrily. "The worst possible man you could get. A fellow opposed to the best interests of the community."

"As my uncle was too, no doubt," she suggested, her voice gently implacable.

"Your uncle made mistakes."

"Do you ever make mistakes, Mr. Mosely?"

He curbed his quick temper. Because of her good looks she was probably spoiled. It would be better policy to conciliate rather than to bully her, at least for the present.

"That scoundrel Silcott has set you against me," he charged. "I hope you will not take his advice. Frankly, I very much want to be friends with you. I want you to join me in my plans to make this a finer community. At least be neutral in this land-grant fight."

"But if I have convictions? You wouldn't want me—"

He cut her sentence in two. "You can't have convictions, because you don't know the facts," he told her, with the finality of a supreme-court decision. "All you can have is a prejudice, instilled in you by a young ruffian who is one of the worst of the claim-jumpers, a man who only yesterday killed wantonly an unoffending cowboy."

"You forget I was present when Mr. Silcott was attacked and had in self-defense to shoot the man," she reminded.

He rode over this roughshod. "You know nothing about it. This fight was forced by Silcott. He was hanging around to kill my foreman. He is a thoroughly bad man who has been a menace to the Hat T for years."

"Are all the settlers under the Aguilar grant bad men?" Anne asked.

"Of course not. But they are all in the wrong, in the sense that they are actually squatters depending on a title that has no just legal basis."

"So you are going to drive them from the small ranches they bought in good faith to add their holdings to the great tract you already have."

His square jaw set. "I'm going to enforce my rights, Miss Eliot. This isn't a matter of sentiment. But I intend to be generous—very generous—with those who have not insisted on becoming my enemies."

"If you win in court," she added.

"If I win in court, which I expect to do."

Both of them had remained standing during their talk. Now Anne made a movement toward the door.

"Some day you will know that I am right and those fighting me are wrong," he told her, with the calm assurance that distinguished him.

"If I do I shall let you know. Until that day, good-by."

"Have you made up your mind to oppose me?"

Her lifted eyes met his without faltering. "Practically," she said.

"If I send you a brief covering my contention, will you read it?" he asked.

"I'll be glad to read it. I want to be fair."

"I doubt that," he replied.

Anne opened the door for him. To be dismissed was a

new experience for him, and he did not like it. Wrathfully he strode out of the house, conflicting thoughts churning in him. Back of his anger was a resolve to bring this proud girl to her knees. He would show her whether she could mock at and defy him.

From the window Anne watched him go down the street, a self-willed man, strong and masterful, good-looking as a Hermes. She wondered if she had done wrong. After all, she did not know Jim Silcott. He might be all Mosely said he was. And it was true her uncle had been given to prejudices and could have been mistaken.

Chapter Eight: TWO BROTHERS

PHIL LAMPREY came into the only room of the little cabin the two brothers used when they were in town. It was one Jesse had built when he first came to Blanco before he started to run cows.

From the bed where Jesse was lying came a sour complaint.

"You certainly took your time. Thought you were never coming back."

The boy did not blame him for being ill-natured and cross. He was still suffering, both physically and mentally. All his jaunty conceit had been flogged out of him, temporarily at least. "Had to wait till Piper came back from dinner and opened his butcher shop." Phil put down on the table the packages he was carrying. "I got you pork chops, sweet potatoes, and corn. Just what you like."

"Hmp! Did you hear any talk uptown?"

Phil knew what he meant. Were people jeering at him for the quirting Prentiss had inflicted? To take his mind from its brooding, Phil told him the big piece of news that for the moment blotted out all else.

"Anne Eliot is in town."

"What?" Jesse raised himself painfully on an elbow and stared at his brother.

"I haven't seen her, but I guess there's no doubt about it. She came in on the stage last night. She was the woman who was with Silcott and Jelks when the Hat T men attacked the *Sentinel* office."

"What's she doing here?" Jesse asked irritably. "Why didn't she write and tell me she was coming?"

The younger brother could have given a good answer, but he knew it was one that would annoy Jesse. The good-for-nothing scamp had been engaged to Anne at the time he left for the West. He had ceased replying to her letters, and after a time she had stopped writing.

"They say she is going to run the *Sentinel*. The story is all over town."

"She always was crazy," Jesse snapped.

"She always was a dandy girl," the boy differed.

"I suppose she's out here to cash in on Carl Rogers's property."

Phil was busy lighting the stove on which to cook dinner. "Expect so. But everybody says she is going to manage the paper."

"She would pull some fool play like that. What was she doing with Silcott and Jelks last night? She had no right to be there."

"Ma Russell says she got Jelks to take her down to have a look at the *Sentinel* building. Natural enough, wasn't it?"

"Just like her. Where's she staying—at Ma Russell's?"

"Yes. I'll have to go see her this evening and find out if there's anything we can do for her."

"I reckon so." Jesse gloomed over her arrival with surly resentment. "This was a hell of a time for her to come, with me laid up in bed."

Phil was about fed up. "She probably didn't know Jud

was going to quirt you," he said.

The older brother looked at him angrily. "You act like you're glad he did it."

"Don't be a fool, Jess. And about Anne—why shouldn't she come if she wants to look things over?"

The man on the bed deflected the conversation for a moment to himself. "What they saying about—about the way Jud treated me?"

"I haven't heard a thing. All the talk is about the killing of Sneve and the rumpus down at the *Sentinel* last night, and about Anne's going to run the paper. The general opinion is Sneve got what was coming to him."

"I wish to hell it had been Prentiss as well as Sneve— and Silcott too, for that matter. He didn't lift a hand for me when the big bully jumped me unexpected."

"Very likely we would all have been killed if he had. By the way, Russ Mosely is in town."

Jesse sat up, a startled look on his face. "How do you know?"

"Saw him going into the Jumbo."

"What's he here for?"

"Don't know. He called on Anne. They say he isn't backing Jud for cutting loose his wolf. I guess there's nothing to worry about."

"Easy for you to say that," the man on the bed snarled unhappily. "You're not the man he's after."

"Russ isn't going to bother with you now, Jess," the younger brother said, filling the kettle from a bucket of water. "I don't suppose he is very well pleased with you, but after what happened last night he has bigger fish to fry. This is how I size it up from what folks are saying. Jud had no orders to go as far as he did. His boss doesn't like to play his hand out in the open. That's not his way. But the milk is spilt now. He'll not forget that Jim Silcott killed Sneve. One of these days Jim will be rubbed out without any witnesses present—very likely drygulched and his body never found. That's the talk, anyhow. Well, Russ is no fool. He won't want to overplay his hand. Best thing for you that could have happened is this killing of Sneve. You get lost and forgotten in the shuffle."

Phil made dinner and Jesse limped to the table. The appetite of the whipped man was coming back. For a few hours he had been very sick from the shock of the lashing he had received. But the pain was subsiding. His legs and his back hurt now only when he moved, or when clothing came in contact with the wheals raised by the quirt.

"I'll have to get out to the ranch tonight to look after the stock," the boy said, pouring coffee. "You can look after yourself now, all right. If I were you, soon as I could ride, I'd get out to the ranch too."

"Of course I will. Think I'm a fool, to stick around here and take everybody's grins when they see me?" He swore a weak, furious oath. "I can tell you one thing. Some day I'm going to settle with Jud Prentiss in full for what he did to me."

"I wouldn't think too much about that, Jess," his brother advised. "Best thing is for you to forget it all as soon as you can."

"Not till I've fixed that damn bully."

After Phil had washed the dinner dishes he tied a silk bandanna round his neck. As he was knotting it, Jesse flung a sneer at him.

"So you're going to make a play for Anne. Don't fool yourself, kid. She won't go in for cradle-snatching."

Phil flushed. He had always admired Anne tremendously, as a youngster does a girl older than himself, with no expectation of a reciprocal emotion. "I reckon you are right," the boy cut back. "She will have had enough of this family."

"Is that so?" The vanity of Jesse drove him to boasting.

"A lot you know about it. I could tell you something would make your eyes pop out."

"You couldn't tell me anything about her that would show her anything but the finest girl I know," Phil retorted loyally. "She was always far too good for you, and she got a lucky break when you quit writing because you had taken up with that girl in the honky-tonk. Now she's through with you."

"Don't be too sure of that," Jesse taunted.

"Anne has too much pride ever to look at you again, after the way you threw her down."

Phil reached for his hat and started for the door.

"Give her my love and tell her I'll be round one of these days," the older brother called after him.

"I'd be ashamed to mention your name to her," Phil flung back by way of a parting shot.

The boy was not very sure how Anne would receive him. She might be done with the whole family. If she was cool to him he would not blame her.

He found her in the garden among Ma Russell's hollyhocks, and as soon as she saw him she flung up a hand in greeting. Her warm and friendly voice relieved him immensely. It swept away the embarrassment he felt.

"I didn't know until an hour ago that you were here," he said. "Are you all settled? Is there anything I can do for you?"

"I can't think of anything, but if I do I'll call on you."

He thought that the years had made her more lovely. There had always been magic in her for him, but she had lost the lankness of her undeveloped teens and now carried her slender fullness with a poised resilience of muscles perfectly synchronized.

"I hear you are going to edit the *Sentinel* yourself," he mentioned.

"I am going to try. It won't be easy on account of this

land-grant feud. Everybody seems to be on one side or the other."

"Not everybody, at least openly. Some do not declare themselves. It does not touch them, and they keep their mouths shut."

"How about you?"

"I'm not really in it. Too young for one thing."

"I heard about some trouble you had with one of Mr. Mosely's foremen. You and Jess too."

Phil was glad she had mentioned his brother in a tone so matter of fact. They could hardly talk and leave his name out of the conversation without awkwardness.

"It was Jesse's trouble, not mine."

"Is he on the Hat T side?"

"Well, he was at first. Russ Mosely employed him to do odd jobs for him. But Jess has been kinda swinging round lately. That's why the Hat T men beat up on him."

"Have you made up your mind which side is right?" Anne asked.

"I don't know which side is right legally," he hedged.

"But you know which side your sympathies are on."

"Yes. But I don't talk about it. I'd as soon tell you. I'm for the small settlers who are fighting for their ranches against the Hat T."

She nodded. "So am I." She changed the subject. "Tell me about yourself, Phil. You and Jess have a ranch still, haven't you? How are you doing with it?"

After the boy had gone Anne's mind reverted to her problem. She was not at all sure that she could run a paper even if there had not been this land-grant feud to complicate matters. Jim Silcott had made it very clear to her that if she opposed Russ Mosely she would have a very difficult time. He owned the bank and could cut off loans. The largest freight outfit from the railroad to Blanco was his, and more than once the *Sentinel* had been faced with a shortage of white paper. In a dozen different ways he had it in his power to inconvenience her and make life unpleasant.

Chapter Nine: A RESPONSIBLE BUSINESS MAN ADVERTISES

ANNE DISCOVERED that she liked working on a paper. It made her feel as if she had some value in the scheme of things. A small town and the surrounding country is a little world in itself, and the center of this is the local newspaper. Nothing happens from a baseball game to a church social without the co-operation of the editor. When a man runs for office he gives thought to the attitude of the home journal toward his candidacy.

Silcott stayed on the job as her mentor. He taught her how to give a friendly, gossipy tone to the *Sentinel's* news, and impressed on her that even trivial events were worth recording to build up interest and good will. She found herself setting down that Hilary Benson, champion horse-shoe-pitcher of the Powder Horn country, had been challenged by Pete Yeager and had successfully defended his title by winning three games out of five. Bar Overstreet, she wrote, had brought in to the editor a basket of the largest potatoes ever grown in the county. Everybody was pleased to know that little Bobby Simpson had recovered from the measles and was back at school. Her advisor drilled into the young woman the importance of getting as many names into the columns of the *Sentinel* as possible.

She decided to write herself the story of the Sneve killing and the subsequent attack on the *Sentinel* building. After she had finished it Anne took what she had written to Silcott for criticism. He finished reading, then slanted a warm, friendly grin at her, white teeth flashing in the brown tanned face.

"My, my, lady, this won't do at all," he told her. "You've turned a news story into an editorial. Just tell what took place. Don't scold the Hat T boys. Be very brief and impartial. The only names you need to mention are those of Sneve and mine. I think your story is much too indignant and much too long."

"But why?" Anne demanded hotly. "You had me write nearly half a column about the school entertainment. There isn't much more than that here, and it's lots bigger news. Or isn't murder news here?"

Jim's eyebrows lifted whimsically. "Murder?" he asked.

"Well, attempted murder," she corrected impatiently. "And it resulted in a death."

"If this story had nothing to do with the *Sentinel* I would say give it a big play," he explained. "But it has everything to do with us. Folks will be expecting you to lambaste the Hat T riders, and if you do they will discount all you say, figuring that you will be telling your side of the story. My idea would be to write a short, impersonal account, giving nothing but facts. This would be a complete surprise. You would gain ground a lot, for fairminded people would see you are an editor not biased by your personal viewpoint."

"They would think I was afraid to tell what I thought."

"Not if your policy about local issues is firm. It doesn't matter what you think about this killing. All that matters in a news story is just what happened." His eyes glanced through the account she had written. "You say here, *Jud Prentiss and his ruffians rode into Blanco with lawlessness and murder in their hearts.* We don't know that. Anyhow, it's only an opinion."

"I suppose it's only an opinion that they flogged Jess Lamprey and tried to kill you and came down here and shot into this building with me in it."

"Let me write the story," he suggested. "You don't have

to use it. But it will give you a line on what I mean. It's important folks should not think you are just an impulsive girl." He gave her again his cheerful smile. "We're going to show them a real editor."

Anne surrendered reluctantly. She liked what she had written, as most young writers do. But her better judgment told her Jim was right. She was on trial, and she had to build up a reputation for impartiality.

She ran the story exactly as Silcott wrote it, though she found a good deal of fault with what it left out. "You don't even say they lay in wait to try to kill you," she complained. "You speak about an unfortunate shooting affray. That's a nice way to talk about a bunch of murderers."

"Everybody in the county knows just what took place," Jim said. "We're not giving anybody information, but just going on record as leaning over backward to be more than fair."

"If they try anything like that again I'm going to lean forward next time," Anne said vindictively. "It's funny about you. From all I can learn you are as wild as young men come."

"Used to be," he corrected. "I'm a reformed character."

"Always gambling, fighting, bronco-busting, and raising Cain generally."

"Some kind friend has sure been giving you the lowdown on me."

"And now after these ruffians try to murder you all you do is turn the other cheek."

He could have told her, what she already guessed, that he did not want her getting into trouble on account of taking up his quarrels.

Later in the week Rufe Jelks drifted into the office, a copy of the latest issue of the *Sentinel* in his hand.

"I dropped in with a news item, Miss Eliot," he said.

"That fine young character, Rufus Jelks, has bought the Longhorn Corral from old man Monk. He has done paid a dollar down, and will settle the balance at some future date unknown after the mazuma begins to roll in."

"Good for you, Rufe," Silcott said. "I didn't know you were a capitalist."

"I wasn't till this morning. I had a run of luck at the Jumbo playing roulette. Couldn't pick 'em wrong. When I walked out in the gray dawn there was thirteen hundred and forty-two dollars of Mr. Russ Mosely's dough packed away in my jeans. He won't like that when he finds it out. Since I'm figuring on settling down soon"—he smiled blandly at Anne—"I decided to be a responsible business man who would be a catch for some nice girl."

"So you bought the Longhorn."

"I bought the Longhorn. And I want a nice little ad put in yore paper, Miss Eliot, about how all the friends of Rufe Jelks will be greeted hearty when they come to my wagon yard."

"Newspaper advertising is the life of trade, Mr. Jelks," Anne said gravely.

"Sure enough? Well, trade is what I want. My crazy kid days are over."

"Mr. Silcott has reformed too. I expect you'll both be pillars of the church soon."

"Jim, he needs a lot more reforming than I do," Rufe said. "Why, I just been reading in the *Sentinel* how he got into an unfortunate shooting affair only this week. He's sure a wild coot."

"I didn't get into it because I wanted to," Silcott justified himself. "It was forced on me."

"I'd never know it from reading what it says in the *Sentinel*," Jelks replied dryly. "I heard Russ Mosely was figuring on buying the paper. Maybe he has done bought it already."

Anne agreed with him warmly. "That's what I told Mr. Silcott. I wrote an article that called a spade a spade, but he talked me into running this milk-and-water one he cooked up. Now I wish I hadn't listened to him."

"Oh, I reckon Jim is right," Rufe conceded. "Russ won't know why you held back. He'll mill it over in his mind, and he'll know that if ever you get riled at him you can blast loose with the whole story."

"Would Mr. Mosely care much if I did?"

"Considerable. He's bull-headed, and he's going his own way regardless. But he likes folks to think he's a good citizen, the way the Big Mogul in the district ought to be. Kinda funny too. You wouldn't expect the boss of a hell-roaring outfit like the Hat T to be thin-skinned. But Russ isn't any Jud Prentiss. When he pulls off his dirty work he likes it to be all nicely covered up if possible."

Anne smiled. "You don't like him much, do you?"

"Not so you could notice it. How about you, Miss Eliot?"

"He's very good-looking," she said judicially.

"Now, looky here, ma'am. Handsome is as handsome does."

"And he told me himself he was a good citizen."

"Don't you believe it for a minute. He's a slick scalawag."

Anne did not commit herself, but she thought that might be true.

Chapter Ten: HAT T DISCIPLINE

FROM THE BUCKBOARD he had just driven into the Hat T plaza, Russell Mosely descended and flung the lines to a young fellow who had moved forward to relieve the boss of the team.

"Send Jud to me—and Pesky Kennedy, if he is here."

"Pesky just rode in," the lad answered.

Mosely did not reply. He strode to the main house, walked up the porch steps, and vanished inside the house, a long, low structure which occupied one side of the square. The bunkhouses of the men and the mess hall faced it. On one flank were the store, the blacksmith shop, and an old adobe building used for piling up saddles, bridles, harness, and ranch implements. On the other more adobe shacks, the stables, and back of these a corral.

The Hat T home ranch was a squalid enough place, entirely without any attempt to make it presentable. Its owner had been too occupied with making money to have any pride about keeping up appearances. Some day he meant to build a big house, marry, and found a dynasty. But there was still plenty of time for that. He was not quite thirty-three, and as yet had not found a chance to enjoy life. Since the age of ten he had been making his own way in the world, and it had been hammered into him that the way to power and place in the land was to hold large possessions in his grasp.

For the first time today, as he had looked down on the ramshackle buildings and their desolate background from the road which dipped in a long slope to the ranch, there had risen in him a feeling of distaste for the ugliness of the scene. He was thinking of how it would appear to the eyes of a young woman used to the neat houses and orderly lawns of a little Ohio town.

The stableboy unhitched the team and turned the horses into the corral, after which he walked across to the blacksmith shop, where Prentiss was supervising the shoeing of one of his string. As he approached, the boy heard the heavy voice of the foreman shouting at the man fitting the shoes.

"Anybody with a lick of sense knows how easy it is to ruin a good horse with shoes that don't fit. I dunno who

ever told you that you are a blacksmith, Dunn. You're not
fit to touch a horse's hoofs."

"Mr. Mosely wants to see you, Jud," the stableboy said.

Prentiss paid no attention. He went on girding at the
smith. Presently the lad mentioned again that the boss
wanted to see him. He was not sure Jud had heard.

The foreman turned on him savagely. "Don't you think
I've got ears in my head, you damn fool?" he snarled. "I'll
go when I get good and ready."

In his heavy, flat-footed way Prentiss clumped across the
square to the house.

"Mean as a bear with a sore paw today," the wrangler
said, his eyes following the heavy, awkward figure.

"Why say today in particular?" Dunn wanted to know.
"Did you ever know him in a decent temper? One of these
days I'll let him have a hammer on that thick skull of his.
To hear him you'd think we were all slaves."

The boy departed to get Pesky. He found the range
rider in the bunkhouse. Pesky was a short, crook-nosed
man with rusty hair and a sulky face.

"What's Russ want with me now?" he demanded.

"Didn't say. Told me he wanted to see you."

Kennedy was disturbed. "He's got a kick about something, that's a cinch. Damned if I stay on a ranch where
you get hauled up on the carpet for every doggoned thing
you do."

"Jud is with him," the boy volunteered.

The cowboy glanced at the bedroll lying on the bunk,
which he had just brought in with him. There was something in it which might come in handy if they started to
ride him too much. He hesitated an instant and then made
up his mind. There was no sense in looking for trouble
before it came.

While he was still a dozen yards from the office he heard
Jud's raucous voice.

"That's a damn lie, Russ. I don't care who told you. Silcott butted in at the Grub Stake before any of us had said a word to him. We were lined up at the bar having a drink. He wasn't in the party. Just horned in, like I said."

The hard, insolent voice of Mosely answered. "Silcott didn't say a word till you started to beat up Lamprey's kid brother. Don't deny it. I talked with witnesses."

"Meaning Kroelling and that bartender Walt."

"They did not want to talk, but I got the story out of them. Listen, Jud." The manner of the Hat T owner was offensively arrogant. "You're just one of my hired hands. Don't forget that. Any time you want to beat up Jess Lamprey it's all right with me, or his brother either, if you want to pick on a kid just out of the cradle. But don't make the play you are doing it for me, not unless I give you orders. I'm running this ranch. Understand? When I want anybody punished I'll let you know."

"I didn't say I was acting for you," Prentiss replied sullenly. "You can't ride me, Russ. I'm no four-bit puncher. I won't take it."

"You'll take it long as you draw wages from me," Mosely told him evenly, his inscrutable eyes watching the other. "I thought you knew I was boss here, Jud."

"That doesn't make me yore slave. I don't come to heel like a whipped cur."

A shadow darkened the doorway.

"You sent for me, Mr. Mosely," Kennedy said.

The ranch-owner did not even look at him. His steady gaze was on the foreman. "I investigated the gunfight too. You told me Silcott began it. That's not the case. Sneve fired the first shot and the rest of you joined in with him. You shot at Silcott while he was crossing the street. He hadn't an idea you were anywhere around. Did you lie in wait for him?"

"No," exploded Prentiss. "Sneve saw him and went

crazy with the heat. We had to back his play, didn't we?"

"Why? If he plays the fool do you have to do it too?" Mosely added with a jeering laugh, "I must say, Silcott made you look like a bunch of amateurs. You're not thorough enough to be a bad man, Jud."

"Make up yore mind one way or another, Russ," the foreman snarled. "First you roast me for shooting at him, then for not rubbing him out. What in Mexico do you want?"

Mosely sat behind the table which served as a desk, his forearm resting on it, his salient jaw thrust forward arrogantly. "I'll tell you what I don't want. One thing is to have to send a nurse along with my hands when they go to town for fear some lone scoundrel will catch them in a huddle and wipe them out. Another is for them to interfere in my affairs without orders and make trouble I have to explain away. I'll decide when Silcott, *or anybody else,* has run on the rope long enough."

Kennedy's gaze whipped from the Hat T boss to Prentiss and back again as they talked. He did not quite get this situation. Russ had not sent for him to cuss him out about the Blanco fight, for he had not been one of the men in town that day. Pesky was uneasy, for private reasons of his own which he did not want to discuss, least of all with Mosely. But why not wait to call him on the carpet, if that was what he was here for, after he had finished laying down the law to Prentiss? The cowpuncher was no fool. His groping mind found the reason. Mosely wanted to humiliate the foreman by putting him in his place before one of the men. Perhaps too he wanted the Hat T hands to realize that they were taking orders from the owner and not from Jud except in details of routine work.

"A man who works for you has to be a mind-reader," Prentiss growled bitterly at his boss. "I reckon you never in yore life came out flat with what you were thinking so a fellow would know what to do."

"When there is anything I want you to know—or do—I'll tell it to you," Mosely retorted curtly. "I'm not dumb." He turned his cold, flinty eyes on Kennedy, let them rest on the man a moment, then flung an abrupt question at him. "Are you working for me or for Bar Overstreet?"

The cowboy floundered mentally, taken aback at the attack. "Why, I'm working for you, Mr. Mosely."

"I'm wondering about that. I sent you to Sweetwater Spring three days ago to drive back any cattle that came there except Hat T stuff. You had grub with you and were to stay there till relieved. Last night you rode across to Bar Overstreet's place and didn't get back till after midnight. Correct me if I'm wrong."

The sulky face of the crook-nosed man flushed. He thought, *This man is a devil. He knows everything. You can't take a step without him finding it out.* He said, "I ran outa tobacco, and after it got dark I figured—"

Mosely cut off his explanation ruthlessly. "You figured that nobody could see you hotfooting it to an enemy of the ranch that pays you to look after its interests. Not after it got dark, if you took the Hardscrabble trail. But you were mistaken, weren't you? And you've been there before. This isn't the first time."

The range rider knew that he had been trapped. Mosely had suspected him and sent him to Sweetwater Spring to give him a chance to ride across to Bar's ranch. With the sleeve of his shirt Kennedy wiped tiny sweat beads from his brow. There was anger in him, but there was also fear. Hard character though he was, he knew better than not to be afraid of Russ Mosely's vengeance.

"You sent me there yore own self, with Pete Yeager, to drive back them strays the muley dun led off!" Pesky cried, worry riding the exasperation in his voice.

"I didn't tell you to stay for supper, did I?"

"Shucks! The bell rang while we was there. We kinda had to eat."

"And you had to go back again, two or three times. Was it tobacco or strays you were after?"

The eyes in the ugly, flat-featured face of the foreman watched Kennedy jealously. He guessed what the magnet was that had drawn the man back to the Tincup Creek country. The pretty face and engaging ways of Betty Overstreet had lured him. Jud had coveted the girl himself, and at a dance on Hardscrabble Creek had been publicly snubbed by her.

"If you think I was tipping him off anything you're wrong," Pesky blurted.

"A man can't work for the Hat T and serve two masters," Mosely told the puncher. "You're through. Here's your check. One thing I won't stand is a two-timer."

"Don't want more than one of 'em around, I reckon," the crook-nosed man flung at his employer resentfully, and was shocked at his own audacity. "Suits me fine. I can get another job. The Hat T ain't the only ranch on earth."

The narrowed eyes of Mosely flashed venom. "For two cents I would thrash you within an inch of your life, you fool. If I wouldn't soil my hands doing it. Get out of here. Don't ever let me see your face again."

Kennedy backed to the door. "I'm on my way, and glad to go," he said. "There ain't a man on the place don't despise you, and yore lousy foreman too."

He vanished from the entrance, but Jud Prentiss was on his feet instantly. It was amazing how swiftly a man so big and awkward could cover the ground. He was on Pesky before the man had reached the porch steps.

All the bilious rage banked in the foreman during the past few minutes boiled up in him and poured out. His

fury at Mosely, his jealousy, his anger at Kennedy for having been present at his humiliation, all worked together
to welcome an outlet of violent action.

As Pesky turned, the hairy fist of Jud lashed out and
caught the cowboy on the jaw. Kennedy shot from the
porch as if he had been fired from a catapult. Before he
could scramble up Prentiss landed on his body with both
feet. The man on the ground groaned, covering his face
with his arms to protect it from vicious kicks. He rolled
away and reached his knees, only to be hammered down
again. Bruised and bleeding, he managed to get to his
feet, after the boots of the foreman had landed on him
savagely many times.

The crook-nosed man could put up no defense. His
legs were buckling beneath him as he staggered back. The
world had turned foggy for him, and it tilted wildly. He
tried to go into a clinch and was driven away by heavy,
swinging blows. Arms dropped and torso sagged. Prentiss
sent home a pile-driver right and Pesky collapsed. He
went down and out.

Jud clenched his teeth and moved toward him.

"That will be enough, unless you want to kill him,"
Mosely said callously. He was leaning against the door-
jamb, his hands in his pockets. "Quite a massacre, Jud.
You never gave him a chance for his white alley."

"You wouldn't care if I did kill him, except for being
scared folks would criticize you," Prentiss said sullenly,
his big fists still clenched, his chest heaving from violent
exertion.

"Don't do it on my ranch."

The foreman glared at him from a face so dark with
blood it was almost purple. "Sure. Not on yore ranch. You
certainly take the cake, Russ. Sometimes I think you have
got yoreself fooled."

Kennedy opened his eyes, realized what had taken place,

and sat up painfully. His swollen and distorted face looked as if it had been pounded with a hammer.

"Roll up your war bag and get out of here," Mosely ordered. "And don't stay in Blanco. Keep going."

The cowboy had taken a terrible beating, but he was no coward.

"I'll stay in Blanco long as I like," he answered sullenly, getting to his feet with difficulty. "This is a free country."

The hairy fists of the foreman tightened. "If you haven't had enough, there's more where that came from," he threatened.

"I've had enough—right now," Kennedy replied, standing his ground. "But this thing ain't ended."

"Fine," Prentiss gloated. "We'll finish it now."

"That will do, Jud," the Hat T owner said crisply. "We'll keep in mind that he is threatening us. Tough men of his sort who look for trouble usually get it. I'm a patient man, but I won't be intimidated by gunmen who try to bully me. Be off this place in half an hour, Kennedy, and keep traveling till you are out of this part of the country. We don't want men of your stripe here."

The cowpuncher went to the bunkhouse, his aching body and face paining him every foot of the way. He took the forty-five from his roll and pushed it down between his shirt and trousers. This was no time to use it, but he did not intend to be caught again in a position where he could not defend himself. A few minutes later he hobbled down the road to the corral and saddled his horse. Prentiss watched him go, without any comment.

Chapter Eleven: ANNE HIRES A DRIVER

A MAN WITH A FACE almost as raw as a pounded steak walked into the office of the *Sentinel* and asked Anne where he could find Jim Silcott. The young woman did

not answer at once. She was a little careful about direct-
ing men to Jim until she had looked them over and decided that they did not mean him physical harm.

"Do you want to see him on business?" she asked.

"On *his* business," the man answered.

Anne thought she had never seen a countenance so distorted from what it must have been before someone or
something had worked it over. There were a dozen cuts
in it, several of them deep and jagged. One eye was nearly
entirely closed, and both of them were surrounded by
green and yellow discolorations. Swollen knobs jutted out
from cheeks and forehead like mountains on a contour
map.

"You have been hurt," Anne said, mentioning the obvious, with intent to get more light on the object of his call.

"Kindness of Jud Prentiss and Russ Mosely," he replied
grimly.

"Oh! Have you come to get something put in the paper
about it?"

"Cripes, no!" the man exploded. "I want to see Silcott
personally, like I said. Is he here—or not?"

"Yes, he's here." Anne raised her voice. "Someone to
see you, Mr. Silcott."

Jim came forward to the front of the building. He had
to look at Kennedy twice before he recognized him. " 'Lo,
Pesky," he said. "Was it a bear or a buzz saw?"

"It was Jud Prentiss, egged on by his boss. He beat me
up plenty with his fists, but most of the damage he did
with his boots."

"He must have been a little annoyed at you," the editor said dryly.

"Yep. Russ gave him what for right before me, and he
didn't like that. When I told him he was as lousy as Russ
himself he jumped me. I was not expecting him so quick
the first time he knocked me down, but he would have

cleaned up on me anyhow, so it doesn't matter much."

"He kicked you when you were down?"

"That's the general idea. He caved in two of my ribs. Doc Head has got me strapped up."

"I reckon you and the Hat T had a little difference of opinion before hostilities started."

"Russ accused me of double-crossing him and gave me my time."

"He ought to know a double-crosser when he sees one," Silcott suggested. "What had you been up to, Pesky?"

"Two-three times I had drifted over to Bar Overstreet's place. It's against orders for any Hat T man to visit with anybody unfriendly to the ranch. Maybe I mentioned to Bar what I thought of my boss, but that's no crime."

Jim introduced Kennedy to Anne. By way of posting her, he explained with a grin that Betty Overstreet was the prettiest girl on Tincup. "Russ ought to get her married to one of his hands," he added. "Then he could keep the boys on the ranch."

"Why doesn't he marry her himself?" Anne asked. "He's a fine-looking man. A girl would think twice before she turned him down."

"Not if she had any sense," Kennedy said bluntly. "At least if she knew him."

"Did Mr. Mosely order his foreman to beat you?" the girl inquired.

"Not in so many words. He let Jud know it would suit him, and since he was feeling mean he jumped at the chance. I had made a mistake. When Russ sent for me I had a kind of hunch it was bad luck, and I had two minds to get my gun out of my roll. But not having anything to back my hunch I took a chance. It will be different next time." Kennedy brushed his own troubles aside. "I didn't come to tell you all this. My system has absorbed beatings a-plenty. I can take care of the guys who handed me this whopping. What I'm here for is to give you a tip. Mosely means to blow up yore dam."

Jim said quietly, "How do you know?"

"I don't know, but I'm sure of it just the same. He freighted a lot of dynamite up to the ranch in boxes labeled groceries and dry goods. Pete Yeager has been up in the rimrock back of yore place for a couple of days. My guess is he is figuring out the best way to do the job."

"Why would he blow up your dam?" Anne wanted to know. "Just out of meanness?"

"Not entirely," Silcott replied. "I built the dam to irrigate some fields where I raise feed for my stock. Mosely claims I'm interfering illegally with the natural flow of the water which he needs for his cattle."

"And what do you claim?"

"That I have a priority right to the water, taken up by due process of law. Also that he has no right to run his stock on upper Tincup and Red Canyon creeks, which range belongs to the Diamond Slash outfit."

"Is that your ranch—the Diamond Slash?"

"Yes. Of course our claims are tied up with the land-grant cases. As it happens, most of my ranch is not on the Armijo grant, but that part of the rimrock where I built the dam on Red Canyon Creek is situated on it. Mosely holds that I am merely a squatter and can be ejected."

"Does he want *all* this country?"

"Not all, ma'am," Kennedy told her. "If a fellow kowtows to him Russ is willing for the guy to have some, if it hasn't any water holes on it and is too dry to feed stock."

"Is this dam very important to you?" Anne asked Silcott.

He explained that it was important now and would be much more so in the future. When the cattle first came up from Texas the longhorns were a poor, bony stock that had run wild in the brush country. But now the cowmen were breeding up their stuff. The price had risen, and ranchers could not still afford to let their herds rough through hard winters with only such feed as they could pick up on the snow-covered range. Raising cows was no longer an adventure but a business. An outfit had to cut a lot of hay if it intended to stay on the map. Many of the oldtimers refused to see this, but to Silcott it was written plain as the words in a primer. A man had to have first-class whiteface stuff, and he must be prepared to feed when the winter winds howled. To do this he must irrigate.

On her way to supper Anne passed the Longhorn Corral and was joined by Rufus Jelks.

"Mr. Silcott has gone out to his ranch," she said.

"Yeah, I saw him. Took Pesky Kennedy with him. I'm thinking of drifting up there for two-three days."

"Because you think there's going to be trouble," she charged.

His white teeth flashed in a grin. "Lady, haven't I told you that I'm a respectable business man with 'object, matrimony' in the back of my nut?"

"I'm glad you are going. Mr. Silcott is too reckless. . . . I want to talk with you about some traveling I'm going to do myself. I do not know anything about this country and very few of the people, and for an editor that won't do. So I'm going to get a driver and go out into the hills where I can meet a lot of my subscribers."

"You've hired yore driver," Jelks told her. "When do we start?"

"We start tomorrow morning early, if that suits you. I suppose we can find ranches that will put me up nights."

"How about postponing yore trip till next week? I'd kinda set my mind on going up Tincup way right now."

"That's the direction I'm traveling, so no postponement will be necessary."

He looked at her suspiciously. "I don't believe I'll take you up Tincup."

"Then I haven't hired a driver, have I?" she said, tilting a smile at him. "The one I hire will take me anywhere I want to go."

"You would want yore driver to give you a little advice, wouldn't you—about the roads and where to go and what ranches are cleanest?"

"Oh, yes! And I would take any of it I liked."

He sighed. "You're not going to turn out one of these strong-minded ladies who want women's rights, are you?"

"Do I look like Doctor Mary Walker?"

"You don't *look* like her. It's yore actions I'm worrying about." He fixed upon her the severe gaze of a respectable business man. "You hadn't ought to be so rambunctious. It ain't becoming in a young lady. Far as that goes, I dunno as it's proper for you to go out into the hills unchaperooned."

The color beat up into Anne's cheeks. "Maybe you had better let me decide what is proper for me to do," she said tartly.

He ran brown fingers through his black hair, to help him think more clearly. "If you was married it would be different, o' course. But a young lady like you has to be careful. She can't traipse all over the country with none of her folks along."

"Not even if she takes a fussy old woman like you along?" she asked.

"You ask Ma Russell. She'll tell you whether you ought to go." Reproachfully he answered her thrust, "I got sisters of my own, and I wouldn't let one of them go."

"Lucky I'm not one of them."

"You been raised right," he told her. "You know what a nice young lady had ought to do and what she hadn't."

"How often have I got to explain that I'm the editor of

a paper and not a simpering little fool sitting under a glass bowl?" she asked impatiently. "I'm running the *Sentinel*, to make a living."

"You don't have to make a living that way. Plenty of men—"

She interrupted sharply. "I've heard that before. Listen, Mr. Jelks. I don't intend to get married. Even if I wanted to I could not. I'm married already."

He stopped in his stride, to stare at her. "You're loadin' me," he said.

There was a hint of defiance in the poise of her head, and in her eyes a bitter self-mockery. "It's true. I'm a deserted wife." She added, a beat of anger in her voice, "So you don't need to be chivalrous about me any longer. Now, if you don't mind, we'll drop the subject."

Her long legs took up again the rhythmic motion of their walk.

Chapter Twelve: A PICNIC DINNER AT TINCUP

AFTER SHE CAME WEST, Anne was particularly glad that she was an early riser. It was an undiluted joy each morning to walk out into a world so warm and sun-kissed. She was feeling this lift when she stepped into the buckboard while Rufus held 'to the lines at which two half-broken young horses strained. The team plunged away wildly, the light rig bouncing and swaying perilously.

Anne clung fast to her seat and hoped there was not going to be a smash-up before they were out of town. They rattled across a bridge, down into a dip and up again, then raced along a stretch of level road in a cloud of dust which concealed everything behind them. In a cut outside of Blanco the sand deepened and made heavy going. The pace slackened.

"Where's the fire?" Anne asked, with a cheerful grin

at her companion.

"They won't be kicking up their heels so much in three-four hours," Rufus promised.

The road went gunbarrel-straight through a sage flat that stretched for miles. The rising sun was streaming across the desert, touching the gray-green foliage to unaccustomed life. Close to the brown ribbon they followed vegetation pressed near, reaching toward the track and threatening to obliterate it. Once Anne caught sight of a file of antelope moving through the brush.

After many miles ·of sage flats the road swung toward the filmy mountains standing against the far horizon. It wandered in casual fashion over low cowbacked hills, which gradually became higher as they rose wave on wave to the misty range.

To feel Rufus out, Anne remarked, "It's a desolate country, isn't it?"

"I hadn't noticed it," the man said dryly. "I reckon some folks like to live in a two-by-four hole all barbered up. I don't."

She laughed. "I thought I'd get a rise. I suppose if somebody gave you a nice slice of New York City you wouldn't want to live there."

"Not if they gave me all of it," he told her promptly. "I want room to breathe."

Anne admitted that the high plains grew on one. "The air is like wine, and you feel glad to be alive. There is something about the mountains too that washes meanness out of you."

"It hasn't taken the meanness out of Jud Prentiss and his boss," Jelks mentioned.

"Jud is a tough old sinner," Anne admitted. "As for Mr. Mosely, maybe he isn't as bad as you think."

"If a guy is good-lookin' he can always get by with women," Rufus said, to the world at large.

"Do you think he really means to blow up the dam?"
the girl asked.

"You can't ever tell what Russ means to do. He's a slick
scoundrel. Offhand I would say he's liable to take a crack
at the dam. If it went out, Jim would lose a lot. And the
Hat T needs more water in the creek below."

"If there is a fight about the dam somebody will be
hurt," Anne said. "That's why you are here—to side with
your friend."

"That bird can get in more trouble," Rufus frowned.
"I never saw his beat."

"You're not so bad at it yourself," she reminded him.

The black-haired young man slanted a suspicious look
at her. "All right. You got me explained. What about
you? Why are you headin' for Tincup, if it isn't to mix
up in this fuss?"

"I don't know." Her eyes were worried. "It's none of
my business, but I feel drawn into it. On account of the
Sentinel. First my uncle, then Jim Silcott. I have to stop
harm coming to him if I can."

"How?"

She threw up her hands in a little despairing gesture.
"I don't know. I thought I would talk with Mr. Mosely.
People obey the law where I came from. Why can't he
wait until the courts decide?"

"That's not the way Russ works."

They were traveling now through a country of high
hills covered with jack pines. The soil was red and the
growth of vegetation not dense. The terrain had the well-
kept look of a mountain park. Following the line of least
resistance, the road wound in and out among the small
trees deviously. Above them was a sky deep blue, cloudless
except for one or two thin skeins drifting high in the air.

"We'll water at a ranch a couple of miles down the
trail," Rufus said. "Then we'll tie up on Tincup and

have dinner."

They descended into a valley and swung from the road to a small ranch house nestling among some cottonwoods. In the corral a windmill clicked cheerfully.

Jelks yelled, "Hello the house!"

Phil Lamprey came to the door.

"Like to water the team," Rufus called, after a word of greeting.

"Help yourself." Phil came forward and recognized Anne. For a moment he was disturbed. He thought she had come to see his brother. But he greeted her warmly.

"We're drumming up subscribers to the *Sentinel*," Jelks explained. "Are you on the list? And have you paid up?"

The boy smiled back at him. "We're subscribers, and we have paid up to the end of the year."

"Fine. Where's Jess?"

"He went up to Bar Overstreet's to get a horse shod."

"Hmp! I've heard forty-eleven different reasons why the boys have to go up to Bar's so often. Some day a guy will break down and tell the truth, that he is taking a *pasear* up there to see Betty." Rufus unhitched the horses as he talked.

Phil opened the corral gate and the team watered.

"We're going to have a picnic dinner on Tincup," Anne said. "Not far from here. Come along and eat with us."

Though young Lamprey declined, there was no heart in his refusal. He was easily persuaded to join them. While Jelks hitched the horses again he roped and saddled.

"Go ahead," he shouted from the corral. "I'll catch up with you."

The road struck Tincup and followed the bank of the stream, the small willows whipping the wheels as they passed through the young growth. The trail rambled up a wide and easy canyon. Beside them the tumbling creek sang a gay song as it raced down over and around boulders on its headlong rush for the river. Indian paintbrushes and columbines bordered the road. Above was an azure-blue sky of deep luminosity.

· Before they reached the little open park which Rufus had selected for a campground, Phil cantered up and joined them.

Anne said, as she stepped out of the buckboard, "I'm ravenous."

"I'm gonna cure that," Jelks promised. He put out an arm to hold her back from the sack of provisions. "You don't have to do a thing, lady. This is to be a camp dinner. I cook, and Phil flunkies for me. You go gather flowers."

Phil unhitched and staked the horses. The black-haired man gathered dry wood and lit a fire. Anne strolled up the creek. When she returned twenty minutes later she saw gray smoke drifting lazily across the open. The enticing odor of bacon and coffee came to the nostrils of the young woman. With the heel of a hatchet Phil slashed the top of a can, obeying the instructions of the cook to "bust open" the tomatoes. Rufe himself was busy with the coffee and the flapjacks.

"Come and get it, Miss Anne," he called presently.

Perhaps it was because the long drive in the sun and the wind had sharpened Anne's appetite that the food tasted so good. She thought she had never enjoyed a meal more, and she said so more than once.

Though she did not talk much herself, she drew out the men to keep up a lively conversation, most of it contributed by Rufe. Occasionally she prodded a question at him. He told of roundups, of night herding under the stars, of camping in cold, drizzling rain on wet and soggy ground. Jelks had the gift of making his story vivid, and ranch dances, battles with rustlers, herds crossing bank-full rivers, rose to life at the call of her imagination. Silcott's name came into one of his stories.

"Yes, ma'am. At Las Vegas. We was all high as a kite. I was with the Flying V outfit then. We drifted into a Mexican *baile* and the boys began dancing with the señoritas. That didn't go over so good. There was a rider called Flea Bite. One young greaser told him hands off his girl. Flea Bite gave him information where to head in at, and the Mexican went for his knife. We had cached our guns at the Eldorado Saloon. I reckon that was lucky. It wasn't any private fight. Everybody was in it. We weren't doing so well, on account of the señors' knives. Then Red stopped it."

"How?" asked Anne.

"He just happened past the place while the rumpus was going on. There was a big tank of water on the roof of the hall to be used in case of fire. The hose was to come down through the skylight. Well, Red grabbed an axe from a wagon, shinned up the stairway, busted a big hole in the skylight and another in the tank, and watched Niagara pour down on the war. Gentlemen, hush! *Muy pronto* we postponed hostilities. That water came down like the cataract at Lodore I read about in my McGuffey's Reader. There was a regular stampede to adjourn. Not any too soon, either. I reckon the Flying V boys lost a total of about a half a gallon of blood from knife wounds."

"Red is a humdinger," Phil said. "I never saw the beat of him."

"Sure is," Rufe agreed. "I don't care who calls himself major-domo. Where Red sits is the head of the table."

Phil rode back to the ranch after dinner. The buckboard climbed to a bench and crossed it. The mountains were still far, though they looked nearer than when they had first seen them in the morning. No longer did they stand out thin and shadowy. In the strong sunlight the range was sharply defined, snowy gulches white against a background of darker spurs and shoulders. Anne had a queer feeling of littleness. She and Rufe were two specks of humanity in a world of vast emptiness. They were alone in a panorama from which all other life was banished.

Jelks understood what she was feeling. "Subscribers to the *Sentinel* are right seldom in this neck of the woods, but when we get down to Tincup again we'll be meeting a few," he promised.

Anne smiled back at him. She was glad she was not alone.

Chapter Thirteen: ANNE TELLS JESSE LAMPREY OFF

FROM THE BENCH they dropped down through a narrow canyon, so sharp that at times there was hardly room on the floor for a tilted, rocky road. Below the mouth of the gorge they could see Tincup Creek, a silver ribbon winding up through rough, broken country to its headwaters. Rufe pointed out a ranch steading set in a pocket of the hills. The revolving blades of a clicking windmill flashed greetings at them.

"The Bar Overstreet Ranch," he told her. "About half a mile as the crow flies, but we'll travel five miles before we get there."

"I understand Betty is worth traveling five miles to see," Anne commented, slanting a smile at him.

"A lot of the boys feel that way."

The Bar O Ranch was set in the prettiest little park Anne had yet seen since her arrival in the West. It was watered by a small stream, and along its borders were fields of alfalfa and native hay. Nearer to the house was an orchard of apple, peach, and cherry trees.

Young Bill Overstreet, still lank and weedy but on his way to be as big as his father, came up to the buckboard to greet them. Rufe introduced the boy to Miss Eliot.

Bill blushed. He was at an age when young ladies embarrassed him. But he led the way into the house, which was built partly of logs and partly of lumber.

From a back room came the sound of a giggle. A high girlish voice was lifted in scolding laughter. "Now you behave, Jess Lamprey, or I'll stick this needle in you. Just because I'm sewing a button on your vest is no reason for you to get fresh."

"Someone to see you, Sis," Bill called out.

Betty appeared in the doorway, a needle in one hand and an edge of a man's vest in the other. Jesse Lamprey was inside the vest.

"Oh! I thought it was just one of the boys." Betty moved forward to meet her visitor. She was a buxom girl, with fine dark eyes and color in her cheeks that came and went easily. Her age might have been eighteen, but she was well developed for her years, and very pretty.

Rufe introduced the two young women.

"I've been hearing about Miss Betty Overstreet ever since I came into the country," Anne said, and smiled as she shook hands.

She had been given a moment's warning, and her gaze did not once stray to the discomfited man in the doorway. Apologizing for coming in without warning, she kept the small talk going until Betty remembered her duty as a hostess.

"Miss Eliot, meet Mr. Lamprey," she said. "He's from the East too, or was before we made a cowman of him."

Lamprey made as if to offer his hand, then drew it back. Anne was looking at him with cool contempt in her eyes.

"I've met Mr. Lamprey," she said quietly.

The man had been taken aback, but he rallied his hardihood. "Why, yes, Anne and I are old friends. We come from the same town. We—in fact—"

"I didn't know that," Betty said. "How nice for you to meet away out here."

"Yes. Isn't it?" Lamprey fumbled for words to put himself at ease. He could not take his eyes from Anne. He had forgotten how lovely were the planes of her face. Time had dimmed for him the memory of her slender, poised grace, the vividness of her personality. Old desires began to stir in him. He cursed himself silently for a fool. Her blue eyes had once been soft and tender for him. He had known the shy surrender of her warm, supple body, and he had flung away wantonly the largesse of her gift. "I heard you had come. Phil told me. I've been meaning to come and see you."

"Why?" asked Anne, the stinging lash of a whip in her cool voice.

It surprised her that she felt no emotion at this meeting. There had been a time when the sight of him had sent excitement strumming through her blood. Now he was a stranger, of less interest to her than Bill Overstreet, whom she had known not ten minutes.

"There are some things I—want to explain," he stammered.

"No," she told him with sharp finality. "The facts explain themselves. There is nothing more to be said."

"I—kinda quit writing because I got hurt and was sick."

She let her gaze rest on the man steadily, and he knew she was telling him without words that he was a liar, and a clumsy one.

"I had bad luck," he blundered on. "Wasn't doing well —lost money."

"Indeed!" Her voice was as cold as the splash of icy water. She turned from him to speak with Betty. "I thought if I was editing the *Sentinel* I ought to drive around and meet some of the people. Rufe offered to bring me, so here I am."

"You'll stay tonight, of course," Betty said.

"It is good of you to ask me, but I don't want to be an inconvenience. If I would be any trouble—"

"Oh, but you wouldn't," the ranch girl interrupted. "Travelers are always staying. They do all through the cow country. I wouldn't think of letting you go tonight."

"Then I'll be glad to stay."

Lamprey walked up to Miss Overstreet and said, "I'll be going now, Betty. Got to see a fellow."

"Did you get yore horse shod, Jess?" asked Rufus, not entirely without malice.

"All right, Jess," Betty nodded. "See you later."

"Like to have a word with you alone before I go, Anne," Lamprey said, with sullen anger.

"What for?" Again Anne's gaze met his with uncompromising hostility. "There is no need for you ever to say anything to me."

"I'm going to just the same," he answered doggedly.

Swiftly Anne made a decision. She had always been honest. It had hurt her while at home to conceal this detrimental runaway marriage, for she did not want any hidden skeletons in her life. Far better tell the truth now and be done with it.

To Betty she said, "I used to be married to this man."

"Married to him?" Betty repeated in amazement. She had noticed Miss Eliot's stiff coldness, but this confession was a bombshell.

Lamprey flushed resentfully. He had wanted to talk this over with Anne and reach a settlement. The blunt announcement did not please him.

"That's not all," he snapped. "You still are."

"No," Anne denied. "Except in name. I want never to see you again."

"You'll see me plenty," he jeered. "I'm your husband. The law says so. And you're my wife. You swore to be mine till death parted us. Talk that away if you can."

Scorn burned in her eyes. "That promise was made for a man who never lived, for a dream man I thought decent and true. You are not that man. You never could have been. If you had an iota of self-respect you wouldn't remind me of that. I'm the woman you married and left at home and deserted."

The weak mouth of Lamprey set obstinately. "I was going to tell you about that, but you wouldn't listen. A fellow has his pride. He can't ask a woman to leave her home to come West and share nothing."

"What about a girl's pride, after she has compromised herself by a secret marriage?" Anne asked. "Waiting for letters that never come—knowing that she has been deceived and jilted—left high and dry neither maid nor wife nor widow."

"I did write at first," he said sulkily.

"Three letters, at wide intervals, and then no more."

"I can't write letters. I never could. But now you are here—"

"We might as well settle this now before witnesses," Anne told him, her slender body straight and her head erect. "If I were a thousand miles away I couldn't be any farther from you. There is no tie between us. None at all. There never will be. Please get that very clear. This is the last time I shall talk with you."

"Oh, I don't know about that," he replied, with jaunty insolence. "I hold to my rights. The law says—"

Rufus cut in, dragging his words. "If Miss Eliot says she doesn't know you any more, why—that settles it," he murmured.

"Not by a jugful. I'm her legal husband and she can't get away from it, even if she has got a devil of a temper."

"I wouldn't talk so harsh," Jelks advised, still in a deceivingly low, gentle voice. "This country doesn't like to hear a man talk thataway to a woman. Some doggoned fool might take you serious and make you a deceased husband."

Lamprey looked at him angrily. "Who cut you into this game, Jelks? This is private business."

"He's right, Rufe," Anne agreed. Her friendly smile robbed the reproof of its sting. "And everything has been said that needs to be. I'd like to wash now if I can, Miss Overstreet."

"You'll find there's a lot to be said yet," her husband boasted. "I'm not going to be thrown away like a dirty dishrag because you've picked up some new fancy friends here."

"Take care, Jess," warned Rufe. "I wouldn't talk any more now if I were you."

"Not here, anyhow." Betty confronted Lamprey. There was a beat of hot temper in her voice. "Leave this ranch, you scoundrel, unless you want my father or one of my brothers to break you in pieces. If you think you can come here, a married man, and play you are single—and make love to me and other girls, you've got another guess coming." She stamped her foot. "I think you are detestable. Get out of my sight, you—worm."

Lamprey realized it was time to be going. "All right—all right, if that's the way you throw down an old friend. Nobody will listen to my side of this. I might as well go."

Anne watched him go swaggering out of the house, a raffish, shallow scamp without pride or bottom. Looking at him now, the marks of deterioration written clear on him, she could not understand the infatuation that had driven her to such folly. He looked not only weak but cheap, and she felt there must be something shoddy about herself to have been deceived by such obvious surface charms. He had not been as bad as this in the old days, but the seeds of degeneration must have been in him.

That she had been very young and credulous did not save her from her own condemnation. She had been brought up right, and had no business letting herself be swept away by a romantic illusion.

Bill Overstreet followed Lamprey to the blacksmith shop. He was only nineteen and he did not quite know what he ought to do about this. His lack of experience hampered him. Was this a case of least said soonest mended? Or ought he to sock the fellow on the jaw and lick the tar out of him when he hit back?

The smith had just finished shoeing the horse. Lamprey beckoned Bill to one side.

"Sorry Anne kicked up such a fuss in your house," he said. "She always was a firecracker. Expected a man to be a little plaster saint and not human. 'Course you and I know we can't all be preachers."

Bill looked at him and said nothing. He was still a victim of his own youth, both unsure and inarticulate.

"I've heard about her goings-on at Blanco with this fellow and Red Silcott and plenty of others. She's got a crust to talk that way to me."

"You'd better hit yore saddle and light out," Bill said gruffly.

"Don't you come that high-and-mighty stuff on me, Bill. I don't have to take it from you like I do from Betty."

"Leave my sister's name out of this. And don't ever mention it again."

"Come off your perch, kid. Betty and I—"

"Look out," warned Bill, his fists clenched.

"Rats! Your sister—"

Young Overstreet let go his right to the chin. Lamprey went down and stayed down.

"What'd you do that for?" he whimpered. "I wasn't saying anything—"

"If you don't want to fight, fork yore bronc and hit the

trail," Bill ordered.

Lamprey climbed to the saddle and rode away.

Chapter Fourteen: AT THE HAT T

ANNE FELT HUMILIATED. She had thought it best to speak openly of her marriage to Jesse Lamprey in order to relieve her of future embarrassment, but she had not intended to be drawn into a quarrel with him or even into a defense of her position. When she learned through the ranch cook, a little Mexican named Juan, that Bill had knocked Lamprey down at the corral she was distressed. It meant more publicity she did not want.

But Betty was distinctly pleased. She told her brother so when he came into the house for supper.

"Good for you, Bill. He'll learn not to go around like a wolf in sheep's clothing making up to girls when he is married."

Bill felt awkward about it. He was not proud about having hit a man who refused to fight.

"I told him I was gonna hit him," he explained apologetically. "There wasn't any fight. I just let loose at him once."

"What had he said?" Betty asked.

He looked at her severely. It was his opinion that his sister was too free and easy with the boys. She flirted with them and led them on, then quashed her beaux when they began to take liberties. If he were in Bar Overstreet's place he would put his foot down.

"Never mind what he said. It's finished. Juan had better learn to keep his mouth shut."

After supper, while they were sitting before the open fire in the big living-room, Anne brought the conversation round to Jim Silcott's dam and asked Bar Overstreet if he thought Mosely would dare destroy it.

Bar eased his big body in the chair which it filled and pointed a question at his guest.

"What makes you think he has got any such idea, Miss Eliot?" the cattleman asked, his voice high and squeaky.

She told him about the visit Pesky Kennedy had paid to the office of the *Sentinel*.

"You don't think Pesky was just trying to stir up trouble?" Bar said. "Russ fired him from the Hat T and Jud Prentiss gave him an awful beating."

Anne was surprised that Bar knew of this so soon. She had yet to learn with what rapidity news spreads in a country where inhabitants are few and far between. She shook her head decisively.

"No, I'm sure he wasn't. He was honestly warning Mr. Silcott. Both of them left at once to go to the Diamond Slash. They must be up there or at the dam now."

Bar drummed with his fingertips on the arm of the chair. "Answering your question, Miss Eliot, I'll say that Russ Mosely has nerve enough to go through on anything he tackles, but usually he is pretty careful what he does."

His oldest son Richard, a tall, broad-shouldered, rangy man, added a dry explanation. "Careful to keep under cover so dirty work can't be proved on him."

"I didn't say that, Dick," reproved Bar. It was his policy not to do much talking about the owner of the Hat T, except privately in the ear of somebody whom he could trust implicitly.

"You don't think, then, that he would blow up the dam?" Anne persisted.

"I wouldn't know about that. He claims he is on the side of law."

"That's one way of putting it," Rufe said. "I'd say that most of the law around these parts is on his side. He has it roped and hogtied."

"I want to see him while I'm up here," Anne told her

host. "Can you get me a guide to take me to the Hat T?"

"I reckon so. You'll have to ride across the ridge. There's no wagon road." He considered for a moment. "Some of us aren't exactly welcome at the Hat T. Dick and I are barred. So is Rufe." His gaze dwelt on the younger son. "Bill can take you. If he wants to go. He hasn't been mixed up yet in any trouble with the Hat T riders."

"Sure. I'll go," Bill volunteered cheerfully. He knew an attractive girl when he saw one.

"After that I want to go to the Diamond Slash," Anne mentioned. "Shall we have to come back here? Or can we cut across to it?"

"Either way. You'd gain some time by going direct."

Anne had brought some riding clothes in her valise. When she appeared in them next morning Rufe thought he had never seen a more attractive rider. She sat her horse well, a trim, light figure of grace.

Jelks rode with them a part of the way. He stopped at a cross-trail to say good-by. "Be seeing you this evening at the Diamond Slash," he told them. "Hope you convert Russ to peaceful and decent ways."

The mountain range ran sharp and jagged back of the Hat T Ranch. In the early morning the peaks were edged with crimson against a sun just beginning to show above the horizon. Later they took on the more sober tints of prosaic day. But when Anne saw them in late afternoon, on her way back from the Hat T Ranch, pools of lilac lay in the gorges, to be succeeded by a flaming sunset of opal and turquoise set in a lake of fiery crimson.

Russell Mosely was at home when they reached the ranch steading. He was very much surprised to see Miss Eliot, but did not let it show in his manner.

"You'll stay for dinner, of course," he said. "It will be ready in half an hour. Till then I'll show you over the place." He turned to a stableboy. "Take care of the horses,

Pete. And afterward see that this young man gets dinner with you and the other boys."

If he was curious about the reason for her visit he showed no sign of it. He was all friendliness and ease. She liked the way he walked, carrying his strong, muscular body with strength and lightness. He went bareheaded, the broad Stetson hat in his hand. Perhaps this was to show better his well-shaped head covered with thick, wavy brown hair.

Anne was surprised at the disorder she saw all around her. The fences were well built and the gates strong. There was a new windmill in the corral. She caught glimpses of expensive machinery in some sheds. The Hat T was a prosperous going outfit, and its owner was very well off. Yet there was an appearance almost of squalor in the place. The buildings had been flung up hurriedly, without any regard to good looks, and there seemed to be no decent pride of ownership. On the porch of the main house was a litter of odds and ends, apparently dropped there by the last user. Her glance picked up a saddle, a pair of muddy boots, a pail half full of water, some rivets, a broken bridle, and an old newspaper. It was the same all over the place—wagon wheels, an empty box, a saddle blanket hanging on a fence, a pair of torn overalls.

Mosely guessed at the criticism in the young woman's mind. "Not very neat, is it?" he said apologetically. "I've been so busy building up the ranch that I haven't found time to curry the Hat T yet."

Since he seemed to ask for a suggestion she made one. "I'd think you could work so much more efficiently with order around you." She did not mention beauty. There was not a flower on the place. Its ugliness was appalling.

He shrugged his broad shoulders complacently. "That will come in time. I'm going to make this the show place of the country." His cool gray eyes rested on her. "The Hat T needs a mistress. I'll have to see about that."

"Make a note to attend to it some day when you have time," she said gaily, and changed the subject by asking him how large the ranch was. He let her deflect his mind, for he liked to talk about his success.

It was as they were returning from their little tour of inspection that he referred to their last meeting. He mentioned it with a smile, warm and genial.

"I'm all the more glad to see you, Miss Eliot, because we parted a little edgeways at each other," he said. "I don't want that. It is important to me to have your friendship. You have come more than halfway to meet me this time. Let me go all the way to you at our next meeting. I know you have heard evil things about me. Let me have a chance to remove that bad impression."

She nodded, smiling at him. "I'm so glad you feel that way. I don't want to be among your enemies. In fact, I wish you didn't have any."

"That can't be helped," he told her. "Any man who is strong makes enemies. It is only weaklings without any backbone who have none. Take this land-grant fight. If I enforce my rights—as I mean to do—I make foes of the squatters who are sitting on the land without valid titles."

"I suppose so." After a moment of hesitation Anne said what was in her mind. "Do you have to take their land from them? I've just been told the old Hat T Ranch is a big one, not counting the acreage in dispute."

"I'm not taking their land but my land from them," he said curtly. "Why shouldn't I, if the courts decide in my favor? I need a big range to carry out my plans. It is not my fault that they bought from those who did not own what they sold."

"Are you going to wait until the court decision is given?" she asked.

He looked at her sharply. "What d'you mean? Of course I am."

"I'm glad of that." She hurried on, before her courage cooled. "I came to see you because I heard a story I don't want to believe."

"Yes?" he said warily, and waited.

"I heard you intend to blow up Jim Silcott's dam."

Astonished, he stared at her. "Where did you hear that?" he wanted to know.

"It doesn't matter where. Word came to me that you had bought dynamite and that you had sent men up there to see how it could best be done."

She faced him, slenderly erect, her eyes demanding of him the truth.

"Did Silcott send you here?"

"No. He doesn't know I am here."

He laughed, harshly, without mirth. "Just came on your own, out of the goodness of your heart, to save me from doing wrong."

"You once came to ask me not to do something," she reminded him.

"And you told me, politely, to mind my own business," he countered.

"Now you can get even." Her smile was shy and placatory. "But I hope you won't. I'm interfering in what isn't my business, but it's because I want to try and bring peace."

"All right. I'll give you an answer. You haven't the least idea as to the right and wrong of this fight. Your misinformation comes from men of no standing—lawless troublemakers. This man Silcott's dam, to take a specific point, has no business to be there. He has impounded water that ought to run freely down the creek. If I want to abate a nuisance I have a perfect right to do so. Mind you, I'm not admitting for a moment that I mean to do so. I'm merely showing you how absurd your position is."

Anne knew she had failed. He spoke with the confident arrogance of one whose decision is not to be questioned. But she would not give up yet.

"I have tried to be fair in the paper," she said. "Did you object to the way the *Sentinel* covered the Sneve killing?"

"No. You might have handled the story worse. But you are against me editorially."

"Not against you personally," she corrected. "Against your policy."

"It comes to the same thing." He brushed the whole thing aside impatiently. "Well, let's go in and have some dinner."

The man interested her, chiefly because of the egocentric force in him. He was masterful, and always would be. Listening to him as he talked, she was convinced that he would go far. No fastidious scruples would restrain him. She guessed that he had political ambitions, national rather than local. Though he seemed to be frank, Anne suspected hidden currents of thought in him not declared. He was impervious, she felt, to a recognition of rights of others which ran contrary to his own. His talk ranged over many subjects. That he was well informed was plain, but out of his rounded phrases dropped queer little hints of moral callousness of which he was unaware.

Standing on the porch with him while the horses were being brought up, Anne made a last attempt to reach the man. "It's been nice meeting you again," she said. "Even though I don't understand you."

"Time enough for that." he told her blandly, with a confident smile. "We're going to know each other very well. By the way, just what is it you don't understand? Perhaps I can explain myself."

"You have large ideas—great ambitions. You are going to travel a long way—if you don't trip yourself."

"What do you mean—trip myself?"

She tilted an impudent grin at him. "You won't like it if I go on."

"Let's have it."

"You're a big man, strong, forceful, dominant. You could do so much for yourself and for this Western country. But I'm not sure you will. You have let yourself get twisted."

"How?"

"By not considering the rights of others. I daresay it's cheeky of me to say so. But it's true. You're going to hamper yourself terribly. A person can't be petty about some things and big about others."

He flushed resentfully. "I'll tell you something, Miss Eliot. You've fallen among thieves. Until you cut loose from them your opinion won't be important."

"I was afraid you would take it that way," Anne said. "Well, good-by. We don't seem to do anything but quarrel, do we?"

Bill Overstreet had come up with the horses and was waiting for her.

Mosely said, recovering his smile, "It's the last thing I want to do with you. A young woman as charming and beautiful as you ought not to be be so wrong-headed. I'm going to make it my business to teach you better."

As Anne gathered the reins to mount she looked back over her shoulder. "Did you ever hear about the blind leading the blind?" she asked.

A moment later she and Bill were moving across the plaza at a road gait.

Chapter Fifteen: A PREMATURE FOURTH OF JULY

JIM SILCOTT AND PESKY KENNEDY sat beside a campfire drinking strong black coffee and eating flapjacks and bacon. On this mountain ledge, far above the valley, the night had been cold. But neither of them complained of that. They were used to extremities of weather. They had many times ridden out blizzards, dust storms, and desert heat. Both of them knew what it was to have been caught on a baked sahara of blistering sand with empty canteens.

After they had eaten they stamped out the fire. In the east the sky was beginning to lighten. Soon the sun would come up and dissipate the mists which blanketed the hills, and they did not want any drift of telltale smoke to warn the enemy of their proximity.

On the previous day they had scouted the country and located Pete Yeager's camp. It was in a hill pocket half a mile from the dam. Stationed among the rocks above it, they had looked down and watched Pete cooking his supper. He had been alone. That he was there for mischief was clear. There were no Hat T stock in this wild region of tiptilted strata. Soon he would be joined by others. No doubt he had spied out the land for them.

The sun showed over the horizon and began to climb the arch. The mists thinned. With a pair of field glasses Silcott scanned the panorama below. There were still pools of obscurity where the haze lingered, but over on Hardscrabble Range the sun had driven away all shadows.

"I see them," Jim called to his companion.

Pesky joined him, and was handed the glasses. "Just coming out of the valley. See? On the second ridge to the left." Jim pointed in the direction indicated.

"I've got 'em, Red," Pesky said, his eyes glued to the glasses. "You were right. Only two of them—and a pack horse with the dynamite. Mosely doesn't want to tip his hand to too many."

"No. When he's made his pile, R. M. is going to turn respectable as hell. He's a smooth worker. Right now he is

a fine example of a good citizen whose right hand doesn't
know what his left does. One of these days he will marry,
a lady who will be a credit to him in the high circles where
he aims to be an ornament, and he doesn't want any
chickens coming home to roost then. I'll bet these lads
coming to do his dirty work can't prove Russ sent them."

"You'd win that bet," the crook-nosed man with the
rusty hair answered bitterly. "He drops a hint to Jud
Prentiss, who works out the details and passes on the
scheme to picked scalawags. If anything goes wrong Mosely
will be grieved in public and will give them fits in private."

"We might as well saddle and drift down," Silcott suggested. "No hurry. We'll take our time."

They traveled a rough country of steep rocky hillslopes,
narrow draws, and high ledges. Both of them knew the
country as well as Jim did the make-up of the *Sentinel,* and
though they changed directions fifty times to follow the
line of least resistance they did not lose an unnecessary
twenty yards. As they came closer to Yeager's camp they
grew more wary. There was no likelihood of any Hat T
men being up here, but they were taking no chances of
being betrayed by their own negligence.

"Better light here and tie, Red," Pesky said at last.

"Yes," agreed his companion. "Not more than two-three
hundred yards from here to our observation point."

They fastened their mounts and moved forward on
foot through a fringe of small pines growing in a boulder
ᵒld. There was a chance that Yeager was to meet his allies
ﾒ e dam, but it seemed hardly likely. The party would
   show there in a body until the place had been scouted
ﾒ ake sure it was deserted. None the less they were
 ·eved to see the fat little Hat T rider busily preparing
ﾒreakfast.

"Getting ready for his company," Pesky said. He spoke
ﾒost in a whisper, though the camp was fifty yards below

them.

"Looks like. They'll be hungry after their long ride in the dark. I reckon coffee and grub will go fine."

Yeager stopped work to roll and light a cigarette.

"Wisht I could have one, but I expect I better wait," Kennedy grumbled.

"Yes, Pesky. As a member of the reception committee you have got to deny yourself that pleasure temporarily."

Long before the Hat T reinforcements came in sight the watchers in the rocks could hear the sound of their horses' hoofs striking rocks. Out of an aspen draw a rider emerged, followed by a led pack horse and a second man.

Pete waved at them a big spoon. "Come and get it, brothers," he called.

The first rider dismounted, turned his horse loose with grounded bridle, and gave his attention to the pack animal. The load was fastened with a diamond hitch, which he released very carefully while the other man held the reins close to the mouth.

"Not taking any chances of jarring the dynamite," Pesky said in the ear of his ally, "Frosty is the fellow at the reins. The other is Roan Judson."

The two men carried the sacks to a grassy spot close to the aspens. The three horses they picketed. After passing a bottle around, from which each of the men took a drink, they sat down to eat breakfast.

No snatch of their conversation reached the two hidden among the rocks above. During the meal the bottle w . from hand to hand more than once. They ate hurri. and as soon as they had finished Judson and Yeager dled and departed.

"The reception committee had better get into ac. now, don't you reckon?" Jim murmured.

They drew back among the rocks and detoured to small gulch leading down to the park. This the scended carefully, Silcott in the van. As they drew closer to the park they redoubled their precautions against being heard. Frosty was cleaning the frying-pan, the coffee-pot, and the tin dishes. He had his back to them and was singing, very much off key, a cowboy song.

Sift along, boys; don't ride so slow.
Haven't got much time but a long round to go.
Quirt him on the shoulders and rake him down the hip,
I've cut you toppy mounts, boys, now pair off and rip.
Bunch the herd at the old meet,
Then beat 'em on the tail.
Whip 'em up and down the side
And hit the shortest trail.

"Why be in such a hurry, Frosty?" Silcott asked gently, drawling the words. "You've got all day, haven't you? And maybe not such a long trail to ride, either."

The man swung round, astonished beyond words. He stared at Jim, jaw slack and eyes dilated.

"Why—why, what are you doing here?" he gulped out.

"That's strange," Silcott said. "I was just going to ask you that."

The trapped man knew the scheme to blow up the dam had met an unexpected obstacle. He must not let Silcott guess why he was here, and he must get him and Pesky out of the way before the return of his companions. There was something about the editor's manner he did not like, a hint of grim purpose that was disturbing. But he told himself he was jumpy without any real cause, even though these men with rifles in their hands were enemies of the Hat T. They were probably just out on a hunting trip. He suggested this to himself and did not believe it. Silcott and Kennedy were not birds of a feather. They were not even friends. Some common purpose other than pleasure had brought them together.

"I knocked off a couple of days to get a buck," Frosty explained. "Got kinda tired of beef three times a day."

"That's fine," Silcott said heartily. "Pesky and I are hunting too. We'll throw in with you. If you're alone?"

The last words were flung out abruptly. The Hat T man hesitated. He did not want to tell too much, but on the other hand it would not do to be caught lying.

"A couple of other fellows with me," he said reluctantly.

"Boys from the ranch?" Kennedy inquired.

"Why, yes. Yeager and Judson. Work is kinda slack right now and we could get off."

Pesky snorted, with harsh skepticism. "Jud must have had a change of heart mighty recent. Mosely too. I worked for the outfit three years and never saw a hand get a day off for hunting."

"If you don't see a buck I reckon you would as soon shoot a dam," Silcott said.

The Hat T man slid an apprehensive eye at him. He was not in a happy enough frame of mind to enjoy puns. Somebody must have got word to Silcott what was afoot.

"I dunno what you mean, Red," he said sulkily.

"No go, Frosty," Jim's voice had abruptly hardened. "You know why we are here, just as we do why you are. Take his gun, Pesky. He might get notions."

Frosty was older than most punchers. He had been riding for fifteen years and had taken many falls. As a result of a broken leg from one of these he walked a little lame. His thin brown face was seamed with wrinkles, and the eyes that looked out of it were faded to a skim-milk blue from squinting at several thousand blazing suns.

"Now looky here, boys," he protested. "You got me wrong. I dunno what's eatin' you. There's no reason for you to take my gun away. I may be a Hat T hand, but that don't mean I'm any friend of Russ Mosely."

"You don't need to tell us that," Kennedy said, relieving him of his forty-five and making sure he carried no other weapon. "That weasel wouldn't be a friend of a thirty-dollar-a-month cowpoke. Or of anyone else except for what was in it for himself, by God."

"You know me, Pesky. You can tell Red I'm all right."

"Yeah, I know you," the crook-nosed man growled. "You're one of Jud's 'Y' betcha' men. Ready to run on any of his dirty errands when he cracks the whip."

"Nothing to that, Pesky," the other cowboy protested. "I don't aim to have any trouble with him, seeing I'm no scrapper. But Jud don't mean a thing to me." He explained to Silcott, with a propitiatory smile, "I'm all stove up with this busted leg and ain't the top hand I usta be, so I got to take any job I can get."

"We'd better get busy," Jim said. "You come along with us, Frosty, and don't make the mistake of trying to light out. If you do, you'll be stove up in both legs. We have no doctor here to dig out the lead. So you'd better mosey along easy just ahead of us."

"I won't be a mite of trouble," the man promised.

"Before we start the fireworks you had better turn loose those horses and drive them away so that they won't get hurt, Pesky."

"That's right." Kennedy walked to the horses and freed them. With a heavy rope across their flanks he started them galloping out of the pocket.

"You're not going to leave me afoot," Frosty said, disturbed at the prospect.

"Maybe your friends will give you a lift, Don't worry about the future, Frosty. Live happily in the present." Silcott pointed to the gunny sacks. "Hoist one of them on your shoulder and carry it to the bluff. Better not stumble, for if you jounce the contents too much we'll both go to Kingdom Come."

Frosty did as he was told. At the suggestion of the Diamond Slash man he repeated the trip.

Jim inspected the face of the cliff. "This spot ought to do," he said, and knelt down in front of a V-shaped hollow at the base of two great boulders leaning against each other.

He packed the sticks of powder carefully and arranged a fuse.

"Better start up the gulch, Pesky," he advised. "I'll be joining you in a minute on the jump. We'll have time to reach the top and take shelter behind some rocks."

Jim lit the fuse and ran to the gulch. He hurried up this, and when he reached the top saw the other two men running into the boulder field. Even though Frosty limped, he was making good time. Silcott caught up with him just as he ducked behind the flat edge of a sloping slab of granite.

They had not been there more than a minute when a terrific explosion sent a hundred rocks hurtling into the air. A shower of them landed in the boulder field.

The sheltered men emerged from cover.

"Tell Russ Mosely we enjoyed his fireworks," Silcott told the prisoner. "Only next time he had better come and enjoy them himself."

"Make that double for Jud Prentiss too," Kennedy add vindictively. "I owe that wolf plenty, and I aim to pay in full one of these days."

Jim led the way down the gulch. He knew that the other two Hat T men would come hurrying back to find out what had set off the explosion, and he wanted to be there to meet them. The three men waited back of a fringe of bushes near the entrance of the gulch.

Presently they heard the sound of galloping horses. Yeager and Judson came crashing through the aspens and pulled up to view the shattered rocks scattered all over the pocket.

"My God!" Judson cried. "The dynamite must have exploded somehow and blown Frosty to bits."

Silcott stepped out from the bushes, rifle in hand. "Glad to relieve your mind, Roan," he said. "Frosty had a grandstand seat where he could see the fireworks fine."

Prodded by Kennedy, Frosty emerged from the brush. The two on horseback stared at them and at Silcott, so completely taken aback that they had not a word to say.

"A little surprised to see us, boys?" the Diamond Slash man said. "We're up here having a look-see at my dam, just as a matter of form. I gather from Frosty that you are hunting bucks—without rifles. It's sure sporting of you to go after them with six-shooters."

"We're lookin' for strays," Yeager said. "Any objections?"

"Did you aim to blow them back to their own range with dynamite?" Jim wanted to know, his drawling voice loaded with sarcasm.

Roan Judson was a long, stoop-shouldered man with a yellow, jaundiced face. "I don't get this," he snapped. "Who set off the powder? And why?"

"Oh, we did that," Silcott told him cheerfully. "Pesky and I. Wasn't that all right? Didn't you bring it here to be set off?"

"It wasn't your powder," Judson persisted, splenetic anger in his voice. "What right had you to touch it?"

"We found it here," Jim answered, bland innocence in his manner. "And when we decided on the fireworks Frosty didn't object. Did you, Frosty?"

The wrinkled little man with the skim-milk eyes yelped an explosive reply. "They kept me covered with their damn rifles."

"It's all right with you boys about us playin' Fourth of July, ain't it?" Kennedy wanted to know, a chip on his shoulder.

Pete Yeager's high-colored face looked apopletic. "Thought Russ told you to get outa this part of the country, Pesky," he snarled.

"Do you think Russ Mosely is God Almighty?" Kennedy inquired angrily. "He never saw the day he could order me to cut my stick."

Frosty volunteered information. "They claim we was going to use the dynamite to blow up Red's dam."

"Who told 'em that?" Yeager quizzed, challenging eyes on the man who had been left at camp.

"I dunno." Frosty glared at the fat, bald-headed rider. "Don't you look at me thataway, Pete. I didn't tell 'em a thing. Ask 'em. Ask Pesky—or Red."

"That's right," Silcott assented. "I wouldn't want to start hard feeling in a happy family like the Hat T. A little bird whispered it to me, Pete."

"Yeah? Well, I want to tell you that you've got yoreself up to the neck in trouble, fellow," Judson predicted.

Jim laughed, undisturbed. "Not news, Roan, but I'm in no deeper than I was before. Friend Pete here was in at a little party where I was the target. There was a little hitch in it, but Russ will try to see it goes off better next time. Pete's intentions were good, but he and the other boys had been tanking up some."

"You were lucky," Yeager said with an oath. "It ought to have been you and not Buck that was carried into the Grub Stake and buried."

"That's right," agreed Silcott. "A man trapped in an ambush, with five men against him, hasn't any license to expect he can rub one of them out and make his getaway safe. It was sure enough gilt-edged luck."

"If you claim it was an ambush, that's a lie," Yeager retorted bluntly. "Buck Sneve saw you crossing the street and started pluggin' at you."

"Seems to me if I was you I'd keep my mouth shut about that fuss, Pete," advised Pesky. "Four-five of you jumped him when he wasn't lookin' and he had the best of it. Why shouldn't he rub you out now when he has you covered?"

Yeager was a hardy ruffian. He continued to chew tobacco undisturbed while he mentally measured the distance between himself and Silcott. Too far for accurate shooting with a forty-five, he decided, but a good shot like Silcott could hardly miss with his rifle. Deliberately he moved his horse closer and drew up eight or ten yards from the Diamond Slash owner.

"Any time Red wants to turn his wolf loose on me it's all right," he said quietly. "The sooner the quicker. But before he begins I'll tell you, Pesky, that when I reach for my cutter I don't need anybody to back my play. Buck went crazy with the heat and started the trouble at Blanco. I wasn't in it till Buck got to shooting."

Silcott looked at the fat, bald-headed puncher and shook his head reprovingly, as if he had been a bad boy. "Naughty, naughty, Pete. If you go around hunting trouble that way some time you'll bump into a citizen who isn't quiet and peaceable like me, and you'll find it sitting right in your lap. About that Blanco business, I'll take your word for it. It was a crazy mix-up. Russ let you know that when he read you the riot act after you got home. He doesn't have his killings done that way. You'll have to get it in your nut that he wants publicity for his support of the church and other civic enterprises and privacy for all the hell he scatters. By the way, you might tell him when you get home, if he starts to ride you for the way this job turned out, that he has nobody but himself to blame. He gave himself away. Pass the word to him that he ought to play his hand closer to his belly."

"How do you mean he gave it away?" demanded Judson.

"Never mind how. He was trying to pull a fast one and wasn't slick enough."

"We'll tell him plenty," Yeager said vindictively. This defeat rankled. It was so unexpected and so complete. He did not see that he had been to blame for the failure, and he intended to tell Prentiss just what Silcott had said. Jud would be furious, and so would Mosely. The big boss had a mania for success in anything he undertook. It would not please him to know that everybody in the district, would be laughing at him. When Russ pulled his lawless, high-handed dramatics he expected to get away with them.

"I expect you are busy. It has been nice meeting you, but we must not keep you too long." Silcott turned his white-toothed grin on them. "If you're going hunting deer with your forty-fives, as Frosty says, you're liable to have a long day ahead of you. Or if it's strays you are after, as Pete claims, you'll probably want to start on a couple of broomtails that hightailed it out of here just before the fireworks began. They were going fast when we saw them last."

"Where are your broncs?" Judson asked.

"Ours? Oh, don't worry about us. We won't have to drag it fifteen miles on foot. Well, *adios,* boys. Don't take any wooden quarters in change."

Yeager went reluctantly. He would have liked to do something to build himself up in his own and others' esteem, but he knew he would have to postpone this. He would gain nothing by a fight. Silcott and Kennedy were watching every move the Hat T men made, and even at this distance their rifles would be far more accurate than revolvers.

"Don't laugh too long," Pete warned. "You're top dogs right now, but this war hasn't begun yet."

Frosty climbed astride of Judson's horse. The Hat T

men disappeared into the aspen draw. The two left in the pocket could hear them threshing through the young growth after they were out of sight.

"Better get back to our horses," Pesky said. "Roan seemed to have them on his mind."

Silcott agreed. They climbed the gulch and crossed the boulder field to the young pines where they had left their mounts. Presently they were in the saddle and on their way back to the Diamond Slash.

Chapter Sixteen: ANNE EXPLAINS

WHEN RUFE JELKS AND BAR OVERSTREET reached the Diamond Slash they found nobody at home except a Mexican vaquero who was topping some colts in the corral. From him they learned that Silcott and Kennedy had reached the ranch on the previous afternoon but had stopped only long enough to get fresh mounts. No, they had not said where they were going. But they carried rifles, so it was possible they were out looking for a buck.

"We better ride up to the dam," Rufe suggested, grinning at his companion. "Maybe we might see a buck too."

They were relieved to find the dam intact and the waters of the lake back of it unruffled.

"Where do we go from here?" Overstreet asked.

"I wouldn't know," Rufe said. "Unless we go back to the Diamond Slash and wait there for a spell. Maybe this is all a mare's-nest cooked up in Pesky Kennedy's imagination."

"Might be," the big man agreed. "Or it might not. I'd hate to have this dam go out. I helped Red build it, and I use water from it for my alfalfa and my orchard. It's just one of the dirty tricks Russ Mosely would pull, to ruin a man's property when he isn't looking and can't prove it on him."

"I reckon Red is scouting these hills to make sure none of the Hat T *lobos* are holed up here." Rufe rolled and lit a cigarette. "But we probably wouldn't find him if we hunted all day. Might as well go down to the ranch."

They jogged down the trail, not very pleased with the situation. They wanted to see Silcott, to offer him help if he needed any. Yet there was nothing they could do about it but wait.

The fences of the ranch were in sight when the sound of an explosion pulled them up short. Jelks and Overstreet looked at each other, the same question in both their minds. Could the Hat T men have blown up the dam after all? This did not look reasonable. It was not a quarter of an hour since they had left the dam, and they had seen no sign of activity. But it was even less likely that somebody was firing dynamite aimlessly in these far hills.

The two riders turned their horses' heads back up the trail. When they came in sight of the dam they saw it had not been injured. The place was as deserted as it had been when they left.

"Couldn't have been a rifle we heard?" Rufe hazarded, and already knew the answer.

"No. A rifle never sounded like that. It sure has got me guessing." The big man looked worried. "I won't be easy in my mind till I see Red safe and sound."

They tried shouting, and their voices echoed back to them. Rufe fired his Winchester and received no answer.

"Maybe we had better ride circle and see if we cut any sign," he proposed.

Before they had gone three.hundred yards they heard the sound of horses' hoofs striking rock. Slowly they moved forward, their rifles across the saddle horns.

Two men came into sight. Rufe flung out a yell· of relief.

"You doggoned old vinegaroon, what's the idea of scaring us to death?" he shouted.

Silcott waved a hand at him. He and Kennedy rode up to the others.

"That you who fired a rifle a little while ago?" he asked.

"Yes." Jelks countered with another question. "That you who blew off a charge of dynamite?"

To his great surprise Jim answered that it was. "You ought to have seen the rocks fly, Rufe."

His friend looked at him suspiciously. "What you been up to, you old scalawag? You look like the cat that has just ate the cream."

"Why, I just told you," Silcott said, very innocently. "We just had some fireworks. Ask Pesky."

Kennedy did not wait to be asked. "The Hat T boys are headin' home with bad news for Jud and Russ," he answered jubilantly.

"You met them?" Overstreet queried.

"Sure we met 'em, and sent 'em home with their tails between their legs."

"Have a fight?" Rufe inquired.

"No. All quiet along the Potomac." Silcott added an explanation, "We were looking for them and they weren't expecting to meet us. That made a difference."

"You jumped them before they got to the dam?" Rufe suggested.

"We located Pete Yeager's camp yesterday in a hill pocket, and early this morning picked up two other riders and a pack horse on the way to join him. So we hung around above the camp till Yeager beat it with one of the Hat T men, I reckon to look the ground over and make sure nobody was there. Then we dropped in on the other man, a fellow called Frosty, and had the celebration right there instead of at the dam. I expect Russ Mosely won't like it. He's a saving soul, and he'll probably think we wasted a lot of dynamite with no results. But you can't please all the people all the time, as Abraham Lincoln would probably have said if he had thought of it. So Russ will have to make the best of it, and charge that powder to profit and loss."

Jim said his little piece with bland innocence. Rufe flung up his hat and whooped. His laughter came back to him from the rock wall in front of the party. When he had sufficiently recovered he agreed with Silcott in a voice weak from mirth.

"No, Russ won't like it, but the Powder Horn country will. Oh, very much. You darned old horn toad, I never did see yore beat. If the Hat T gets rambunctious any time, a fellow will just have to suggest it go blow up a dam. That ought to put the snuffer on it."

Bar Overstreet's merriment had been less exuberant than Rufe's, and it did not last as long.

"That would be fine if Russ Mosely felt so about his little defeat," he said, rubbing his stubby chin reflectively. "But I've noticed that Russ hasn't much of a sense of humor except when he is at the right end of the joke. This is going to hurt his prestige. A dictator has got to win every time. He'll be mad all the way down to his boot heels. What he is liable to do is put the snuffer on Red. I'm not making any charges, gentlemen, but—don't forget what happened to Carl Rogers when he got too annoying."

Jim said blithely, "The bullet hasn't been molded yet that can kill me. And anyhow, we'll not get anywhere worrying about it. If there's no new business I move we adjourn to the Diamond Slash."

They ate a late dinner at the ranch. When they had finished, Overstreet said he must be getting home. He had just swung his heavy body to the saddle when two riders came round the corner of the pasture fence. One of them was a young woman. Silcott stared at her incredulously.

"I forgot to mention that Miss Eliot came up with me to Tincup to drum up subscribers to the *Sentinel*," Rufe revealed.

"What for?" Jim scoffed at the assigned reason for the visit. "She already has everybody up here. Does she want us to subscribe twice?"

"She didn't tell me about that." Jelks drew his friend aside. "Say, something funny came up yesterday. We met Jess Lamprey here, making up to Betty Overstreet. When he saw Miss Eliot he was plumb confused. He sure had a license to be, for it came out presently that he is her husband and that he deserted her when he drifted to the Powder Horn country."

Jim could hardly believe it, though he saw that Jelks was serious. "Jess Lamprey's wife. Are you sure?"

"That's what she said. She told Jess she didn't ever want to see him again. I'm putting you wise so you'll understand if anything about it comes up."

Bill Overstreet helped Anne to dismount. Her eyes swept the group and rested on Silcott.

"Mr. Mosely told me he doesn't intend to do anything about making trouble for the claimants under the Aguilar grant until the courts have decided in his favor," she announced.

"That's nice of him," Jim answered, with gentle irony. "Did you see him in town?"

"No. At his ranch. Bill and I had dinner there today. We just came from the Hat T."

"So he promised you not to molest any of us, unless and until he beats us in court," murmured Silcott.

Pesky laughed, with bitter disbelief.

"He didn't exactly say that." Anne frowned, trying to find words to convey precisely the impression she had received. "I wasn't very well satisfied with what he said about the dam. He made the point that he has a legal right to abate a nuisance, but he wouldn't admit that he meant to do it."

"By jiminy, he has his nerve!" Bar Overstreet exploded. "Why, the smooth rascal had already sent his men up to dynamite it."

Anne looked at the big ranchman, startled. "Has he blown up the dam?"

"Not his fault he hasn't. Red and Pesky stopped them."

The gaze of the young woman swept back to Jim. "Was there a fight?"

The owner of the Diamond Slash shook his head. "Nothing like that. Everything peaceable. We had a little talk."

Since she was now a newspaper woman, Anne did not rest content with that tame explanation. She asked questions and learned the facts.

"He'll try again, won't he?" she said.

"We don't think so," Overstreet replied. "He knows now we are on our guard."

"Mr. Mosely doesn't look to me like the kind of man who will give up because of one defeat," Anne persisted.

"Probably he'll try something else next time," Silcott contributed lightly.

"Such as what?"

"Nobody knows." He diverted the conversation in another direction. "It is pleasant to see you here in the Tincup country, Miss Eliot. We hope you find the scenery all we promised."

"Yes, it's fine," she said automatically, her mind not on the answer.

She was thinking of Russell Mosely as she had seen him two hours earlier, a man strong and ruthless, intent on driving to his ends without regard to others' rights or the difficulties in the way. These men were trying to cry down the danger because she was a woman and must not be alarmed. She was not going to be fubbed off. As well as they did, she knew that the Hat T boss would be furious at this setback and would not rest until he had regained his prestige.

Apparently she dropped the matter from her mind. But she contrived to have Rufe Jelks ride down with the Overstreets to their ranch on the pretext that she wanted to see the dam. Jim would escort her there later. Rufus took the hint and departed. Pesky Kennedy was to stay at the Diamond Slash.

It was not until they reached the dam that Anne moved to the attack. "It's a little humiliating after I told you I didn't need your help any longer, Jim," she said. "Bu' I don't know enough yet to bring out the paper alone. I can see I'm going to get all worried and disturbed about it, because I do so want to make a success of the job. I want you to give another month to teaching me. Of course that's asking a great deal of you. I know that."

A whimsical quirk twisted Silcott's lips. "Now, I wonder what this song and dance means," he mused aloud. "Two-three days ago she was quite sure she could get along without me, and she was eager to try her hand alone. But now it's the other way. Without my advice she is sunk. There's something that doesn't meet the eye, Jim. Watch out."

"Can't I change my mind when I find I was wrong?"

"You can and you have, but not because you think you need me so much. I reckon it's Mosely that's on your mind. You still feel responsible for not letting him get me. Just to put you at ease I'll mention that I don't intend to let him rub me out."

"How can you help it when you ride around the country unprotected, as you are doing this very minute?" Anne flung out. "For all you know somebody may be standing back of that mound waiting to shoot you."

"I noticed the back of it when we came round the bend," he demurred with a smile.

"You're perfectly reckless, if you want to know what I think. That's why Rufe came up here, to watch over you."

He took several minutes to show her this was not the case. An oldtimer, by reason of long usage, saw everything in the landscape that was suspicious. If a bush looked too dense, if there was a fresh hoofprint on the trail, if birds rose in a flurry, he was instantly on his guard. Moreover, this particular spot was just now entirely safe. The enemy had been driven away, and there would be no return until the Hat T riders had consulted with their employer.

All of which did not convince her in the least. But she dropped that angle of argument and reverted to her need of his help.

"All right," he promised. "I'll come down two or three days in the middle of each week until you feel more sure of yourself."

This was not very satisfactory, but it was the best she could do. She knew he really was very busy with ranch affairs. If she had not been worrying about his safety she would not have considered drafting him for the paper.

On the way down from the ranch Anne asked him if Rufe had mentioned her marriage.

"Yes," he answered. "Just as you and Bill arrived at my place. He didn't have time to say much."

Her blue eyes looked directly at him. "I wasn't trying to deceive you into thinking I am a spinster," she said. "I'll explain, if you don't mind. Jesse and I ran away and got married one night. Nobody in town knew it, for he left to come here next day. I kept it a secret, meaning to tell people when he sent for me. But instead of doing that he stopped writing. My wounded pride kept me silent. I meant when I came West not to sail any longer under false pretenses. But I wasn't going to take Jesse's name, and I did not want to go around shouting that I was his wife. Folks might think I was trying to fasten myself on him. So I waited till I met him."

"That all seems quite reasonable," Jim told her gently.

"None of it is reasonable!" she cried. "I was a silly little fool ever to fall in love with him, if that is what it was. My people brought me up right. Why did I let him persuade me into a secret marriage? Looking back at it now, the whole thing seems incredible. Usually I'm a sensible person. Did you ever do some one wild thing that was perfectly crazy?"

"A score of them," he answered. "Something gets into my blood, and off I go at a tangent."

She rode in silence for a minute. He thought her the loveliest creature under heaven.

"Why have I told you this?" she went on. "After so many years of complete silence. I suppose I have to talk with someone about it just once, and you are the unlucky victim. Poor man!" She laughed, a little wildly, not sure whether she ought not to be scornful of herself for wearing her heart on her sleeve.

He said in a low voice, "I'm honored that you can tell me, Anne."

"Anyhow, you know I'm not trying to entrap you," she told him, the color beating into her cheeks. "I'm out of the market, for good. My bargain with destiny has been made. For as long as life lasts, Jesse told me yesterday. That's true, even though I don't intend that he will ever be more than a stranger to me again."

"Nobody can blame you for being bitter," Jim replied. "Bad luck like that ought not to come to any girl. I can only say that everybody here will respect you very highly, and that I hope you will take me for your friend."

"I would like that," she said simply, a little shyly.

Her slender, graceful figure, shoulders and hips in a straight vertical line, looked well in the saddle. Watching her, the delicate breathing color in her cheeks, the beautiful line of the round throat sweeping down to the shoulders, Silcott knew a sudden panic. The blood was pounding stormily in his veins. The glamour of her provoking beauty swept over him. Almost he pulled up his horse, in the sudden realization that he was in love.

Chapter Seventeen: RUSSELL MOSELY IS ANNOYED

DURING SUPPER at Ma Russell's boarding-house, all the paying guests present, Anne told the story of the dam dynamiting which didn't come off. Rumors of it had reached town, but this was the first authentic account. It was the sort of joke which the cow country relished, the defeat by shrewd mother wit and audacity of a grasping man who had overreached himself. The tale went all over town, and spread to the most lonesome ranch in the district. Jim Silcott had scored heavily, but the general opinion was that he would have to pay for his victory with his life. It might not be immediately. In spite of his intolerant arrogance Russell Mosely could be patient. He might decide that it would be good policy, on account of public opinion, to wait until after the laughter had died down and the dam episode was not in the thoughts of everybody.

Anne ran a squib in the *Sentinel:*

Three Hat T riders have invented a new way to hunt deer. They took a load of dynamite with them into the hills to frighten the game down into the lower country. Unfortunately they met two ranchmen who persuaded them to use the powder as fireworks for a premature Fourth of July. We hear the Hat T men will do their hunting in the good old way in future.

That was all, but most of the readers of the *Sentinel*
chuckled over it. One of them who did not was Russell
Mosely. He knew Anne Eliot was aware that this was his
defeat, that the Hat T men on the scene had been merely
his agents. She was rejoicing at his discomfiture, as were a
good many others. A pent-up fury boiled in him. He could
not take failure gracefully, even a temporary one. To feel
that he had lost prestige was galling. About popularity he
cared little, but he had to bolster the legend of his invin-
cibility. He had to let men know that those who dared
fight him went down to disaster. Particularly he wanted to
impress Anne. In spite of his flinty hardness, she had built
a fire within him. He wanted her gallant loveliness for his
own. There were a lot of fool ideas in her pretty head, but
he would sweep aside all that rubbish after he had won
her. Back of the hot desire burning in him was the assurance that her fine poised beauty would be a great asset to
him. She had the social graces he lacked. Her charm and
spirited vitality would make her immensely popular in
Santa Fé, Denver, and even in Washington, which would
react very favorably on his success. To lose ground with
her now was annoying. He would make it up with her
later, of course, since she was no fool and must know where
her bread was buttered. But even so it irritated him.

He was brooding over his setback, a heavy frown on his
handsome face, when Jud Prentiss came in with news.

"That fool woman—the one that runs the *Sentinel*—it
seems she's married to Jess Lamprey."

Mosely stopped jabbing the point of his pocket knife
into a piece of blotting paper and looked up.

"Who told you that lie?" he demanded, his eyes bleak
and cold.

Jud scowled at him. He did not like the manners of his
boss, any more than the Hat T hands liked his.

"All right," he growled. "If it's a lie, I'll drop the subject."

"Of course it's a lie. She would not marry that weak fool. I said, who told you?"

"Rusty. He just got in with supplies from Blanco. The whole town is talking about it. She told the boarders at Ma Russell's. But, like you say, she was probably lying." Jud gloated over his employer. In the back of his mind was a suspicion that Mosely was interested in this young woman. Jud had seen her, and was of opinion that she was not in a class with Betty Overstreet for looks. The foreman liked his girls big and bouncing and blooming. But if the Hat T owner fancied this Eliot woman, Jud was glad to hand him a jolt.

"Send Rusty here," Mosely ordered. "I want a report on his trip."

Rusty confirmed the story of Anne's marriage. He had heard it from several people. One of them was Kroelling, who boarded at Ma Russell's. The gambler had got it first hand from the girl herself in a public announcement at dinner.

"When did they get married?" Mosely asked, still incredulous. "Some lunkheads must have been running a sandy on you, Rusty. How could Jess have met her, except for a few minutes? He's been out on his ranch ever since she came to town."

"The story is they was married back in Ohio before Jess came out here." Rusty added details. "They have done separated. Seems Jess deserted her after he got here. There was a girl in a dance hall he fell for. Anyways, this editor woman says she's through with Jess for good and all."

"If any woman hasn't got any better sense than to marry Jess Lamprey she deserves what she got," Mosely said with finality. "Did you see Carter and arrange with him to take care of that Hereford bull when it gets here?"

"Why, no, Mr. Mosely. I thought you told me—"

The Hat T owner slammed a fist on the table. "I can't get anybody who works for me to carry a straight message without getting it balled up. You thought! Never in your life did you think, you thick-headed mutt. I suppose that bull is out in the yards starving to death because you had to go and lush at the Grub Stake. Get out of my sight, you dumb fool."

Mosely was not as angry at Rusty as he pretended. He knew that the station agent would notify Carter when the animal arrived and that he would be looked after. His flare-up was a reaction to the news he had heard about Anne Eliot, and he had let himself go so that Rusty would remember the dressing down he had got rather than his employer's interest in the young editor.

It was characteristic of Mosely that he adjusted his mind cynically to the changed situation. As a matrimonial prospect Anne's value, assuming that she divorced Lamprey, had declined very greatly. She would be damaged goods, he considered, and he had no intention of saddling himself with a liability. But his mind still concerned itself with her. She was no longer a girl who could pick and choose by reason of her charm and beauty, but a woman who had made a foolish mistake that cheapened the price a man must pay for her. Definitely she had lost caste, in his opinion, by her elopement and subsequent separation from her husband.

He felt it would be a good idea to see her soon. Probably she was humiliated and ashamed. In that frame of mind she would be more accessible.

The demands of the ranch held him at home for two or three days, but as soon as he could he drove to town. There was always sufficient business there demanding his attention.

In the late afternoon he dropped into the office of the

Sentinel. Jim Silcott came forward to meet him. Mosely flushed angrily. The sight of this man's mocking smile, so cool and undaunted, filled him with a passionate rage.

"Anything I can do for you, Mr. Mosely?" Jim asked, with affable politeness.

"Not now or ever," the Hat T man returned, his bearing stiff, his voice curt. "I came to see Mrs. Lamprey."

Silcott strolled toward the back of the room. "Mr. Mosely to see you, Miss Eliot," he called.

"Be there in a minute," she answered, and when she appeared explained to her caller that she had stayed to wash from her fingers the ink stains of a leaky pen. "You warned me I would get inky, and there never was anything more true," she concluded.

"Why do you keep that man hanging around?" he asked bluntly. "I told you it would do you no good to be friendly with him."

The rather thin smile that had been on her face faded. "Are you still arranging my life for me, Mr. Mosely?" she asked, resentment etched in her voice.

"From what I hear you have needed someone to arrange it for quite some time," he retorted brutally.

A pulse of anger beat in her throat. "If you have any business with me perhaps you had better get through with it, since you are leaving so soon," she said, with deceptive quietness.

He knew he had gone too far. Like most dictators, he did not always know when to use the velvet glove. The sight of Silcott had started him off wrong, and it had annoyed him that her step was still elastic and her pride still untamed. The deserted wife of Jesse Lamprey ought to be humble with him and eager to propitiate.

"Sorry," he told her gruffly. "You get my back up. Ever since you came here you have been doing the wrong thing. I never saw a more contrary woman. This man Silcott, for instance—"

"Do we have to go into that again?" Anne cut in sharply.

"Why do you have to be so obstinate? Why must you pick on my enemies for your friends?" he demanded, unable to keep his dudgeon wholly down.

Her beauty, tempered like a fine sword blade, both inflamed and irritated him. It was so independent and aloof. She was her own woman, impervious to his power and force and impassioned intent. Soft outside, she was like steel within.

"It seems impossible for you to understand that I am the mistress of my own life," she said. "I go my own way. I make my own friends. When I am unwise, sometimes I suffer for it. That is the way life is."

"Why can't I be one of your friends? This Lamprey business won't do you any good. I'm the most powerful man in this district, and you need me."

"I don't choose my friends because I need them," she replied. "You and I go different ways, Mr. Mosely. We don't think alike about anything in the world. How can we be friends when we haven't any common interests?"

Her point of view baffled him. The only common interest he knew between men and women was the ancient one which had existed since the beginning of the world. To a woman's opinions, to her intellect, he gave no weight. Her business in life was to keep the home fires burning if she was a wife; if not, by all the wiles of sex at her command to trap a man into marriage as soon as she could. He detested a strong-minded woman. She was a pest and a nuisance, he thought. But it was impossible to escape the delicate, penetrating fragrance of this girl's personality by classifying her as undesirable. Suffragettes and their like did not have voices like a silver bell with a low, haunting timbre in them. They did not have dark silken lashes over blue eyes that reminded him of wood pansies.

Pesky Kennedy walked into the office. His face was still marked with the scars left by the beating Jud Prentiss had given him.

Mosely scowled at him. "Thought I told you to leave this part of the country," he snapped.

The eyes of the crook-nosed man narrowed. "I aim to stay where I'm at," he said sullenly. "If you have any objections, Mr. Mosely, cut loose yore wolf."

"Not here," Anne said swiftly. "I'll have no trouble in this office."

The lean, whipcord body of Silcott moved rapidly across the floor from the rear of the building. Evidently he had noticed the entrance of Kennedy and thought it a good idea to be among those present.

"I'm sure Mr. Mosely has no objections to your being here, Pesky," Jim said evenly. "He probably knows you are working for me now and came to report."

The muscular jaw of the Hat T man hardened. "I can do my own talking," he retorted, frosty eyes fixed on Silcott. "I told him to keep traveling, and I still say that's good advice."

Pesky ignored what his former employer had said. He spoke sneeringly at Mosely.

"Sure, Red, I came to report. The dam was still there when I left. It's being watched. I haven't seen any more miscreants with dynamite around since you and me kicked the last bunch back to the hole from which they crawled."

"Please," Anne pleaded.

Silcott backed up her request. "Remember that there is a lady present, Pesky," he said trenchantly. "No talk of that sort here."

"That's right," Kennedy admitted, and took the hat from his rusty head to bow apologetically to Anne. "I plumb forgot myself, Miss Eliot."

Figuratively Mosely brushed the other two men from the map. "I came to have a talk with you alone, Miss Eliot," he reminded the young woman. "Without the presence of this riffraff. If we can't have it here, where can we meet?"

Anne looked at him with level eyes. "I know nothing that needs discussion between us," she replied. "When I saw you at the ranch you told me you would wait for the law to settle these land difficulties. I went to see you about the dam—to ask you not to do anything that would precipitate war. You chose to refuse what I asked. There is no more to be said."

Anger burned in his face. "I told you then that you were a little fool, interfering in what you knew nothing about. I say now what I said at the ranch, that the dam is a public nuisance which I have a right to abate if I wish. However, I knew nothing about what those numbskull boys of mine were doing. I'm explaining this to you, Miss Eliot, not to these two worthless scamps."

"That's right," Pesky flung out. "Save yore breath far as we are concerned. We wouldn't believe you. Where did Yeager and his sidekicks get that giant powder? I'll tell you where. Outa the root-house where you had it put after it was hauled to the ranch."

"I'll see you later, Miss Eliot," Mosely said stiffly.

He turned and walked from the building. They watched him cross the street, straight-backed and strong, his long stride eating up the yards.

Silcott ran a hand over his crisp red hair. "Russ would be a great man if he was not blind," he said.

"What you mean, blind?" Kennedy growled. "That guy can see what his hands are doing when they are five miles away. Trouble is he's dirt mean, and so greedy he wants to hog everything. Likewise, he's crooked as a dog's hind leg. And also, doesn't value a man's life at more than a coyote's."

"You don't think highly of him, do you, Pesky?" Anne said, laughing.

But she had understood what Jim meant when he had called Mosely blind. He had no sense of moral values. He could see nothing except what was to his own advantage. When he thought of right and wrong, he twisted the meanings of the words to suit himself.

Chapter Eighteen: BLOOD ON THE SADDLE

ANNE WATCHED JIM SILCOTT ride out of town, with Pixie on the saddle in front of him. She did not like to see him go, for she felt there was no safety on the road for him. Usually he traveled at night, but today he was in a hurry to get back to the ranch. He had promised her, as soon as he was a few miles out of town, to cut into the hills and follow a little-traveled trail. This did not relieve her anxiety greatly, and when an hour or two later she met Rufe Jelks she discovered he was as worried as she was, though he tried to conceal it from Anne.

"I was uptown when he come for his horse and didn't get back till right now," he explained. "I sure wouldn't have let him go off alone if I'd been here. He's the most reckless guy I ever did see. Why couldn't he have waited till after dark anyhow? Doggone his hide, he certainly gives his friends plenty of worrying to do. Not but what he's all right. Red can look after himself. You don't need to be scared about that." He added, after a moment, "I'd ride after him if I thought I could catch up before he got home."

Anne thought he did not make a very good business of reassuring her. He was as distressed as she was and could not help showing it.

"They're going to get him, Rufe," she said hopelessly. "If not today, next week or next month. I try to make myself believe differently by thinking that men can't be so murderous. But I can't convince myself. They killed my uncle, and they didn't hate him half as much as they do Jim."

The boss of the wagon yard leaned an elbow on the fence, taking a moment to find an answer. "About the killing of your uncle: There have been lots of rumors scooting around. Some Hat T men were in town the night he was killed. They left right afterward. Jud Prentiss was one of them. It's claimed he did it personally. I wouldn't know. But Rogers had been riding him hard in the paper for mistreating a poor family of homesteaders who had taken up a spring the Hat T wanted. Jud beat up the man and his son, then drove them out of the country. Carl Rogers had sand in his craw, God rest his brave soul."

"And there have been others killed besides my uncle."

"Yes. Two nesters disappeared. Everybody thinks they were drygulched and their bodies buried in the rocks."

"By the Hat T men?"

"By nobody else. The personal belongings of these two birds were left in their cabins, so they couldn't of moved out of the country. No evidence as to the guilty parties, you understand. But Russ Mosely had claimed publicly that they were rustling his stock and that he wouldn't stand for it. Maybe they were. Lots of rascals have squatted close to a big outfit and built up their herds to beat the band."

"Mr. Mosely once told me Jim is a rustler," Anne said.

"He lied," Jelks answered bluntly. "I've never met a squarer man than Red."

Anne nodded, smiling at him. "You don't need to tell me that. I know it. If he weren't, I wouldn't worry so much about him."

The owner of the Longhorn Corral looked at his watch. "Five minutes to twelve. I reckon we had better mosey along to Ma Russell's and see if she made that apple pie she promised me."

"She didn't," the girl told him.

"How d'you know? She told me she would."

"She got a substitute. I made the pies today."

He looked at her suspiciously. "Can you cook, on top of everything else?"

"Wait till you taste one of those pies," she said, and smacked her lips.

After dinner Anne went back to the office of the *Sentinel*. It was a fine, warm, sunny fall afternoon. Walking along the street, she could see at the end of it the hills turned golden with the foliage of the aspens getting ready for winter. Already she knew the charm of the high plains country, which drew back the hearts of men separated from it by many years and thousands of miles. The air was like wine. It made mere living a glorious thing. But today she did not feel the lift of it. There seemed to her something cruel about these wide-open spaces. So many high and valiant hearts had gone down to defeat here. So many had spent their energy and strength in vain. Back in Massillon people had the safeguards of a settled and organized life. They went their humdrum way free of danger. If they fell sick, nurses and doctors looked after them. If they were poor, somebody saw that they were fed. But in the West every man was on his own. He had to stand or fall by the force that was in him. The protection of law was here a frail thing, much less potent than the forty-five strapped to the hip. Human life was considered of so much less importance than it was in Ohio. Men committed homicide, and if they had killed in a fair fight walked the streets unmolested by officers. They shot others down from ambush and were never brought to trial for lack of proof.

Anne sighed. There was no use fretting. It would do no good. She tried to concentrate on work, but her mind wandered. Pictures jumped to it of a lean, brown man on horseback winding his way into the hills, of sinister figures crouched among the rocks waiting for their prey, of the crack of a rifle breaking the stillness. The girl told herself she was a fool. Her mother had seen a lover go to war and for three years had not set eyes on him. As a million other women had done, she had waited hopefully for the return of the loved one. This man was nothing to her but a friend. She had given herself a hostage to ill fortune and was through with lovers.

She picked up a letter from her desk and re-read it. The stage had brought it from Santa Fé. The writer had gone to school with her, had married a young army officer, and was stationed in New Mexico. The letter urged Anne to pay her a visit.

Anne's mind lingered on one paragraph:

The streets of Santa Fé are so narrow and so quaint. My dear, it is like being in a foreign country. Our house is a fine old adobe one with a lovely patio inside. It used to belong to an old Spanish family named Gandara. None of them lives here now, I am told. The man who built it was Don José Gandara, if you please. Rummaging in the attic the other day, I found an old leather trunk bound with steel at the corners. It is the dearest thing you ever laid eyes on. I am going to have it dusted off and brought downstairs. There are a lot of papers in it—letters in Spanish, documents of one kind and another, I suppose. I'll make a bonfire of these.

Maybe it would be a good thing for her to go to Santa

Fé and forget her worries for a few days. Henrietta promised her plenty of dances and horseback rides and young
army officers to pay attention to her. It would be good
fun to have a gay time and forget that she was a married
woman, at least in name, and that she was editing a
struggling newspaper, besides worrying for fear her
friends would be sniped at by hired killers. She could be
a courted young lady instead of just a harassed woman.
She could get Jim Silcott to run the paper while she was
away. This would keep him in town, where he would be
safer than out in the hill country. Not that he would be
very much safer, if she was to judge by what had occurred
to her uncle.

Anne decided to go. When Jim came in next week she
would take off. It would be partly a business trip, since
she wanted to make arrangements with a bank there for
credit with which to buy paper. The Blanco bank was
controlled by Russell Mosely, and she did not want to be
dependent on him in an emergency.

She dropped into the office of the stage company to re-
serve a seat for next Tuesday, but before she could say a
word the agent, Hilary Benson, blurted a question at her.

"Have you heard about Red Silcott's horse coming into
town alone?"

The blood drained from her face. "What do you mean
—alone?"

"Without him. It showed up ten minutes ago at Rufe
Jelks's Corral."

Anne stared at him. He was excited, and the Adam's
apple in his scrawny throat was jumping up and down
wildly. But she did not see that. She did not see the man
at all, consciously. Her whole being knew only one dreadful certainty. Jim was dead. They had killed him.

Benson thought she was going to faint and did not
know what to do about it. He ran to the pail and brought

back a dipper of water. The young woman pushed it away.

"I'm going down to the Longhorn Corral," she said in a low voice.

"I'll go with you," he said.

She did not object. She did not care whether he went or not. Though she knew the bottom had dropped out of her life, she moved in a sort of numb, dead vacuum.

Rufe was busy saddling a horse. He bawled to the boy who helped him at the corral to bring his rifle from back of the door. Two other men were on horseback waiting to go.

Anne said to Rufe, "It's true, then." There was despair in her dead voice.

"We don't know what is true yet," Jelks said. "Red's horse came back. Maybe he had an accident."

"You don't believe that."

"He might be alive," Rufe said doggedly. "There's a chance." His eyes picked up the other two riders. "All set, boys. Let's go."

Jelks let his companions pass through the corral gate ahead of him. "You are sure he told you he was going to take the Swanson cutoff," he said to the white-faced girl at his stirrup.

"Yes. And from the summit he was going to leave the trail and strike through the hills." She added, in a flat monotone, "What do you think, Rufe? He's dead, isn't he?"

"Don't quit hoping, girl," he comforted, his voice rough with feeling.

With that he swung his horse and went through the gate, lifting it to a gallop as soon as he reached the dusty road.

Half a dozen men and boys were in a stall looking at the horse which had come in alone. Someone raised an excited yelp.

"Look here, Bill. There's blood on the saddle."

Anne felt sick. She moved forward, her hands reaching for the fence to support her. When she got to it, her fingers clamped themselves around two palings. She must not faint. She was not going to be so silly. . . . The building across the street tilted up to meet the sky.

Chapter Nineteen: PIXIE BARKS

BLAZE WAS A HORSE OF SOLID COLOR. Red he was from the tip of his nose to the tail, except for the one splash of white on his face. Jim had been keeping him at the Long-horn lately during his stays in Blanco, and Blaze liked the good feed and the lazy life of town. That was why when he found himself turned loose later, terrified at what he had seen, his head pointed for Blanco rather than for the ranch on the Tincup.

Pixie snuggled down in front of Jim. Accustomed to the saddle, he was quite contented to be a passenger. Occasionally he turned his head to lick the hand of his master. Like most canines, he had supreme confidence that all would be well with him while he was so near the lord of his world.

Silcott sat the saddle lightly, at loose ease, following the gunbarrel road across the safe flat. He was a man fearless by nature, at times reckless, but never foolhardy. As he traveled, his gaze searched the brush on both sides of the sand ribbon which stretched before him for many miles. It was not likely that any of his enemies would lay for him here. Too many settlers rode or drove this way going to or from town. The chances of being seen would be over-much.

When he came opposite a gap in the hills, Jim swung from the road through the gray vegetation. His horse be-

gan to climb, for the country was now a rolling one as it
rose in waves toward the ridge in front of him. Blaze made
good going. He would break no speed records, but he had
the stamina to keep going all day at a road gait without
showing distress.

Silcott followed no trail, for he knew this country as
he did the palm of his hand. Detouring widely, he moved
up and down the slopes, taking such cover as the country
afforded. Nobody could be looking for him in these huddled hills. If he met an enemy, it would be by chance.
Farther ahead there would be danger points, Rabbit Ear
Gap for one, and after that the canyon below. Anybody
who took the Swanson cutoff had to go through the Gap.
There was no escape from it, since peaks rose sheer on
either side. It was as if in the morning of the world some
titanic axe had slashed a passage through the mountain
mass.

The sun was high above Rabbit Ear Peak. A breeze
stirred and swept across the hilltops. It was cooler here
than it had been down on the sage desert. The land swells
grew more rugged. Rocky ridges rose steeply toward the
pass. Jim pulled up, to rest his horse and to let Pixie down
for a run.

The Gap was looming just above him now. A short,
stiff climb would bring him to the entrance of the defile.
Looking up at it, a faint chill ran down his spine. He
wondered if this was a warning, if that sixth sense of
awareness to imminent danger, common to men who lived
on the perilous frontier, was telling him to be vigilant.
Lightly he dismissed the thought. The Hat T men could
not know he was taking the cutoff, and at this particular
hour.

None the less he traveled more slowly, scanning every
rock and shrub to make sure as possible that it did not
hide a foe. Smiling at the precaution, he drew the rifle

from its boot.

"We'd hate to be caught not ready, Blaze," he murmured apologetically. "I reckon we'd better send Pixie
on a scout."

A silence that seemed eternal brooded over the mountains. No sound disturbed it but the occasional click of
one of the horse's hoofs striking a stone. Peace brooded
over the land and mocked Jim's shadowy doubt.

Silcott stopped Blaze and sent Pixie forward to the pass.
He knew that if the pup met anybody there or scented anything suspicious he would stand and bark. He might do
that if he saw a chipmunk or a rabbit, in which case his
master would have to make up his mind what to do about
it. But if the collie, ranging over the ground, raised no
alarm he might be pretty sure the cut was safe to travel.

Pixie ran forward, nosing the ground for scent, and
turned to the right. Called back by Silcott and directed
to go straight toward the Gap, the dog advanced another
fifty yards before he went off at a tangent. A third time
the rider headed the pup for its objective. Apparently
Pixie now caught the idea, for he trotted steadily to the
summit. Just before reaching the gateway he pulled up
and lifted his head. He was looking and listening, as dogs
do, uncertain as to what this unknown quantity in front
of him was, some presence which he sensed might be an
enemy. He cocked his head and waited, then began to
bark.

A rifle shot shattered the stillness and echoed back from
the rock wall. Startled, Blaze leaped wildly to one side.
Silcott, unprepared, caught at the saddle horn but could
not save himself from being unseated. As he went down,
he knew he had been hit and that the bullet had come
from the quartz boulders at his end of the pass. His
shoulder struck the ground hard, but he did not stay
there. Swiftly he was up again, rifle in hand, heading for

the granite slabs at his left.

Guns crashed, either two or three of them, and the sound beat back at him as he zigzagged for cover, limping while he ran. He reached the slabs and dropped down back of the nearest.

There was no chance to reach Blaze, for at the first alarm the horse had turned and was galloping down the hill up which they had just climbed. He had to make his stand for life here.

Already his mind was working in stabbing brain flashes. One of the ambushers had fired too soon, forced to it by the dog's discovery of them. Otherwise he would have been killed at the first blast. His opinion was that the wound in his leg was not too bad. No artery had been hit, though the leg of his boot pressed soggy trousers to his flesh. He was back of pretty good cover. The enemies would have to come out from the pass to get at him, unless they waited where they were to peck at him whenever he showed his head. If he could stop the blood flow he might be able to hold his own for a while.

The situation might have been worse. If the Hat T men had concealed themselves back of these slabs he would not have had a chance, for lower down the hill there was no protection. He could have been picked off as he made his run for safety. That opportunity they had missed, probably because they had been too confident. Except for his wound and the disparity in numbers he was as well off as they. They held him prisoner where he was, but by the same token they could not easily leave the spot where they were forted, at least not to move forward and attack. One advantage more they held over him. In case they decided to ride away without finishing the job they could do so undiscovered. But Jim did not expect them to go. They were hardy ruffians and they must know he was wounded. They would stay and do their best to rub him out. His guess was that they would very likely succeed. But not, he thought grimly, without paying a price.

There was one chance, but a slender hope to rely upon. A frightened horse has the homing instinct. Blaze might make a bee line for the Longhorn Corral. If so, Rufe Jelks would immediately organize a search party. He would probably call up Anne Eliot, who knew that he was going to take the cutoff. Given the breaks, Silcott might look for help in about three hours. But there was a catch even to this. The horse is a dumb animal, far from intelligent, and dependable only under routine circumstances. Blaze might meet some other horses on the range and wander off with them.

Jim drew the boot from his wounded leg and examined the hurt. The bullet had passed through the leather of the upper part of the boot and the flesh of the calf. A nice clean wound, if infection did not set in from lack of attention.

In his pocket he found a cord. Using a splinter of rock for the screw, he made and fastened a tourniquet to his leg. Around this he wrapped the bandanna taken from his neck. While doing this, he had peeked around the edge of his shelter every few moments to make sure that his foes had not come into the open to charge him.

A bullet flattened itself on the rock slab and went off at an angle on a ricochet. Jim thought it time to let the Hat T men know he was still alive and still active. He fired a shot at the rock pile where they were concealed.

Pixie had vanished into the brush, probably to follow the old scent of a rabbit. Now he reappeared and trotted down the slope.

Somebody in the Gap took a shot at the dog. A spurt of dirt to the front and a little to the right of the collie showed where the lead struck.

Jim whistled sharply to the pup, which barked joyfully and came frisking across the open toward his master. Again a rifle cracked. The dog leaped or was flung into the air, turned heels over head, and landed hard on the ground. He moved once, feebly, then collapsed into a still, lifeless huddle.

Resentment blazed up in Jim. He had felt none at the attack on himself. That was all in the way of business, and since these killers were of the wolf variety he had not expected them to give him a chance for his white alley. But the shooting of a little collie pup out of sheer wantonness was something else. Only somebody with a black heart callous to all human decency could have done that. The fellow had probably done it in exasperation, because the little dog had been the means of frustrating in part the surprise.

A man slipped out of the Gap, rifle in hand, and made for a sand hummock fifty yards away. Jim fired at him and missed, took a second shot and hit. The rifle fell from the man's hand. He clutched at his forearm, turned, and scuttled back to the Gap. Meanwhile the guns of his companions had been drumming at Silcott. Sand spurted to the right of Jim. Bullets spattered against the slab.

The Diamond Slash man grinned wryly. His leg was sending telegrams to his brain reporting pain from the wound. But this last exchange evened the score. "I reckon they'll be a little careful how they try to outflank me again," he murmured aloud.

Long shadows began to reach from the rocks toward the east. The sun was far on its way down. In a couple of hours darkness would fall. Then the Hat T men would crawl out from the Gap and surround him. After that there would be a short, sharp battle, and they would ride away to report victory to Russell Mosely. But not all of them. Jim did not mean to pass out of the picture alone.

Chapter Twenty: A RESCUE

RUFE RODE WITH A HEAVY HEART. There was little hope in him. He had no doubt that Silcott had been ambushed and shot from the saddle. No other hypothesis would explain the return of Blaze with an empty, bloodstained saddle.

Yet he traveled fast. There was no need to cut trail. Better head straight for Rabbit Ear Gap and road-sign there. If Jim had not reached the pass they could ride back and try to pick up news of him between there and town. When they found the place where he had been unhorsed the story of what had occurred would be found written in the surrounding terrain.

The rescue party left the gunbarrel road not far from the spot where Silcott had deflected from it. All three of the riders were oldtimers, though young in years, and they guessed Jim had not followed the trail to the Gap but had taken to the brush in a short cut where he would be safe until he reached Rabbit Ear. This was what they would have done under similar circumstances.

Not until they came to the long stiff climb to the pass did they find evidence that their judgment had been good. Here and there they picked up tracks that Blaze had made while laboring up the steep mountainside.

"Look!" Rufe cried out.

He stopped and dismounted, as did his companions. They examined fresh tracks of a horse headed downhill. The length of the stride showed that the animal had been going fast.

"Blaze on his way home," one of the men commented. "And hell-bent to get away from here in a hurry."

"Looks like," Jelks agreed.

He looked up the sharp slope at the Gap, and a chill

foreboding swept over him. Not far from here his friend had been shot down from cover. His face set grimly.

"They waylaid Red from the rocks," the third man said. He was a cowboy in shiny leather chaps and a polka-dot bandanna.

"That's right, Chips. Red never had a chance."

Rufe said nothing. A lump had choked up into his throat. He looked away, so that the others would not see his face.·

The crack of a rifle snatched them from the gloom settling over them. They looked at one another, startled at the implication of that shot.

"Someone shooting, and not at us," Chips said.

Again a gun roared, this time from the slabs of sandstone to the left of the trail above them.

Rufe let out a yell of relief. "Red's alive! They haven't got him yet. He's forted back of those rocks. Come on, boys."

Before he mounted he fired his rifle, to let Silcott know help was at hand. They left the trail at a sharp angle, taking advantage of cover as they made a half circle of approach. Some scattering shots were fired at them, but at a distance·too great for accuracy. When they came out into the open at last it was at a spot sixty or seventy yards below the sandstone slabs.

They left their horses out of sight and climbed the last stretch on foot, dodging from one scrub pine to another as they advanced. The enemy did not interfere with their progress.

"Looks like they have done lit out," Chips said. "That's what they would likely do, so as not to be recognized."

Rufe nodded agreement. "I'm gonna make·a sprint for the rocks," he said. "You boys cover me, in case they're playing 'possum and show up to fire."

Silcott called down to them, "1 think they have hit the

trail, boys, but don't take any chances."

His friend did the last thirty yards in a rush. Jim was sitting on the ground, his back against the stone wall.

"Better light, stranger," he said with a grin, "and if you have a spare cigarette feed it to me."

Jelks did not speak for a moment. He was still panting from the run uphill. With a look of disgust he masked the apprehension that fear had etched on his face. "Hell, I might a-knowed you would be all right, you old moss-horn," he said presently. "We bust a trace to get here in time, and you're camped here peart as a jack in a mes-quite patch." As if by an afterthought, he added, "Don't tell me they didn't pump a single hole in you."

"One," Silcott answered, and pointed to the improvised tourniquet.

Rufe looked down at the leg. "Bad?" he asked.

"The patient is resting comfortably," Jim said, with a wry grin. "Unless complications set in he will be helling around in a few days."

"Didn't hit an artery?"

"No. I got one of them in the arm. So it's even steven. How about that cigarette?"

"Hmp! You don't deserve it." Rufe's voice was sharp, a reaction from his great relief at the outcome. "Of all the durned crazy galoots I ever saw, you take the cake. One of these days the Hat T warriors will bump you off slick as a whistle, and we'll pat you down with a spade where we won't have to worry about you any more." He tossed a sack of smoking-tobacco and a book of papers at the wounded man, then wigwagged the news to the two men below that all was well, after which he gave his attention to the leg.

"Lemme have a look at it," he said gruffly.

From his canteen he gave Jim water to drink before using the rest of the contents to wash the wound. The others of the rescue party had arrived and were watching operations. They huddled back of the sandstone slabs in order not to expose themselves to any possible bullets.

"You were lucky, Red," Chips said. "That leg won't keep you from riding far as the Berry place, will it?"

"Far as Blanco," Silcott corrected. "Yes, I sure was lucky."

They guessed he was suffering a good deal, but they offered no sympathy. Broken limbs were common on the range, and gunshot wounds were not rare. It was expected of a cowman that he be a stoic when occasion called for endurance.

"Spill yore story, fellow," Rufe growled. His hands had been deft and gentle while dressing the wound, but none of this consideration reached his manner. "And it had better be good."

Jim told them briefly what had taken place.

Chips was watching the pass above for signs of the enemy. It was getting dark, and the sharp outline of the rocks was blurring to a more vague, black mass. "They have done lit out, don't you reckon?" he said.

Silcott thought they had. "Soon as they saw you fellows, after firing two-three shots at you as a warning not to crowd them. Couldn't afford to be identified. But I think we'd better not investigate too closely. Some of them might be there. No use for us to get on the prod."

"Soon as it's dark I'm going up there," Rufe said.

"Why?" Chips wanted to know. "They're roosting up there, or they ain't. If they are holding down the claim you don't want to meet them. If they've gone, they haven't left a thing to tell you who they are."

"How about that rifle the buzzard dropped when Red hit him?"

"Trouble about getting that rifle is that one of them may have the same idea as you, Rufe," Jim said. "He and you might meet up there."

"That would be tough on one of us," Jelks said. "But I'm going after that Winchester. I'll promise to be a regular Injun and not throw down on myself."

The protests Silcott made were brushed aside by his friend. "You're a fine guy to talk about playing safe," Jelks jeered.

Rifle in hand, he slipped away into the gathering darkness.

"I would like to bury my dog, Chips," the wounded man said. "The body is out there about forty yards. Do you reckon you could find it? They can't see you from above now."

"Y'betcha!"

With his pocket knife Jim scooped a shallow grave. When Chips brought in the body Silcott buried his canine friend. They heaped stones on the grave as a protection against coyotes.

"He was a good little scout," Jim said, his voice empty of feeling. "If it hadn't been for Pixie, I would have been ready for burial myself. The little cuss got a bullet they had been saving for me."

They talked, as casually as possible, to conceal their anxiety as to what was happening above them just outside the Gap. Two or three times Chips suggested that he was going up to look for Jelks. Silcott vetoed this. He did not want any more of his friends in the danger zone.

"Rufe knows what he is about," Jim said. "He'll keep under cover same as an Apache would. I reckon no news is good news. If you went you would only double the danger of discovery, Chips. That is, if there is any danger. My idea is that their horses are throwing up dirt miles from here."

He wished that he felt more sure of that. What stuck in his mind was that dropped rifle. Somebody was going to

stick around and try to recover it. Maybe all of the attackers were still in the Gap, waiting for the darkness now
descending over the hills. If it were not for his bad leg
he knew he would be up there with Rufe now.

Two rifle shots sounded, with scarce a second between
them. Chips was on his feet instantly.

"I'm on my way," he said, and was gone.

There was another intolerable wait. The men below
were in a fever of foreboding.

"Someone has been shot," the cowboy said. "Maybe
Rufe. I reckon I'll drift up too."

A few minutes later Jim heard the murmur of approaching voices. Rufe and the cowboys came out of the
darkness.

"Everything all right?" Silcott asked.

Rufe was enjoying the excitement of danger met and
now gone.

"Fine as silk. You were right about another guy wanting
the rifle. But I got there first and scared him off. Here's the
gun. Let's go, boys."

Chips gave Jim his horse and rode behind Jelks. They
rode a mile out of the way to pick up another mount at
the Berry Ranch. While they were waiting for the horse
to be caught and saddled Rufe fired a question at his
friend:

"Red, are you able to travel in the saddle or not? We
can get a buckboard to take you in tomorrow. Don't ride
just to show how tough you are."

"I can take it all right," Jim said.

His leg was hurting more than he wanted to admit.
Both the jolting of the horse and the perpendicular position of the limb pained him, but he intended to endure
whatever agony there might be without a fuss. He knew
a dozen cowboys who would have done the same.

Rufe looked at him suspiciously. He guessed it was

hard.going for his friend. "Might be better to leave you here tonight and send Doc Head out to you," he suggested.

"I'll go in with you," Silcott said curtly. "It's only four miles from here."

"All right." Jelks shrugged his shoulders. He knew there was no use arguing if Red had made up his mind.

One of these days he meant to break loose with a few well-chosen sentences loaded with bristling epithets, conveying the general idea that Red was a dad-blamed fool. But this did not seem the right occasion. His solicitous gaze had observed Silcott a good deal on the way down to the flat. The tight-shut lips and the white face had told him as much as words could have done. He reckoned he would wait to make oration about lunkheads who went out into the hills alone and invited enemies to drygulch them.

Chapter Twenty-One: AN OLD LETTER IS TRANSLATED

MA RUSSELL THREW OUT one of her transients to make a place for Silcott while he was convalescing. The long ride to town had not done him any good, but, like most cowmen, he had built up such a hardy constitution that a mere flesh wound could not keep him in bed long. Soon he was hobbling about the house, and within two weeks was back at the office of the *Sentinel.*

The Court of Public Opinion, meeting not *en bloc* but in small groups, found the Hat T guilty of inefficiency. Twice it had made a gesture, with all the odds in its favor, and twice failed. This gay, light-hearted brown man had mocked the efforts of the big ranch to destroy him. He had roughed through, somewhat damaged, to be sure, but with his flashing, reckless grin still working. A suspicion began to seep down into the consciousness of the Powder Horn country that Russell Mosely had been overestimated, or else Red Silcott had not been judged at full weight.

In front of the courthouse one sunny morning Jim and Rufe met the owner and the foreman of the Hat T Ranch coming out of the building. They came together, face to face, so abruptly that there was no chance for either party to turn aside without giving way. Taken by surprise, Prentiss stopped, a scowl on his ugly flat face.

Jim smiled blandly. "A news item for the *Sentinel*. Blanco is honored by a visit from Messrs. Mosely and Prentiss." He reverted to reminiscence. "I have met recently several Hat T riders, but I don't think either of you two gents were present. Some of your boys were over on the Tincup hunting, and we celebrated together the Fourth of July a little prematurely. Since then we ran into some at Rabbit Ear Gap, looking for big game, I reckon. Did they get any, Russ?"

Anger in his eyes, Mosely answered curtly, "You talk too much, Silcott."

"He does more than talk, Russ," suggested Jelks, with splenetic laughter.

The mouth of the foreman had become a thin, cruel slit. The devil that Silcott stirred in him was dragging at his temper. "Some guys make a heap of a little luck," he taunted.

"And others don't have any to brag about," Rufe countered.

"I wouldn't need any luck to handle some guys I know."

Silcott lifted a monitory hand. "Tut, tut! No acrimony, if you please, Mr. Prentiss. Smile and the world smiles with you."

"You may go slap-dab to hell!"

Jelks tossed out another remark, also designed to irritate. "By the way, Jud, I have a rifle down at the corral which belongs to one of the Hat T boys. Whoever owns it dropped the gun in a hurry at Rabbit Ear Gap. If it is yours, Jud, you can have it any time by coming down to my place and claiming it."

"I don't drop guns," Jud snarled.

"Fine," Rufe answered cheerfully. "I didn't think it was yours. The fellow that owns it has a game arm. From the gossip I hear that description fits Roan Judson."

Prentiss almost foamed at the mouth. He ripped out more staccato oaths.

"I'll do any talking that's necessary," Mosely told his employee harshly, and strode on his way.

The *Sentinel* made no reference to the visit of the Hat T men to town, but there had been a story with a sting in it about the fight at Rabbit Ear Gap. Anne had also run an editorial headed *Hired Assassins,* in which she had charged that a certain ranch known to all was using murder as a weapon in its struggle to control the range.

Anne was not at peace with herself these days. Emotionally she felt upset, and her pride rebelled at it. Already she was a sufficient subject of scandal without making it worse. She had almost betrayed her concern at the corral when she came near fainting. Though Rufe Jelks had given no indication of it, she was sure he guessed that she was in love with Jim. If she was not careful, Silcott would discover it too.

Severely she told herself she was a married woman, through with all such foolishness as love. But to say it did not make it true. She could not be near Jim without being always aware of his presence. When his shoulder brushed hers by chance a heat ran through her blood.

This would not do, she decided. She was making a fool of herself. The thing to do was to accept Henrietta's invitation to visit Santa Fé and to get hold of herself while she was away. Abruptly she told Jim she was leaving and asked him to look after the *Sentinel* during her absence.

She took the Santa Fé stage next day, but it was not until the second afternoon that they came into the red hill country studded with piñons and cedars which surrounded the old town.

The stage dropped down to narrow streets lined with one-story adobe houses and swung into the old plaza which had been the center of life in this district for hundreds of years. The long, low Governors' Palace faced them as they drew up at the stage office. On the plaza were a score of burros laden with firewood, in charge of Indians who had brought them in caravans for twenty or thirty miles.

Henrietta and her husband, a young lieutenant just out of West Point, were on hand to meet their arriving guest. He was a fresh-faced lad named Raleigh Windom, and Anne liked him very much from the first moment of meeting. He carried in his open countenance a certificate of warm-hearted integrity.

Anne was whisked away in a surrey, leaving her baggage to be brought later by a soldier with a wagon. Henrietta was a vivacious blonde, and she was delighted to see her schoolmate. She chattered gaily, italicizing words that seemed important, making them stand out from the surrounding context by voice stresses. Since she had so much to say, and wanted to say it all at once, she never hesitated to interrupt herself to toss in extraneous comment.

Though Anne listened, she also kept her eyes open. Never before had she seen a town like Santa Fé. It bore little resemblance to the raw frontier outposts of the West she had passed through. Here was the dignity, the gentle indolence, born of a background crowded with history. There were ten Mexicans to one Anglo-Saxon, and there was about them a friendly courtesy which greatly impressed her. She was to learn from oldtimers that they

were excellent citizens, and very easy to get along with
if one did not insult their pride.

The old Gandara house where her friend lived delighted Anne. The thick adobe walls and deep windows
made for coolness, as did the patio with its wide porches
and lounge seats. A good deal of the furniture was an inheritance from the regime of the old Don. The quaint
kitchen, equipped with shining copper pots and pans and
with built-in ovens, was a joy to behold, and nothing
could have been more restful than the bedroom to which
Anne was taken. The gaily painted bedstead was charming, though there was a crack in the woodwork of the
headpiece.

Henrietta broke off an animated description of a *baile*
she had lately attended to toss a nod of her pretty head
at the bedstead. "It's more than two hundred years old.
Don José brought it with him from Barcelona when he
came to Mexico, and then hauled it *thousands* of miles
across the desert. Lots of the old Gandara heirlooms are
still in the house. Tables and chairs and bellows, heaps
of things. You'll like it here. We have lots of fun. Some
of the officers are very nice. Of course they will all fall in
love with you. I had forgotten you were so—so *devastat-
ingly* pretty."

Her guest stuck a pin in that balloon. This seemed as
good a time as any to tell of her foolish marriage. Henrietta listened, wide-eyed. Anne Eliot was the last girl she
would have picked among all her friends to mess up her
life in that way.

"It's very romantic," Henrietta commented, her big
blue eyes bright with interest. "But it doesn't seem like
you, darling. You were always so—so sort of sensible. I was
always the crazy one. Don't you remember how when we
roomed together I was always having cases with the boys
of the military school?"

"Yes, and I was always warning you." Anne smiled
wistfully, with a touch of nostalgia for the old school days
when an unknown future lay before them filled with
knights in shining armor just around the corner. "But
it seems I was the one who needed warning. I'm dread-
fully ashamed of having been such a fool. I was in love,
of course, or thought so."

"And you're not now?" Henrietta inquired. "Not the
leastest little bit? Your heart didn't flutter when you saw
him the other day after so long?"

"Not a flutter," Anne continued reluctantly. "He looked
—cheap. And of course I must be, or I wouldn't have married a man like that."

Mrs. Windom denied the conclusion indignantly. "You
were awf'ly young. How were you to know?"

"I knew well enough that I hadn't any right to marry
him secretly, even when I was doing it."

"Are you going to get a divorce?"

"No. If he wants one he can have it. I am through with
him. He knows that."

Anne was introduced to the friends of her hosts as
Mrs. Lamprey.

"I haven't seen Anne for *ages*," Henrietta explained
airily. "I didn't even know she was married. So many letters are lost between here and the river." (In frontier
times "the river" always meant the Missouri. It was the
dividing-line between civilization and the unknown
West.)

There was plenty of social life at Santa Fé, and Henrietta saw to it that her friend was kept busy. They rode a
good deal in the afternoons, and the evenings were filled
wi h gatherings of one kind and another. Sometimes the
young people danced. Occasionally they played cards. One
nigh they had a picnic in the moonlight. A costume ball
was si ggested and enthusiastically accepted.

Mrs. Windom decided that Anne must go as a Spanish señorita. "There is a lot of stuff in the garret—old dresses in boxes," she said. "Maybe we can find just what you'll want."

It was while they were searching for a suitable costume that Henrietta pointed out the leather trunk she had mentioned in the letter to Anne.

"I've been meaning to have Felipe take it downstairs and dust it off," she said, and added impulsively, "I'll have him do it now. He can burn the trash inside it."

Anne opened the trunk. In it were papers, parchment documents, Spanish newspapers fifty years old, a book or two, and some bundles of letters wrapped up and tied with string.

"Is it all right for me to look at these letters?" Anne asked, after Felipe had brought the trunk downstairs.

"Yes. But they are in Spanish. You can't read them."

No, she could not read them. But as Anne looked at the faded ink, set down on that paper more than sixty years earlier, her imagination kindled. By the signatures she guessed that some of these letters had been written by the wife of Don José Gandara to him, and others by him to her and to one of his sons. Without being able to read a dozen words of them there began to rise before her glimpses of that vanished life when Spain was lord and master of this whole Western country. She saw a semi-feudal system, the land parceled out by the king to aristo-cratic soldiers who were to hold the territory against the Indians for Spain. These yellowed documents told a story of high-pulsed hope, of love, and romance, and adventure. Back of them she saw pictures of the fascinating days when the Spanish dons on the frontier dispensed a prod-igal hospitality and ruled over hundreds of dependents with firm but fatherly benevolence.

"These letters ought not to be destroyed," Anne said.

"The ~ may be records here of great value to historians. I would i. ~ to get them translated, if you don't mind."

"Goodi. s me, no! Do anything with them you like. I didn't know you were interested in such musty old papers, dearie."

Anne explained that her paper was involved in a land-grant fight connected with this same Gandara family which had built the house where the Windoms lived. The lawsuit's issue, she mentioned, would determine the ownership of hundreds of thousands of acres and the property of scores of settlers.

"So it is important that I get an honest translator and one who understands both Spanish and English thoroughly," she said. "There is a chance that Don José or his wife in their letters may say something about his grant. I am going to sit there while they are being translated, to make sure none of them are taken."

It turned out that Lieutenant Windom knew an old gentleman named Antonio Castro who exactly filled these requirements. He took Anne around to the office of the man and introduced them. Castro was a small, neat man past sixty. His clothes were shiny from wear, but he was immaculately clean. He had gentle brown eyes, and his manners were punctiliously courteous. That he was a man of good family fallen on evil days was as apparent as that he clung to an unblemished integrity.

Castro translated the letters, out loud, while Anne sat and listened to them. Occasionally the Spanish-American explained bits that referred to customs or articles not familiar to the young woman. In spite of the somewhat flowery language, there were homely touches and flashes of emotion that wiped out the intervening years. This was especially true of the letters sent by Donna Maria to her husband. It was as if she had written them yesterday. Her bones had been dust since long before Anne had been

born, but the sweetness, piety, and love of this Spanish
lady stood out from those faded pages with startling vividness. It came to Anne that the essential character of
women had come down through the generations un-
changed. She had always thought of Helen of Troy and
Cleopatra and Joan of Arc as historical characters. Now
she saw them for a flashing moment as one with herself
—little children who ran crying to their mothers after a
fall, young girls moving shyly out of adolescence, women
tortured by the complexities of life that overwhelmed
them.

The letters of Don José were brusquely masculine.
They were objective—dealt with affairs local and national. Most of them held orders to be given some of the
numerous subordinates who were managers or foremen
of his ranches. One brought Anne to sharp attention:

In answer to the question raised by Señor Torres (so
the quiet voice of Antonio Castro translated), *you may
tell him that he has no need of a paper from me to make
his title valid. As you know, I have relinquished the great
grant made to me by His Majesty for services rendered in
the wars. I have more than I can use—more than any of
our sons will need as a range for their cattle. The grant is
an agricultural one, and I have no mind to turn farmer
in my old age. Nor is the land fit for anything except as a
range for stock. Have Miguel explain to Señor Torres
that by not complying with the conditions of the grant I
am releasing it back to the King.*

The other paragraphs in the letter related to other matters. Anne paid no attention to them. She had Castro read
the paragraph a second time, and once again, slowly, while
she wrote it in English word for word as the old man
translated the meaning.

There could be no doubt of the effect of this plain
statement on the land-grant claims. In his own handwriting old Don José had written that he no longer held
a valid claim to the estate. All that would be necessary
would be to prove the handwriting in court. This ought
to be easy, since the Don had left his bold, stiff signature
on fifty extant documents.

Anne walked back to the old house, a strange excitement in her blood. She wrote a letter at once to Jim Silcott and asked him to come to Santa Fé by the first stage.
The reason she gave was that she had run across a letter
written by Don José Gandara which seemed to her to have
a vital bearing on the land-grant case.

After she had dropped the letter into the slot at the post
office Anne walked through the twisting streets to cool the
commotion in her. She was greatly elated. If the courts
accepted the old letter of Gandara as genuine, Silcott and
all his friends would win their cases. To be a factor in the
victory pleased her very much.

She wandered to the old church of San Miguel by an
unpaved road which ran between century-old houses. In
the yard a thin-faced priest was clipping some roses. He
offered Anne one, and when she stopped to thank him
asked if she would not like to go through the church. It
was, he assured her, the oldest one in the United States.

"San Miguel was built, so many claim," he informed
her, "in the year 1540, though Bandelier incorrectly sets
the date much later. The Pueblo Indians destroyed the
roof in 1680 during an attack on the town."

The walls were of adobe, from three to five feet through.
Penuela restored the church thirty years later, as the
señorita could see by reading the inscription carved on the
gallery beam. One of the paintings was done by Cimabue.
The padre was particularly proud of the bell, cast in
Spain in the year 1356. It weighed seven hundred pounds,

and had been dragged a thousand miles across the desert
by pioneer priests in the early days of Santa Fé.

Anne walked out of the old church into a world that
basked indolently in a glow of warm sunshine. Her excitement was calmed. Here time stood still. For the moment
it did not seem to matter so greatly who triumphed in the
quarrels of landowners. It would be all the same in a
hundred years. The little town had been a battlefield since
the time of its founding. It had been the seat of power
for Indians, Spanish, Mexicans, and Americans in turn.
And all of the lusty warriors had passed away. Onate, de
Salivar, Penalosa, Baltazar Fuentes, Armijo, Stephen W.
Kearney: all of them had played their historic roles and
vanished, forgotten except for the records in musty vol-
umes. Into her mind flashed a quotation from Charles
Kingsley, one she had recently read:

So fleet the works of men back to the earth again;
Ancient and holy things fade like a dream.

But life flowed too strongly in her for such a view to
predominate long. The sight of some brown Mexican
babies playing on the ground, with a background of red-
pepper strings hanging down the adobe house wall,
snatched her back to the present. She smiled at them in
answer to their toothless grins. They brought back to her
a sense of personal value. No doubt time flowed on forever, and she would vanish as all the generations of the
past had done. But while she was here she could make the
most of beauty and laughter and friendship.

Chapter Twenty-Two: A VISIT TO A LAWYER

JIM SILCOTT READ both the original and the translation of
the letter Don José Gandara had written to his wife, in

which he had mentioned renouncing the land grant made
him by the King. He was elated at the discovery, and proposed that Anne join him in an immediate visit to D. L.
Stratton, the lawyer in charge of the legal fight in behalf
of the Armijo claimants.

"I believe this letter will win our case for us," he told
her jubilantly. "It confirms in the old Don's own words
the claim we have always made, that he not only slept
on his rights but actually relinquished them."

A warm glow poured through her. "I do hope so. We
ought to win with this, if there is any justice in the
courts."

"I think we'll get fair play," Jim said. "Mosely doesn't
control the United States courts. Of course technicalities
sometimes decide suits. But this letter certainly helps us
a lot."

Through the narrow streets they walked side by side to
the office of the lawyer, which was in a low adobe building
a stone's throw from the plaza. Jim liked the way Anne
walked, with ease and grace, shoulders and hips in a
straight vertical line, back flat, breasts firm. There was a
breath of wind blowing, and as her long legs moved
rhythmically the skirt of her dress clung to and modeled
the knees and swelling thighs.

In front of the office hung a sign suspended from an
iron support attached to the wall. One side of it bore the
legend, *Despacho de Daniel L. Stratton.* On the other side
was the English translation, *Law Office of Daniel L. Stratton.*

Anne was disappointed at the coolness with which
Stratton received the news of the letter. He showed interest but very little enthusiasm. The lawyer was a neat
little man, immaculately dressed. He wore a long black
mustache, perhaps to make up for the thinness of the
hair which was carefully draped in long strands over the

bald head. Before speaking he seemed to weigh and measure his words.

"The letter may be quite useful if admitted as evidence," he admitted guardedly.

Anne would have no such tepid reception of her discovery.

"I should think it would blow up Mr. Mosely's case. Don José admits it is not his land. He says he does not want it and that he is not taking it." Hotly she concluded, "He couldn't have put it stronger, could he? What more would the court want?"

Stratton smiled blandly. "My dear young lady, the lawyers of Mr. Mosely will not read this letter as you do. If it is admitted as evidence they will contend this was written in a mood which his later actions show was not his settled intent. They will take his own words, *By not complying with the conditions of the grant I am releasing it back to the King,* and try to show that he negatived this by later complying with the conditions. Still, undoubtedly the letter will greatly help our case, if we can get it admitted as evidence."

"Why can't we get it admitted? I found it in a bundle written to his wife."

"Handwriting experts employed by the other side will cast doubt on the genuineness of the letter."

Silcott made the point that there was a great deal of Don José's writing extant, which would give plenty of basis for comparison of the letter with other specimens of his chirography.

"But Don José wrote the letter," Anne broke in. "There is no doubt of it. You believe that, don't you?"

"I haven't the least doubt of it," Stratton said. "But it will not be admitted without a fight."

"We read six letters from him and even more from his wife," Anne explained. "The letters tie up ¬ith each

other. In this one he answers a question Donna Maria had
asked in a previous letter, which is among those I found.
In it she mentions having followed some instructions
given in an earlier letter from Don José. There's a—what
d'you call it?—runs through them."

"A continuity," Jim suggested.

"That will strengthen our position, if the connection is
quite clear," Stratton agreed. "It will be more difficult to
throw out this letter without throwing them all out. We
are under obligations to you, Miss Eliot."

"Don't you expect to win the case?" Anne asked bluntly.

"If I didn't think we had a good case I wouldn't be engaged in it," the attorney answered dryly.

Before they had left the office thirty yards behind them
Anne flung a query at her companion. "Do you think he
is honest—that he is really fighting to win?"

"I'm sure of it. He is an absolutely straight lawyer."

"Anyway, he has ice water in his veins."

"He does seem a bit desiccated, until he begins to try a
case. You should see him then. He is as keen as a fine
blade."

"Hmp! A bit desiccated. Why, a rotting old sahuaro
on the desert has more blood in it than he."

"Cases in the higher courts are not won by oratory,
lady," Jim mentioned. "There won't be a flaw in D. L.'s
logic."

She laughed. "I don't suppose I ought to have expected
him to throw up his hat and shout. But I do think he'd
make a fine undertaker, with that soft, studied voice of
his. Is he married?"

"Yes, ma'am. And you don't need to pity his wife. They
are very happy together."

"You caught me out that time," she admitted, mirth in
her eyes. "The fact is that I'm a bad judge of character at
first sight, and sometimes at second and third. Now, take

Mr. Mosely."

He shook his head. "Let someone else take him. I don't want him."

"I don't think I do either. But he is certainly impressive. When I first saw him I thought he was about the finest-looking man I had seen, so big and masterful, with that Greek-god face of his, and in a way likable."

"Likable," he repeated. "I'll grant you the rest, but I stick at that."

"My notion was that he had just got off wrong foot first, the way a blundering boy does, and that all he needed was to have his eyes opened. I couldn't believe he was responsible for the death of my uncle and other terrible things. But I know better now. Morally he's color-blind. It's funny, too. He doesn't seem to me as handsome as he did. His eyes are a little too close, and even when he smiles they are as cold as a frozen lake."

Jim answered with an understatement. He did not want to talk too harshly of a man he disliked so much.

"Russ isn't just what you could call warm-hearted," he agreed.

"It would be awful to be the wife of a man like that," she said.

Silcott slanted a look at her. He wondered why she had said that. In his mind there had been a suspicion that Russell Mosely was much taken with her. Anne was the kind of woman likely to interest him. There was the fine racehorse look about her beauty that he would think ought to belong to him. Jim guessed Anne was aware of the cattleman's admiration.

He said, tentatively, "Russ would probably spend money on a wife of whom he was proud."

"Yes, and she wouldn't have the slightest influence with him. She would be just one of his possessions."

Jim thought that was a shrewd judgment.

Chapter Twenty-Three: MRS. WINDOM DECLINES AN OFFER

WORD CAME TO MOSELY by the grapevine route that a letter written by Gandara had been found which would greatly prejudice his case. He wasted no time in getting to Santa Fé, where he was met by his informant. The spy had talked with a clerk of Stratton, who had not seen the letter but had heard mention of it in the office. The clerk knew that Silcott and a young woman had brought the document to his employer and that it had been found in the old Gandara house where Lieutenant Windom was now living. Of the contents he could speak only by hearsay.

The cattleman called on Windom at once. The officer was not at home, but his wife was quite willing to talk with this bronzed Westerner who looked like a Greek Hermes. He gave his name and mentioned the letter.

"Oh, the letter Don José wrote to his wife! Isn't it *amazing* that it would lie here in an old trunk fifty years and be found by accident just in time to be of use in some lawsuit about land? Anne was pleased as Punch. She wrote a letter to a friend at Blanco and he came right up here. A Mr. Silcott—lots of fun. He's in town now. I don't suppose you know him." Henrietta slanted a smile at him. She was thinking that he would be a nice new man to take to the dance tomorrow.

"Yes, I know him." His answering smile was grim. "Do you know what Miss Eliot did with the letter?"

"They had it photographed. Heaven knows why. The original they left with Mr. Stratton."

"I'm interested in old Spanish records," the Hat T owner suggested. "Do you happen to remember what the letter said about the land grant?"

"Oh, nothing much. Just that Don José had all the

land he needed without bothering with this grant the King had made him."

"Sometimes they worded their phrases very quaintly, Mrs. Windom. I don't suppose you recollect the exact translation."

"Goodness me, no! He just told Donna Maria to tell somebody or other not to worry about some land he had bought, since he had given up his claim."

Mosely disentangled the' pronouns in her sentence and found small comfort in the information. If Don José had actually put it down in black and white that he was relinquishing his claim, this would tell heavily against the Hat T interest.

"Since you are a friend of Mr. Silcott I expect Mr. Stratton would be glad to let you see the letter," Henrietta said helpfully.

"I'm sure he would," the cowman agreed, with a tight-lipped smile. "Thank you for the information you have given me, Mrs. Windom."

"I'm glad to help you," she said, smiling at him. "If you live near Blanco you probably know my friend Anne Eliot. Mrs. Lamprey, she is now."

"Yes, I know her too," Mosely replied, a little curtly.

He was greatly annoyed at the whole business. The finding of the letter was a blow, but to know that Anne was responsible for it and that she was co-operating with his most bitter enemy was gall to his soul.

Henrietta showed surprise. "You don't sound very friendly, Mr. Mosely. I'm very fond of Anne. She's a scrumptious girl, the very nicest I know."

"She won't let me be friendly," he answered bluntly. "For some reason she has joined in with my enemies—with this fellow Silcott, for instance."

"I thought Mr. Silcott such a nice man," the young woman murmured.

"You thought wrong. He is a menace to the country, opposed to those who are trying to build it up. In fact, he is a miscreant and a ruffian of the worst kind."

"I'm so sorry to hear that. Anne thinks—"

"Miss Eliot doesn't think," he interrupted. "She is guided by her emotions entirely. Because she has taken a fancy to this young man she is letting herself get into serious trouble. The fellow is an outlaw."

Mrs. Windom was distressed. What he said might be true. In the old days she had not thought Anne unduly impulsive, but she had made one bad judgment of a man already, and might be making another. Not that Jim Silcott looked like a bad man. In fact, she had not met one so charming and attractive in a long time. Of course it was possible Mr. Mosely might be prejudiced. He had said Silcott was his enemy. A flash of light came to her.

"Are you a party to this land-grant suit, Mr. Mosely?" she asked.

"As it happens, I am," he told her stiffly.

"I see. Naturally you are interested in old Spanish records." Her cool voice held an edge of sarcasm. "I have you placed now, sir. You are the owner of the big ranch. No doubt you are a very busy man. I must not detain you any longer."

She rose, erectly dignified, to dismiss him. Anne had given her a vivid account of the outrages his men had committed.

He lifted a hand. "Just a minute, Mrs. Windom. I suppose a young army officer isn't paid any too well. A little something on the side might be a welcome addition. If you will get that letter back from Stratton, I'll give you one thousand dollars cash on the barrelhead for it."

The young woman looked at him, eyes quick with anger, blond head thrown back. Before she could speak, horses clattering down the road stopped in front of the house.

She waited, listening.

They heard footsteps on the porch, and a moment later voices gay with laughter in the hall. The door of the living-room opened, to let in Anne and Jim Silcott.

Henrietta's visitors stared at one another with surprised hostility. Since she was not taken unaware, she was the first to speak.

"I think you know Mr. Mosely," she said in a cool, stinging voice. "He is an antiquarian, interested especially in old Spanish documents. I've just had an offer from him of a thousand dollars for one of Don José's letters."

"Why don't you sell him one, Mrs. Windom?" Silcott said, mockery of his enemy in the smile he flashed. "I don't suppose he cares which letter. Any one will do."

"I warn you, young women," Mosely said harshly, "that the penitentiary yawns for people caught in a forgery conspiracy."

"Don't fool yourself, Mr. Mosely," Anne said quietly. "This letter is not a forgery."

There was anger in his cold gray eyes. "I warned you to keep out of this," he snapped. "You'll remember that too late." He snatched up his hat and strode out of the room.

Chapter Twenty-Four: JIM DROPS IN ON AN OLDTIMER

JIM SILCOTT AND ANNE ELIOT came out of the dark old Governors' Palace and stood blinking for a moment in the untempered New Mexico sunlight. They walked along the front of the long one-story adobe building, which occupied an entire side of the town plaza. Already the historic walls were crumbling with age.

"It's amazing, isn't it, how chock-full of history this old place is," Anne said. "Very likely Onate started from this very building three hundred years ago to cross the plains."

"Maybe," Jim said. "I doubt if the Palace is that old,

but certainly Penalosa held the commissary general of the Inquisition prisoner here during the latter part of the seventeenth century. From that time to this stirring events have happened often in the building and on the plaza. There have been battles and murders and executions. Most of the men famous in the struggle for the West have walked along the path where we are going now. Priests, soldiers, trappers, Indians, explorers, and settlers. All of them have come and gone.

> 'Their swords are rust,
> Their bones are dust,
> Their souls are with the saints, we trust.' "

They had turned to the left at a right angle and were strolling past the stores on the adjacent side of the quadrangle. In front of a saloon Silcott pulled up sharply. His gaze was fixed on some horses at a rack close to the sidewalk. Anne said, "What's the matter?"

He stepped into the dusty road to examine the brand on one of the horses. His first glimpse of it had been cut off by a movement of one of the hitched animals. Swinging the cow-pony round, Jim pointed to the design burned on its flank. "The Hat T brand," he said. "On a horse Jud Prentiss rides. I'm wondering what it is doing here."

Her eyes found his and held to them. "You think he is here to make trouble?" she inquired.

"He might be here on ranch business."

"Or Mr. Mosely may have sent for him to finish what the Hat T men failed to do at Rabbit Ear Gap."

Jim shook his red head. "No. I'm not that important at the moment. And Russ is too smooth to call attention to his deviltry by pulling it off here. He likes to stage his killings in the wide-open spaces."

"You don't think that man Prentiss is here on legitimate business, do you?" Anne asked scornfully.

"Why not? He's a bad egg, but he can't stick on the job of being wagon boss to Satan all the time." Silcott looked over the other three horses at the hitch-rack. "This roan is a Hat T bronc. The others may be too, though they haven't Mosely's brand."

"The riders must be inside this saloon. We'd better go. They might come out and find us here."

"I don't reckon they would bother me while I'm with you," Jim said easily. But he fell into step with her. He did not want even a verbal battle with Prentiss while he was with Anne. If Jud or one of his men was drunk enough he might let drop some remark that would annoy her. The cast-off wife of Jesse Lamprey did not rate as much consideration as Anne had met with before her married state was made public, at least not with men like the Hat T riders.

"If Jud Prentiss came here on ordinary ranch business he would not have brought other men with him," Anne insisted.

"If he came to drive stock back he would need help," Jim mentioned.

"Oh, you can talk!" she scoffed. "Just the same, I know they have some meanness in their minds."

Silcott dropped around to report the latest development to Stratton. They discussed the situation.

"When Mosely offered Mrs. Windom a thousand dollars for the letter he was making his first move," Jim judged. "He won't stop there. What will his next step be to get the letters?"

"I don't know." Stratton thought it over. "Do you think he will try to bribe me?"

"No. He knows you are not for sale. My guess is that he will stand back and let his foreman, this Jud Prentiss, deal with you."

"Make his offer through him, you mean?"

"Yes." The face of the Powder Horn man was grim. "But there won't be any cash involved. This Prentiss is a bad man, a killer. I think I'll take the letters with me."

The lawyer pointed to an iron safe. "They are locked up there. Mr. Mosely's handy man would be good if he could get them out of that steel container."

"You don't know Prentiss," answered Silcott. "There's Indian blood in that scalawag. He might try Apache tricks on you."

Stratton was startled. "You mean torture me to get the lock combination?"

"Jud would enjoy that. He's a born bully."

"If you had the letter would it be any safer?"

"I can put it where he wouldn't know where to find it."

"Can you put yourself where he wouldn't know where to find you?" Stratton asked dryly. "You mentioned his Apache tricks."

Jim gestured that off lightly. "I'll have to take my chance with Mr. Prentiss. He and I are old acquaintances."

This was not very satisfactory to the attorney, but neither was the alternative. He did not quite believe that Mosely would let his men go as far as the Diamond Slash owner had indicated, but dark rumors of his methods had for some time been bruited about the town. Also, Silcott had told him of the recent attacks on his life. After all, this was the fight of the Armijo grant purchasers. Their lawyer was employed to handle only the legal end of it. Stratton unlocked the safe and handed the Gandara letters to Jim.

"I don't need to tell you how important these are to our suit," he said. "You'll be careful of them, I know that."

"That's certainly my present intention," the cattleman told him.

"Will you take them to the bank? You can't tonight;

it's closed."

Jim smiled. "If you knew where I was going to put them they might as well be in your safe. When Prentiss inquires, just refer him to me."

"If he does," corrected Stratton, more hopefully.

The attorney watched his client going down the street, his slim, compact figure erect and jaunty. There was something about this cool and reckless youth that inspired confidence. Stratton told himself he did not need to worry about his friend's safety. He was able to take care of himself, and had done so very adequately up to date.

As he moved down the street toward the plaza Jim became aware that he was followed by a Mexican vaquero. The man might simply be going in the same direction as Silcott, or he might have been deputed to trail him. Jim decided to find out. He stepped into a dry goods store and bought a shirt. When he came out the vaquero was looking in the show window at some gay bandanna handkerchiefs displayed there.

Jim crossed the plaza, his shadow in attendance. At a second store he bought some wrapping paper and a ball of string. From there he went to his hotel and wrapped two packages. In one were the Gandara letters, and in the other a folded copy of the latest issue of the *New Mexican*. With a pencil he marked one of the little parcels in order not to make a mistake.

He had been invited to the Windoms' for supper, and he made himself as presentable as possible. There was a young woman there before whom it was important to him that he appear at his best. One of the packages he concealed inside his shirt. The second one he put in his coat pocket. To be fully dressed he took out and tested the revolver strapped in a holster underneath his left arm, then replaced it carefully.

The vaquero was still on the job. He sauntered after

Silcott to the post office, and from the window outside
watched him take the parcel from his coat pocket and address it. His black eyes observed the Diamond Slash man
hand the package in for weighing, buy stamps, and leave
it with the clerk to be sent to its destination.

Jim had one more call to make before he reported at
the Windoms'. He stopped at a saddlery store just below
the plaza to see its proprietor, an old friend who had ridden the brush country of Texas with his father.

From the doorway Jim called in cheerily, "How you
making it with that saddle I ordered, oldtimer?"

Homer Caldwell was a big, lank man close to sixty, with
a long reach of well-muscled limb. He had a lean, bony
face with a hawklike nose and deep, piercing eyes gleam-
ing out beneath grizzled brows. Except when he talked
his lips were close shut. Even in the store he wore a wide
sombrero and cowboy boots, into the tops of which the
legs of his jeans were thrust.

If he was surprised at this reference to the order for a
saddle never mentioned to him before, he gave no sign of
it. Perhaps Silcott's wink tipped him off. He knew there
was something here he did not understand, but it would
be made clear to him in time.

"Why, I'm makin' right smart progress," he said. "But
I didn't expect you here so soon. I had some trouble fixing
up the skirt with the *sudadero* just the way you wanted it.
You're such a particular buzzard, Red. Come along in and
have a look-see."

Jim walked into the store and pretended to examine the
tree of a saddle which rested on a frame and had not yet
been completely draped.

"It's shaping fine," he said. "Listen, Homer. I'm being
watched. Keep up talk about the saddle."

Caldwell talked, his eyes on Silcott, who had drawn a
parcel from under his coat and was apparently studying

a pair of saddlebags close at hand.

"Tell me if I'm being noticed right now," Silcott murmured.

"No, sir," Caldwell told him, after a swift look toward the door. "I claim you're wrong about that. What does a kid like you know about the fit of the *basto*? I've not only made saddles. I've rid 'em a-plenty before you were weaned."

Jim's hands, moving swiftly, transferred the package to one of the pockets of the saddlebags. "All right. All right." He seemed to concede the point. "You don't need to get on the prod, Homer, because I like a saddle the way I like it. I've forked a'few in my time, if I ain't an old Methusalah like you." His voice dropped a note, but not too obviously. *"I'll come and get it myself* when I'm ready."

"That's all right." They had begun to move toward the front of the store. "I could sack the saddle and ship it, but if you're gonna be in you might as well pick it up."

Jim stopped a moment at the entrance. The vaquero and another man were lounging outside the door of the adjoining saloon. That they had been closer until the past few moments seemed to Silcott a reasonable guess. The companion of the Mexican was Pete Yeager.

"You're looking some peaked, Homer," the Diamond Slash man suggested. "You want to remember you're an old man and cut out cavorting at so many dances."

"I don't go to dances," protested Caldwell indignantly. "And I'm not so doggoned old if I wanted to go. You talk like I was a stove-up old vinegaroon." He added sharply, "You're the one that looks peaked. I done heard how you was shot up couple of weeks ago."

"By amateurs," Jim explained, and pretended to catch sight of the fat little cowpuncher for the first time. "Why, hello, Pete! I was just talking about you. Mention an angel and you hear the rustle of his wings. How are cases? You been hunting lately?"

The bald-headed man retorted promptly, "Don't worry about my hunting, Red. And I'd advise you to drop that notion about me being an amateur." There was resentment in his heated voice.

"Amateurs are all right in their place, Pete," Jim told him soothingly. "Maybe you'll do better after a while. They say practice makes perfect."

Yeager snorted. "Hmp! One of these smart galoots who knows it all."

"Sometimes I think you don't like me, Pete. Well, I got to be moving. Supper at Lieutenant Windom's house. Can't keep my friends waiting." Silcott turned to the Mexican vaquero. "Let's be going, young fellow, if you're trailing me. See you later, Pete. Don't take any wooden nutmegs."

He sauntered down the street, leaving Yeager fuming behind him.

Before he had gone fifty yards a voice hailed him. "You doggoned old buzzard-head!"

Two riders were coming up the street. One was Rufe Jelks, the other Pesky Kennedy. Rufe swung from the saddle and bowlegged to the sidewalk.

"What are you doing here?" Silcott asked in astonishment.

"Why, can't a couple of cowboys come to see the elephant?" the owner of the Longhorn Corral asked hilariously.

"They can, but they didn't," Jim said. "Spill it, Rufe."

Jelks grinned. "Word reached us that the Hat T had moved headquarters to Santa Fé, so Pesky and I drifted along to see if we couldn't get a job."

"You might, at that, before we are through," Jim admitted. "Rest your saddles, boys, and come into the Green Light with me for a powwow."

They walked into the saloon and took a small table. Each ordered what he wanted. Their heads close together, they talked almost in murmurs. Jim told them the most recent developments.

"Hmp!" grunted Jelks. "Thought something was doing when the Hat T hands collected Jess Lamprey and lit out with him. Knowing you were here, we figured Santa Fé would be the center of the storm. So we hightailed it to the city."

Silcott rose. "I'm due at Lieutenant Windom's for supper. Miss Eliot is staying there. Later in the evening I'll meet you at the hotel. *Adios,* boys."   •

Kennedy spoke for the first and last time during the conference. "Don't let them knock yore block off, Red," he said.

"Not if I can help it. Be back about ten."

They watched him moving lightly down the street. He was whistling "Good-by, my lover, good-by."

Chapter Twenty-Five: STRATTON RECEIVES A CALL

JUST AS STRATTON closed his desk and rose to go home two men walked into the office. At sight of them his heart lost a beat, for both his visitors were masked and one of them had a .44 in his hand.

The lawyer's right hand fluttered down toward a drawer still open, but stopped abruptly on the way. The man behind the revolver had said curtly, "Don't you, D. L."

He was a big, heavy man with long arms and thick, rounded shoulders. His resemblance to an ape was enhanced by the growth of hair that matted his throat and the backs of his hands.

"What does this m-mean?" the lawyer stammered, the color fading from his cheeks. He followed peaceful paths and was not used to war's alarums.

The big man padded across the floor and pushed home the bolt of the back door. His companion turned the big key in the front door and pulled down the windowblind.

"So we can be comfortable and not be interrupted," he explained, his white teeth flashing below the mask in an ironic grin.

Frightened though he was, Stratton noticed that the man's height was below the average and that he was of plump build. Where his face showed it was high in color.

"If it's money you want—"

The ape man cut off the attorney's protest. "Can the chatter, D. L., and do as you're told. You know what we want. Cough up that letter."

As the man shuffled forward the revolver in his hand looked as large as a small cannon to Stratton. From the hairy wrist back of the hand a quirt hung. The muscles of the lawyer's stomach collapsed. This was a danger more menacing than any in his experience. He remembered what Silcott had told him of the foreman's Apache tendencies. But he made an attempt to push back the panic sweeping over him.

"Wh-what letter?" he asked.

"Don't play horse with me," the hairy ape said, a threat in his harsh voice. He stood with his feet well apart, his head thrust forward. "If I once start I'll rip the white flesh from yore bones with this quirt."

Stratton gave up. "I haven't the Gandara letters, if that's what you mean," he answered.

"Open that safe."

The attorney opened it. The fat man went through the papers inside, scattering them on the floor after he had examined each. He rifled the desk.

"If it's here and you're lying to us, I'll skin you alive," the big man promised viciously.

"I haven't got the letter."

"We know better. Red Silcott left it here."

"He took it away again. This afternoon."

A hairy hand reached out and caught Stratton by the throat. Sinewy fingers closed on the flesh. "So you're gonna get funny with me, eh?"

The face of the lawyer grew black and his eyes glassy.

"Hey, Jud, cut that out!" the fat man warned. "You'll strangle the guy before we get what we want."

Prentiss flung his victim into the chair from which he had risen a few minutes earlier. The lawyer coughed and sputtered. Slowly he recovered enough to gasp out a word or two.

"Don't! P-Please don't do that."

"Come clean, then." The man towering over him cursed the choking man angrily. "Damn quick, too. Or you'll taste this quirt."

Again the plump man interposed. "We don't want to raise a row, Jud," he reminded his companion. "I don't reckon this bird has got the letter."

"He knows where it is. Open yore trap, fellow. Where's that letter?"

"S-Silcott took it."

"What did he say he was going to do with it?"

"He wouldn't tell me. Said if I didn't know I couldn't tell."

"You're lying to us."

"It's the truth. He said if you asked for it to refer you to him. I would give you the letter if I had it."

"He's speaking truth, Jud. No use jouncing him around any more. Let's get out of here. I told you how it was before we came."

"You always know so cursed much," Prentiss snarled. He turned on Stratton. "Clamp yore mouth, fellow, if you know what's good for you."

The Hat T men clumped out of the office.

Without waiting to gather up the scattered documents on the floor, the attorney locked up and went home. He was weak and sick, and his throat ached from the pressure of the iron fingers that had closed on it. His wife put him to bed, sent for a doctor, and meanwhile tried to relieve the pain in the throat.

"We've got to get a warning to Silcott," he told his wife.

She was a competent, motherly woman. "Don't worry, dear. I'll take care of that. This has been a dreadful experience, but you are through with it now. I'm going to see Russell Mosely."

He was alarmed at the anger in her eyes.

"You mustn't say anything that will annoy him, Jane," he told her. "You don't know what he would do."

She nodded. "He will be reasonable, Daniel. I'll promise that, and so shall I." Mrs. Stratton did not explain what she meant by reasonable.

Jane penned a note to Jim Silcott and sent it to the Windom house by a Chinese servant whom she could trust. She wrote the word "Immediate" on the envelope.

A Mexican maid handed it to Silcott while he was at supper. He asked permission of Mrs. Windom to read the message.

Two masked men came into Mr. Stratton's office just as he was leaving. They brandished revolvers and forced him to open the safe. When they did not find what they wanted they almost strangled him. He is now sick in bed. One of the men called the other Jud.

My husband has asked me to warn you to look out for yourself. He thinks you had better get out of town at once.

The signature on the note was *Jane Stratton.*

"I hope it isn't bad news," Henrietta said.

"Mosely has made his second try for the letter," he replied. "Two of his ruffians assaulted our lawyer, Stratton. He is at home sick. The note is from his wife."

"Is Mr. Stratton badly hurt?" the hostess asked.

"I don't think so."

"Did they get the letter?" Anne wanted to know.

"No. Stratton did not have it."

Anne did not ask any more questions. She knew the answer to that one. As soon as she was alone with him for a moment she put a more direct one to him. "What have you done with the Gandara letter?"

He grinned at her. "Stratton didn't know, so he couldn't tell them."

"They wouldn't dare touch me, if that's what you mean."

"Not unless they have gone clean daft, but you can't be sure what Mosely would do. Safer for you not to know."

"Are you carrying it with you?"

"No."

"Why didn't you show us that note you got from Mrs. Stratton?" she asked, shifting the attack.

"I told you about it." Jim was a trifle disconcerted by her acumen.

"You told us what you wanted to tell us," she corrected sharply. "I'll have a look at it, if you please." Her small hand was outstretched for the paper.

"You're some bossy," Silcott commented. "That note was written to me, young lady."

"I'm in this as much as you are. Hand it over. Unless you would rather I'd go to Mrs. Stratton and ask her."

"You sure do ride herd on an idea until you have it roped," he said, a hand coming slowly out of his coat pocket with the letter.

Anne moved closer to a lamp and read it. "So that's why you didn't read it aloud, because you didn't want us to

know they would be after you right away. Do you think
I'm dumb? I didn't need Mrs. Stratton to tell me that.
What do you intend to do?"

"What would *you* do?"

She told him promptly. "I'd take a train, no matter
where it was going, and drop off at the end of the line."

Jim shook his head, smiling at her. "No, you wouldn't
do that. You'd stick around, as I am going to do."

She drew a deep breath of surrender. "There's no use
talking to you. You'll gang your ain gait, as my Scotch
grandfather used to say. What will be Russell Mosely's
next move? It wouldn't do him any good to have you shot
and then see the Gandara letter bob up later."

"No. Just now I'm more valuable on the hoof than
slaughtered. I think the next thing he will do will be to
rob the post office."

She stared at him. "Why?"

"Because he thinks I mailed the old Don's letters."

He explained to her how he had been followed and had
maneuvered to throw the spy off the track.

"You mean you didn't mail the letter but have it hidden somewhere?"

"Go to the head of the class."

"And you won't tell me where it is hidden?"

"No. Little girls mustn't be too inquisitive."

A sense of despair swept over her. He was moving in
the valley of the shadow of death and she could do nothing
about it.

"Men like you ought to live alone on a faraway island,"
she said bitterly. "Then their friends couldn't see them
strutting around inviting death."

"I don't want to distress you," he said gently. "I take
all the precautions possible. My own opinion is that I am
going to live to a ripe old age. Don't worry about me."

Her eyes fell away from his. "That's easy to say. How

can I help it—since we're friends?"

He plucked a hope from her unhappiness, even though he knew malign Fate had built a barrier between them. How much her emotions were involved he could not guess. There had been exultant moments when he had read gifts in her eyes, but he felt he might easily be mistaken. A man in love could let his judgment interpret kindness for something deeper.

Even if she cared for him there was no way out for them to find happiness. She had been brought up, as he had, in the narrow convention of a puritanic age which looked upon divorce as a disgrace. A woman who had made her bed, no matter how unwisely, must lie in it. From this Anne had revolted. She would not live with Jesse Lamprey, but neither would she ask for a divorce.

Henrietta's eager voice came to them from the adjoining room.

"Come on, everybody. We're going to play charades."

They drifted back to the group.

A few minutes later Anne, all excited, drew Silcott aside again.

"If you think they are going to rob the post office why don't you set a trap to catch them at it?"

Jim grinned. "You're ahead of schedule. I gave you five minutes to work out that idea. It took only three."

"Oh, you've already thought of it." Her eyes asked for information.

"It did occur to me, so I mentioned the matter to Lieutenant Windom. Since the government is owner of the post office, he has stationed half a dozen soldiers in the building to protect its property."

"Perhaps they will catch Russell Mosely!" she cried.

"No. Russ is too smart for that. He'll be working by deputy."

"Some of his Hat T men, then."

"That would be right interesting."

Henrietta came across the room to them. "The word is 'artichoke.' We do it in four acts, each syllable separately and the whole word in the last scene. You're in the first scene, Anne."

She began to explain the business of it.

Chapter Twenty-Six: TRAPPED

SILCOTT DID NOT LEAVE the Windom house by the front door. It seemed better for him to slip out inconspicuously through a kitchen door leading to the garden.He climbed a paling fence and dropped down a short slope to the bank of the Santa Fé River. Along this he moved through the brush to the Cerrillos Road and crossed the river by a rickety bridge. A dusty, winding wagon path led to the south side of the plaza.

The crackle of shots pulled him up in his tracks. A quick excitement stirred his blood. He guessed that there was trouble at the post office. Swiftly he moved forward along a narrow street flanked by one-story adobe houses. The shooting had died down after the first sharp volley.

To him there came the slap of running feet and the sound of voices. Figures emerged vaguely out of the darkness, heading in his direction. Jim ducked into a deep doorway and crouched low, waiting for them to pass. He did not expect them to notice him or, if they did, to pay any attention. They had more urgent business on hand than to bother with some sleeping *trabajador* who had drunk too much tequila.

Three men passed, moving fast. Silcott came out from the doorway and followed. He had recognized Jud Prentiss. The Hat T overseer was bringing up the rear heavily. Not used to running, the pace was getting his wind.

That these men had tried to rob the post office and been

repulsed was a safe surmise. Jim meant to find out where they were going to hole up until the danger was past. They swung to the right, into a street less packed with houses. From back of the scudding clouds a moon came out. Silcott dropped farther back. He did not want Prentiss to discover that they were being followed. This had its disadvantage, for if they could not see him he could not see them, except as dark, blurred objects moving in the night.

The fugitives left the road and crossed the shadowy slope of a hill. The terrain was sown with piñons, and it was very difficult to distinguish the small trees from human figures. Jim lost and found his quarry, then missed his men again as the moon went under a cloud.

He counseled with himself as to whether he had better go on and try to pick up the trail or go back and let Windom's men carry on the hunt. In his throat the pulse of excitement was beating, which always signaled the exhilaration of danger. That he ought to return to town and report he knew, but he wanted to have something definite to tell. It would be a great *coup* if he could find the hideout of the outlaws.

An arroyo opened out of the darkness on his left. He stopped to listen, but no faint rumor of sound reached him. Had they gone up the gulch or had they swung to the right? It was a toss-up. He chose the arroyo only because of an obscure feeling that hunted men run to the hills. A stone's throw from the lower exit the canyon widened to a little park, and in this was a house built close to a rock wall. Cautiously he drew near, making the most of such cover as there was. He wished that Rufe and Pesky were with him.

The building was more a Mexican *jacal* than a house. It was built of upright poles daubed with clay. Sloping poles waterproofed with grass sod formed the roof, which sagged in places from long-time neglect. There were two

windows in front, and most of the panes in both of them
were broken. The corral fence was only a feeble memory
of what it once had been. Altogether there was an air of
decay about the steading. Externally the evidence pointed
to abandonment, but in Jim's brain rang a bell of warning that told of close and immediate danger. Again his
sense of wisdom advised retreat, or at least observation
from a distance. He rejected this in favor of a bolder
policy. Before he turned his back on this adventure he
meant to find out whether the little ranch was as deserted
as it seemed to be.

He slipped forward, from a clump of Spanish bayonet
to a scrub cedar, and from the stunted tree to the corner
of the *jacal*. His heart jumped, for a man had come out
of the house and was standing in front of the doorway.
The thick, rounded shoulders, the heavy-set figure with
the long arms, told him the man was Jud Prentiss. Jim
was in deep shadow. He pressed close to the wall, scarce
daring to breathe. The Hat T foreman walked away toward the arroyo without seeing him.

Heavy sacking hung over the nearest window, to prevent any light from being seen. Jim edged closer, and very
gently slid a hand above a jagged segment of broken glass
to draw aside the improvised curtain so that he could look
inside. Three men were in the room, which was entirely
empty of furniture. The light came from a lantern hung
on a nail driven into the wall.

Two of the men were seated on the floor. The one with
his back to the window was Pete Yeager. Jim identified
him by his bald head and plump torso. Opposite him sat
Roan Judson, dragging at a cigarette, his yellow, jaundiced face turned toward Pete. On a roll of bedding spread
out on the floor lay the third man. The Diamond Slash
man was surprised to see him. He had not expected to
find Jesse Lamprey an ally of Prentiss.

Before Lamprey opened his mouth to speak Jim knew by the sullen, frightened face that he was no willing one.

"I knew how it would be," Jesse whined. "I told you so all the time. I wish to Heaven I had got out of the country a month ago."

Pete looked at him, no friendliness in the round, rubicund face. "That would have suited everyone, I reckon," he answered. "But you didn't. And here you are, right in the middle of the damndest mess you ever did see."

Jesse shuddered. It might just as well have been he instead of Juan shot down by the soldiers. "I told Russ Mosely I didn't want to come, that I couldn't help him any, even though I am married to that crazy girl."

"She sure got a jim-dandy man," Judson said sourly. "They must be hard up in Ohio for guys who will go through."

"How come those soldiers to be waiting for us at the post office?" Yeager wanted to know. "Someone must have blabbed, that's a cinch. They weren't there sorting the mail." His cold eyes rested on Lamprey.

"Don't look at me that way," Jesse snapped irritably, masking his fear with temper. "I didn't tell 'em. Even if I'd wanted to, I haven't had a chance. I haven't been away from you fellows for a minute."

"What makes you so jumpy, Jess?" Pete asked gently, his hard gaze on the man who had been lying down. "Did I mention you?"

"Cripes' sake!" Lamprey cried. "You can't stick it on me. I didn't want to come. Russ made me."

"That's right. You didn't want to come." The narrowed eyes in the red face mirrored suspicion. "I'm wondering if this is another of Mosely's mistakes. He has been making plenty lately."

"She don't even speak to me. Why would Russ expect to make her dig up the paper on my say-so?"

"That ain't the mistake I'm thinking of, Jess," the fat man said, almost in a murmur.

Lamprey flung a startled look at him. "Don't jump to fool conclusions, Pete, when there's nothing to them. I'm with you till the cows come home. You know that."

"Sure we know that. Don't we, Roan?"

Terror choked up in Lamprey's throat. "Goddlemighty, I wouldn't do that. You know I wouldn't, Roan."

Judson turned his jaundiced eyes on the unhappy man. "Don't try to ring me in for a witness. I dunno what you would or wouldn't do. But somebody spilled the beans. If not you, who?"

Abjectly Jesse spread his hands. "How would I know? Maybe the soldiers just happened to be there." A sob choked in his throat. He was close to a breakdown.

Jim reflected that in this frontier country a man had to be strong to make the grade. A weakling could survive by attending strictly to his own business. But if he aspired to leadership, whether for or against the law, he had to have iron in his blood. That was where Jesse Lamprey had made his error. His vanity had wanted to sun itself, and he had talked big. Like a fool, he had thrust himself into the land-grant feud fight without having the nerve to back his claims. Now he was in deep water and ready to cry for help. Because he had been a sly and slippery customer he might very likely have to pay the price of guilt, though in this case innocent.

It was time to be gone. Jim turned from the window, to see two men coming toward the *jacal* from the direction of the arroyo. They could not miss seeing him. He was trapped. Instantly he made up his mind what to do.

"That you, Jud?" he called out easily, and started walking away at a right angle toward the brush.

"Yep!" The foreman barked a question. "Who is it?"

"Roan," Jim told him. "Be back in a minute."

He did not hurry his pace. From his voice he had kept
all trace of anxiety. But something in his gait betrayed
him. Whoever he was, he could not be Judson. For Roan
had a gangling, jerky walk, different from this light ease.

"Stay where you're at," Prentiss ordered, and moved
swiftly to cut off his escape.

Silcott started to run and stumbled over a bucket in his
path. He went to the ground with a crash. Before he could
rise Prentiss flung himself on top of the interloper. They
threshed over the ground, each trying to get on top. The
second man hurried forward. His revolver barrel crashed
down on Jim's head.

Chapter Twenty-Seven: TORTURE

JIM SILCOTT CAME BACK to a world shot with flashes of
light, out of which voices came to him hazily as from a
great distance.

"He's coming back to the party," somebody said. "He's
a hell-a-miler for punishment. A little crack with the barrel of a gun won't faze him long."

The first visual impression of Silcott was that he was
surrounded by heads detached from bodies. The eyes of
all of them were focused on him, some with malignity,
others with alarm.

A domineering voice rode down another that started to
speak. "He's saved us the trouble of dragging him in here.
Suits me fine. I'll have it out with Mr. Silcott."

Jim's head was clearing. He recognized Russell Mosely.

"Maybe he didn't come alone and the other fellow got
away," Lamprey said timidly. "If so, the soldiers will be
swarming all over us right soon. We'd better light out."

The cold, stony eyes of Mosely rested on Lamprey for a
moment. "You'll stay here." That one curt remark wiped
Jesse from consideration. The Hat T boss gave his atten-

tion to the captured man. "You're going to dance to my music, you interfering fool. Make up your mind to that."

Jim found a handkerchief in his pocket and held it to his bleeding head. "Looks like you're worried considerably, Mosely," he said. "We've got you out in the open at last instead of hiding behind your dummies."

"You'll have plenty worrying to do for yourself without bothering about me," the big cattleman retorted. "I'm going to get those Gandara letters from you. Where are they?"

"Didn't you find them in the post office?" Jim inquired blandly.

"Let me handle this bird," Prentiss said brutally. "When I get through with him he'll talk."

"Presently, Jud, if necessary," his employer answered. "First off, search him. We'll make sure he hasn't them on him."

They stripped Silcott to the skin and examined every inch of his clothes. The foreman went over them himself.

"No letters here," he announced unnecessarily.

"Maybe I ate them," Jim suggested.

"If you did we'll rip you open and get them," Prentiss snarled.

Lamprey was white as a sheet. This was not a business to his liking. Moreover, the fear was in him that his turn would come. He said nothing, but terror showed in his eyes.

"If you're looking for helpful advice, Mosely," Silcott said, "I would advise you and your gang to light out *muy pronto*. The soldiers ought to be here any minute now."

Roan Judson slid a quick look at his boss. That might be the truth, even if the warning came from an enemy.

"Don't try to fool us, Silcott," the Hat T owner snapped. "You came here alone. We're as safe as rabbits in their burrow. But since you have mentioned the sol-

diers you might tell us how they came to be planted in
the post office."

"Oh, I thought that out," Jim answered coolly. "Soon
as I found that vaquero on my trail I decided to give him
something to report to you. So I made the post-office play,
and you swallowed it hook, line, and sinker. Naturally I
figured you would try to get the package back soon as it
was dark."

"You haven't a spy among us?" Mosely asked, his hard
eyes trying to beat down those of the prisoner. "Jess Lamprey, maybe?"

"No." Silcott shook his head. "Don't need one. You're
too obvious, Mosely. Any kid could guess you out."

Anger flamed up in the big stockman. "Maybe you can
guess what I'll do next," he said cruelly.

Jim was putting on the trousers that had been tossed
back to him. He knew he was in a desperate situation, but
no sign of it appeared in his easy manner. He was going
to be tortured, but no matter what they did to him he
must keep his mouth shut. It was not a matter of obstinacy,
but of life or death. For if he told them where the letters
were and Mosely got hold of them his life would be
snuffed out beyond a shadow of doubt. He must bite on
one fact and let no agony deflect him from it: that
Mosely would not kill him until the letters were in his
possession.

"Some things I don't need to guess about," he said
hardily. "For instance, I know that when you get in a
jam, as you are now, you'll slide out if you can and let
some of the boys here pay the price. You've got the government on your neck now, but maybe you'll be slick
enough to fix it so the boys can go to the pen instead of
you."

Pete Yeager laughed mirthlessly. It was quite likely
that what Red Silcott said might turn out to be true

prophecy. The Hat T boss was playing his own hand strictly, and there was no loyalty in him. If it ever paid him to toss overboard his tools he would do it without hesitation. Pete knew that.

"Looks like he knows you, Russ," he jeered.

"He'll know me better before I'm through with him," Mosely answered in cold rage. "And you may too, Pete, if you're not careful."

"Hell, if I was careful I wouldn't be here pulling yore chestnuts outa the hot coals for you," the fat little man flung back at his employer. "And while we're talking turkey I'll mention that I don't scare, Russ."·

"That's too bad, Pete," Silcott cut in. "Because your boss is getting near the end of his crooked mile and he's liable to drag you down with him. I would be scared if I were you."

Jim picked up his shirt to put it on, but Prentiss snatched it from him. "You're not going to need that right away," he sneered, with a savage laugh. "We're gonna have a little fun first, you'n me."

From his waist he unstrapped the heavy leather belt he wore. "Better gag him, boys, so he won't sing too loud," Jud said.

Silcott lashed out at Judson with his right as the man tried to seize him. In the mêlée that followed Yeager met a flying fist that landed on the eye. But the odds were too great. Jim was flung down, gagged, and stretched out face down. The belt hissed through the air, buckle end out, and landed on the bare back of the prisoner. The white flesh winced, but no sound came from the tortured man except his heavy, broken breathing. Each stroke left an angry, bleeding welt. After a time Mosely stopped his foreman.

"If you'd like to give any information about those letters hunch your shoulder," he said.

Silcott made no sign. He was suffering the torments of the damned, but his mind was fixed.

Again the leather thudded down on the crimson, lacerated back. An agony like that of flaming fire poured through Jim. His teeth clamped into the handkerchief that had been thrust into his mouth. He felt that he had been enduring pain for dreadful, endless days.

At last Lamprey cried out a protest. "For God's sake, Russ, that's enough! You'll kill him."

There was a convulsive shudder of Jim's body and then slack limpness. The mercy of unconsciousness had come to him.

Yeager stopped chewing his quid of tobacco. "He's done fainted. No use, boss. You can strip the rest of the flesh off'n his body, but he won't talk. Too game." Sharply he added, "And by God, I say too he's had enough."

A bitter savagery in his face, Mosely looked down at the torn and bleeding flesh crisscrossed by wheals from the belt and ripped by gashes of the buckle.

"I've got a way to make him talk," he said. A devil looked out of his eyes. He had gone too far to retreat now. He was no longer a wise and crafty leader, but a man driven and harried to desperate chances.

Jesse Lamprey rose to his feet, sick and trembling. Under orders from Prentiss he had been clinging to a wrist of Silcott, his gaze averted from the quivering flesh. He noticed that a spurt of blood had stained the back of his hand.

"Oh, God!" he moaned, and leaned his head against the wall to hide his face.

Harshly Mosely gave an order, still frowning down at the prisoner. "Leave him alone. Till I come back. I'll be here—soon as I can."

"Where you going?" Judson asked suspiciously, his jaundiced eyes fastened to the face of his employer.

It was evidence of how far Mosely's star had declined that his men dared challenge him as first Yeager and then Judson had done. He was angrily aware of it and stored his resentment for future expression. Just now he had to tread softly. In good time he would quell rebellion, but not while he was in this jam.

"I'm going to make him tell me where that paper is without laying another hand on him."

"How?" asked Yeager flatly.

"Don't worry about how. I'll do it. After we get the paper, we'll vamoose. There will be big pay in this for you, boys."

"Where will we spend it—in the pen?" Judson asked sourly.

"Keep your shirt on, Roan," the Hat T owner said. "Everything is all right. Come on, Jud. I want to see you."

Mosely strode out of the room, the foreman at his heels.

"So everything is gonna be all right. That's fine." Yeager's face was a picture of sarcastic skepticism.

Jim opened his eyes. Waves of pain and sickness ran over him. His gaze went round the room and he picked up understanding of what had occurred.

The gag had been removed from his mouth. Feebly he asked, still unbroken, "Where's—Mosely gone—to sell you out?"

Yeager slapped a hand on his thigh. "By thunder, Red, you take the cake!" he cried. "Don't you know you'd ought to be yelping for mercy?"

The eyes looking up at the bald-headed man were those of one who had been in hell, but there was no surrender in them.

"Mercy from wolves?" he said scornfully.

"You said it, fellow. That's what we are. A pack of wolves dragging down meat for Russ."

"Probably you'll swing for it—most of you," Silcott

prophesied. "A good riddance of fools. There's not a lick of sense in any of you. Russ sure must laugh his head off when he's alone."

"Keep yore mouth shut, fellow," Judson snapped.

What Silcott said disturbed him. It might be too true. He did not like to listen to the derisive warnings of this indomitable man.

Chapter Twenty-Eight: ANNE RECOGNIZES JIM'S NECKTIE

PRENTISS WALKED WITH MOSELY to the head of the gulch where the Hat T boss had left his horse. On the way his employer outlined what he had in mind. The foreman asked questions until he understood the plot clearly. There were two parts to it, and he was assigned the lead in the more dangerous one. Juan had been wounded and taken to the hospital. Jud was to find out where he had been put and to arrange it so that he would not talk.

"Why shove that off on me?" he grumbled. "I'll get the girl, and you take care of Juan."

"Don't be a fool, Jud," Mosely snapped. "How could you get the girl? Anyway, you won't have any trouble. It's an adobe building—only one floor. You don't have to go inside the hospital at all. There will be a window to the room, won't there? Do your job from there."

"Yeah, and if they catch me before I make my get-away?"

"They can't, if you are smart. All you have to do is fork your saddle and light out."

"Hmp! You make it sound like stealing nickels from a kid. All right. I'll go through, but if there's a slip-up I'll see you're in the mess too."

"There won't be a slip-up. Give the other boys their instructions before you go."

"They're to have him hogtied and gagged before you

get back. That the idea?"

"Yes," Mosely assented. "And all lights out. She isn't to know there is anybody in the house."

"I get it. How long before you are back?"

"If I pull it off I oughtn't to be much over an hour."

" 'If'? What makes you think she'll come?" Jud's ugly face was creased by a thin, unpleasant smile. He liked to hand his boss a mean dig when he felt it safe. "She don't fancy you any better than she does dirt."

Mosely strangled an impulse to knock him down for his impudence. "That will be my job," he answered curtly. "You attend to yours, and see you don't slip up."

He swung to the saddle and rode down the arroyo, flat-backed and strong, a man arrogant and proud, even with the prescience of defeat riding his shoulders. Events had moved too fast for him in the past few days. They had forced his hand, made him come out into the open. Though justice meant nothing to him, he had never told the world so. He had moved always under cover and had concealed his stubborn lawlessness under a smug and smiling mask. Now he had let his anger rule judgment. Bitterly he blamed himself for not having destroyed Silcott long ago. He would have to do it as soon as he got the letters. There could be no safety with the man alive. But in doing so he would put himself in the power of men he no longer trusted. Well, that was a bridge he would have to cross later.

Russell Mosely rode to the Windom house and tied his horse to the hitching-post in front of the sidewalk. The lower part of the house was dark, but there was a light in one of the upstairs bedrooms. He circled the building and came back to the lighted apartment. More than once a shadow was flung on the blind, that of a woman crossing the room. No voices came to him. He thought the chances were that it was the room of Anne Eliot and not that of her host and hostess.

From the walk he picked up a little gravel and flung a small handful against the pane. After a moment somebody came to the window, raised the blind, and softly lifted the window. It was Anne.

"Who is it?" she asked in a low voice.

"Russell Mosely," he answered. "I must speak to you about something that is very important."

Her vast surprise did not express itself in her cool, whiplash voice. "I know of nothing you can have to say to me important enough to need discussion at this time of night, sir," she replied.

"It has to do with your friend Silcott. I fear some bandits have made him prisoner."

The shock of it held her silent for a moment. He pressed his advantage.

"I think I know who they are and where he is. If you will go to the place with me I can perhaps buy his release."

Her thoughts raced. She put into words the conclusion of them.

"You hate him. Why would you buy his freedom?"

"Perhaps to show you that I am not as evil as you think, I might do my enemy a favor just this once," he responded.

She did not believe him. He was trying to trick her somehow, but for what purpose she could not see. The thought of kidnaping occurred to her, and she discarded it at once. Mosely was not fool enough to put himself outside the pale by anything so desperate. It would mean the end of him forever in New Mexico.

"I'll see Lieutenant Windom and ask what he thinks," she said, not knowing that the officer had been called from the house on urgent business.

"No," the Hat T man told her curtly. "That won't do. Windom would take soldiers. The outlaws would kill Silcott and escape while troops were approaching."

She was greatly troubled. It might be true that Jim Silcott had been taken prisoner. If so, of course it had been by Mosely's men. Perhaps he had come to make some kind of bargain with her. To win his case he had to get possession of and destroy the Gandara letters. Maybe he still thought she might have them or at least know where they were. Perhaps he had come here to trade Jim's life for the documents.

"You say he is a prisoner," she called down in a low voice. "How do I know it is true?"

"I didn't say it was true. I said I thought so. Would you recognize the necktie he wore tonight?"

For the moment she was not sure. "I don't know. Why?"

He took something from his pocket, rolled it into a ball, and said, "Catch." Anne looked at the tie he had thrown her and the color ebbed from her face. She had seen it encircling his throat scarcely an hour ago. The pattern was a novel one impossible to mistake.

"Where did you get this?" she asked.

"I picked it up on the street. There were signs of a struggle. I thought I had seen Silcott wearing the tie. The way it is torn makes it look like it had been snatched from his neck."

She tried to crush down the rising panic in her, but she could not keep back the urgent fear in her heart. "Is he dead? Have you killed him?"

He lifted a hand in a gesture of rebuke. "That won't do, Miss Eliot. If I am to help you—if we are to work together, you will have to trust me." He added, in a moment, "I don't think he is dead. If he hadn't been alive they would not have taken him away. But he may be wounded. Perhaps you heard shots some time back."

Anne did not trust him in the least. All this was false as Satan. He knew where Jim Silcott was. The men who had captured him were Hat T men and they had done it

at the orders of Mosely. But she had to go along with him.
She could not leave the man she loved to his fate. Nor
could she appeal to Lieutenant Windom for help. He
would call his soldiers, a sure way to bring disaster to the
prisoner. Swiftly she made up her mind.

"I'll be down in two or three minutes." Her eyes picked
up the horse tied to the post. "Are we going far? Do we
walk or ride?"

"You ride. I'll walk. We won't have time to get another
horse."

She changed swiftly to a rough walking-dress, put out
her lamp, and tiptoed downstairs. Mosely had untied the
horse and was waiting impatiently. He helped her into
the saddle and walked with long strides beside the animal.

"Where are we going?" she asked presently.

"Into the hills. Maybe we're on a wild-goose chase. All I
can say is that I'm playing a hunch as to where the hide-
out of this gang is."

"Why will they give him up to us?"

"For money. Outlaws will do anything for that. I have
five hundred dollars with me. That ought to be enough—
if we are in time."

"In time?" she echoed. "You mean—"

Her words died away. To put so dreadful a thought into
words was to make it more real.

"If I am right, this is a gang of outlaws with whom Silcott used to work. He sold out, or just quit them—I don't
know which. But one was killed by officers and two went
to the penitentiary. They blamed Silcott and have always hated him. Now they mean to get even."

He told his story smoothly, and Anne did not believe a
word of it. But there was no use telling him so. She had to
play along with him until he showed his hand.

They went through quiet, narrow streets to the edge of
town and came to the hill country above the saucer in

which Santa Fé lies. After a time they came to an arroyo, into which Mosely turned. He led the horse along a stiffly rising trail strewn with stones. The gulch widened to a little park. In the moonlight Anne made out a fence and some buildings. As they drew closer she observed that it was a place that must have been long deserted.

Mosely stopped the horse, apparently to rest it after the steep climb.

He began to speak, abruptly, as if what he was saying followed the line of their talk. "But I tell you, Miss Eliot, that Silcott is not only a scoundrel but a fool—and a dangerous fool to follow. He has led you into trouble, so that you have played with fire as a child would. And now—here you are. I warned you, but you would not listen."

Anne looked at him, surprised at this outburst. It did not make sense, unless hatred of Jim Silcott had been simmering in him all the time and had suddenly broken the barriers of reticence.

"Let us not talk of this now," she said. "Let us find and free him. Perhaps then a compromise may be possible, if we first drop this bitterness."

"You take his side and follow him!" he cried. "Whatever that rascal says is right to you."

"I do not follow him," she denied. "I take the side I think just. What else can I do?"

"Black is white when he calls it so. The fellow has cast a spell over you. Do you think I am a fool and do not know you are in love with him?"

He flung the charge at her violently, and she declined to discuss it. "You brought me here to find Jim Silcott. You told me you felt sure you knew where he was. Are you going to take me to him?"

"Not until I have told you that he is responsible for dragging you into this. Nothing you can say will change that."

There would be no profit in a quarrel, Anne reflected. In her mind was only one thought, to save Jim if she could. "I have flung away my life foolishly. That is true. Some day I will talk of that with you, but not now. Help me save Mr. Silcott, and all my life I shall be grateful to you."

"Grateful!" he repeated harshly. "And what will that buy me?"

Mosely caught the horse by the bridle and started to go. To them there came a faint sound of knocking.

"What's that?" Anne cried, tightening the reins.

He kept the horse moving. "Only a New Mexico night woodpecker. This country is full of them." His next words reverted to her suggestion. "Perhaps you are right, Miss Eliot. We may be able to compromise this quarrel. The first thing is to find Silcott."

"Yes," she assented. "Let us do that. It is not too late to arbitrate the feud."

But in the back of Anne's mind there was a feeling of something that had gone wrong, of a warning that she had missed. A thought was knocking at the door for admission, and it was as elusive as a moving figure in a heavy fog. All that had happened in the past few minutes was off key. It did not fit into the picture. She had the queer feeling that it had been some sort of stage rehearsal, but if so she could not see any possible reason for it.

The impression of failure grew on her. It seemed to Anne that they began to wander around in the hills to no purpose. Until they had reached the deserted homestead Mosely had known exactly where he was going. Now he headed first one way and then another, as if his object was to kill time. Yet there was a driving impatience about him, an anxiety to be done with what appeared to be a wild-goose chase. Why had he brought her here? What reason could there be for this ride? As time passed her distress sharpened.

"Afraid I'm lost," he said. "I thought I knew where this outlaw hide-out was. The location was described to me, but I can't find it."

"Please!" Anne implored. "Don't torture me. Take me to him."

He threw out his hand in a gesture of defeat. "I can't. The description was not accurate enough. Maybe I'm all wrong. Maybe he is in town at his hotel. I think we had better go back."

They had come to a knoll from which they looked down upon the lights of the town.

"I can't go back—and leave him to die," Anne cried, a sob in her throat.

"The more I think of it the more I believe we jumped at the wrong conclusion," he said. "That necktie might mean nothing. It may not have been his."

"But it is his. I'm sure of that. If you know where he is take me to him, Mr. Mosely."

Over and over he told her that he did not know, that he had been trying to serve her and had failed. She was not satisfied. A dreadful fear weighted her heart. But there was nothing to do, except take the weary way back to town.

Chapter Twenty-Nine: A BARGAIN

SILCOTT LAY ON AN OLD BLANKET, only vaguely aware of what was going on about him. He was weak and a little delirious. Waves of pain and nausea swept him. He felt like an old, broken man who had lived centuries. Just now he was letting himself float light-headedly in a world inclined to come and go. Later he would have to buck himself up to endure more agony, but he was too weary to think of that at present.

He opened his eyes, to note that Mosely had left. Prentiss was giving directions to the others, after which he too vanished. Jim made out that the others were dissatisfied. There was some grumbling, not unmixed with curses. What the resentment was about he did not know. It did not seem worth while to concentrate his attention on finding out. The lapse of time meant nothing to him, not in a universe so filled with physical misery. So far as he knew he might have lain there one hour or six.

Lamprey brought him water in a tin dipper. He drank it and asked for more, but he did not know that Jesse was trying to convey to him a message of friendliness without putting it into words. His captors showed their restlessness. First one and then another of them went to the door and looked out into the darkness. Sometimes they disappeared for a few minutes, to come back and spit out bitter comment about Mosely and Prentiss. A suspicion was in their minds, though they had no evidence to back it, that they were going to be left as sacrifices to the law.

Roan Judson came in hurriedly, after one of these expeditions into the night, with a warning to the others.

"Some folks are coming up the arroyo. I heard voices."

Swiftly they gagged Silcott, then tied him hand and foot. He was tossed into a corner and the light was put out. Jim roused himself, to consider the meaning of this.

The clip of a horse's hoof on stone came to him. Somebody was approaching the house. A voice lifted, clear and distinct in the silence. Mosely back again. The bound man heard his own name mentioned, coupled with the assertion that he was a scoundrel and a fool. But it was the words which followed that snatched Jim to close attention.

"He has led you into trouble, so that you have played with fire as a child would. And now—here you are."

Then in answer Anne's voice. For an instant he thought this was part of his delirious thoughts. He shook his head to clear it and knew that this was actually her voice. But what was she doing here, in the night, with Russell Mosely?

He could find only one answer for that. She had been brought here by his enemy on account of her knowledge of the Gandara letters. Her friendship for him had brought her trouble, just as Mosely was now reminding her. The sound of the horse moving away reached him. He lifted his bound feet and knocked on the floor. A moment later Yeager's arms went round his legs and held them fast.

It was not until several minutes later that they untied and ungagged Silcott.

Judson upbraided him for trying to make his presence known. "Ain't you got any sense, Red? If anyone finds you here we got to bump you off and light out, haven't we?"

"Yeah, and think of the girl," Yeager told him righteously. "If she had figured you was here we'd have to hold her prisoner till everything was fixed up. You don't want that, do you? But Russ fixed it slick. Told her you was a New Mexico night woodpecker. That's sure a new one on me."

"What did that devil bring her here for?" Jim demanded. "What does he aim to do with her?"

"I wouldn't know about that," Yeager replied casually.

"Are you so low you are going to sit here and let him hurt a woman who has done nobody any harm?"

Yeager had made up his mind on that point, but he did not care to tell Jim so. She had been brought for the specific purpose of making him talk.

"I don't reckon Russ would hurt her—much," Yeager answered, indifference in his voice. "I'd like to borrow the loan of a chew, Roan."

Judson tossed him across a plug of tobacco. "It ain't ladylike to butt in on men's affairs," Roan pronounced oracularly. "Not that I'm sayin' a thing against yore wife, Jess. She's pretty as a new-painted wagon. And I sure don't blame her none for giving you the go-by after the way you treated her. But who ever heard tell of a woman running a newspaper? It's in the Bible how she had ought to stay home and tend to her own business. I reckon it's in the constitution too, come to that."

"Where has Mosely taken her?" Silcott asked, sitting up awkwardly.

Every movement of his body was a torment, but he had forgotten that now. He was in desperate plight, with fever beginning to burn him up and the shadow of death creeping toward him. Yet these considerations he brushed aside. What Mosely had said was true. It was he, Jim Silcott, who had brought her to this. If she had never met him, had not thrown in with him against the Hat T, she would not have been snatched up into this peril. Had Jim been quite himself he might have reasoned that Russ Mosely dared not lift a hand against her. But the fearful punishment he had endured shook his faith in the strength of the traditions of Cattleland. He was seeing things from a distorted angle. Mosely would stop at nothing. He would destroy her, if it was necessary to his plans, just as he was going to rub out Silcott.

Jim tried to rise, some vague idea in his head of going out into the night and trying to find Anne and the man with her. Yeager restrained him.

"Hold yore horses, Red," he said. "No need to push on the reins. The boss ain't a-going to hurt her any till he's had a talk with you first. You show a little sense about those letters and she'll be all right."

"Where is she? Where's he keeping her?"

There was in his eyes the wild, glazed look of high fever.

"Out there." Yeager made a wide gesture which told nothing. "No use you getting all worked up, Red. See how nice Jess is taking it, and she is his wife."

Lamprey's fear broke out in a protest. "I think this whole business is damnable. Has Russ gone crazy? He isn't God Almighty. What right has he to beat the life out of a man and to drag a woman like Anne into his rotten schemes?"

Judson's lip lifted in a sneer. "Tell that to the boss when you see him, Jess. You can bet yore boots he'll thank you nice when you've said yore little piece."

"And what right had he to make me come here, just because I'm Anne's husband and he thought that would give him some excuse to force the letter from her through me?" Lamprey continued, his voice rising almost to a scream. "I'm not one of his hired hands. Why can't he let me alone?"

"Quite an orator, ain't you, Jess?" Yeager said dryly. "When you get back to Blanco—if that's where you are heading for—you had better hire a hall and run for Congress."

"I wish to Heaven I was at Blanco," the harassed man cried.

"Why, I reckon you're not alone in that," the fat, bald man commented. "Red, here, wouldn't mind being there, and by gum! it would suit me all right too. I've been drug in on this business further than I ever aimed to be. I don't like it a lick of the road."

"But you haven't guts enough to stand up for a woman against those wolves Prentiss and Mosely," the prisoner flung at him.

The cold, bleak eyes of Yeager met those of Silcott. "Don't worry about how much sand I've got in my craw, Red. I already told you that the young lady is safe as if she was in a church—providing you crash through with the info Russ wants. It's up to you. You are stubborn as a government mule, but get it into yore thick noodle that soon as you talk she will be returned home right side up with care."

"Where is Mosely? Go get him. I'll talk now."

"He'll be around after a while." A blank film veiled Yeager's expression. "What's yore hurry, Red? You had better wish him a thousand miles away He's bad medicine for you."

Nearly an hour later Mosely arrived.

At once Silcott flung at him the question that filled his mind. "What have you done with Miss Eliot?"

The challenge of this foe whom he had tortured but had not broken stirred the angry hatred in Mosely. He covered it with a manner of insolent scorn.

"Are you interested in Miss Eliot?" he asked.

Jim had gone too far in anguish to bandy repartee with him. "You damned scoundrel, what have you done with her?"

"Keep a civil tongue in your head, you fool. And remember that I'm asking the questions here."

Jim gripped a peg in the wall and pulled himself unsteadily to his feet. His burning eyes met those of the Hat T man unflinchingly.

"If you have done her any harm—" he began wildly, and stopped for want of words adequate to cover his meaning.

"I thought Jess was her husband, not you," Mosely jeered.

"Cut the talk and get down to cases," Yeager snapped. "Red has got information for you now, Russ."

"Then he had better spill it."

"How do I know you will free her if I do?" Silcott demanded.

"I could give you my word," the big cattleman said.

"Not worth a straw. You're a liar, and the truth isn't in you."

Mosely's face went dark with rage. "You want some

more leather poured on you, I see."

"Nothing doing," Yeager cut in sharply. "He's had plenty."

"If he wants to tell where the letter is and you want him to tell, why don't you get together, Russ?" Lamprey asked irritably, his nerve near the breaking-point.

"I'll handle this," the Hat T owner said curtly. His sullen gaze swung back to the prisoner. "Are you ready to talk, fellow, or aren't you?"

"Not till I know Miss Eliot will be taken safely back to the Windoms' house."

"If you won't believe Russ, will you believe me?" Yeager asked

"Are you boss of this outfit spawned in hell?" Silcott said contemptuously.

"I'm enough boss of it to know I won't hide behind any woman's skirt," Yeager retorted. "If it's the last thing I ever do I'll get her back home safe."

Jim's eyes searched the man's face. He was satisfied. Pete was a scoundrel, but he was a hardy one. If he said he would fight for a woman his word could be depended upon. But Yeager's promise did not bind his employer. Silcott pointed a finger at Mosely.

"If that damned villain doesn't stand in your way. That what you mean?"

"I'll go through hell and high water to get her back," Yeager promised. "Russ couldn't keep me from it any more than Jess here. Not if I was alive and could travel."

"Pete Yeager, Galahad," Mosely said, irony in his bitter laugh.

"There's no call to gimme names, Russ," the fat cowpuncher told him evenly. "It goes like I've said."

The chill, hard eyes of Mosely fastened on his victim.

"If you're talking, Silcott, I'll listen," he said.

The two men looked long at each other. Both of them

knew that if the prisoner told where the letters were he was signing his death warrant. Jim stood with one hand against the wall, to steady himself. He was beyond fear now for himself. Nothing but a miracle could save him, and God did not work by miracles in this lawless land. But his strength had been greatly sapped by what he had been through.

"I'll have to write a note to a man telling him to deliver the letters to your messenger," he said.

"To Stratton?" the Hat T boss asked harshly.

"No. The understanding is that this man is to give them only to me. It's a cinch he won't turn them over to you or to one of your crew."

"Maybe I can find a way to handle that. Get this, Silcott. I'm not bound by any agreement if I don't get the letters."

"You can't bully this man into doing anything he doesn't want to do," Jim answered. "He'll go through to a finish."

"I see." Mosely's thin smile had no mirth in it. "You would like to go on this errand yourself. Is that it?"

Silcott went on as if he had not spoken. "He wouldn't give the package to Yeager—nor to Judson. That's sure. He probably would to Lamprey, if I wrote a letter telling him to do so."

Mosely's nervous fingernails drummed on his teeth. Silcott had made a valid point. The question was as to Jesse Lamprey. Could he be trusted? The man was in this affair against his own wishes. He would throw down his employer if he dared. But that was the crux of the whole thing. He did not dare. The fear of vengeance was planted too deep in his weak soul.

"Write the letter," Mosely snapped. "Make it short—and convincing. Say you have need of the package right now, and for him to deliver it to Jess. That will be enough.

No undercover stuff with a double meaning."

From his pockets he produced a pencil and a notebook, which he passed to Jim. "Who is the man?" he demanded.

"The man isn't in this row," Silcott replied. "He doesn't know what is in the package. I handed it to him because I was in a jam and had to get rid of it."

"That's all right. We won't hurt him if he makes us no trouble. Who is he?"

"Homer Caldwell. An old cowboy who has a saddle shop on the plaza."

Russell Mosely dictated the note, but Jim shook his head at the wording. "Better let me do it. I stuck the package in a pair of saddlebags. I'll mention that, so that he will be sure the message is from me."

"He had better be sure," the big cattleman said ominously. "For your sake. And I'll say this, Silcott. If you are pulling any shenanigan on me you'll wish you had never been born before I'm through with you."

Roan Judson was chosen to ride to town with Lamprey. The instructions given him in the presence of Jesse were explicit.

"You'll stay with him until you get close to where you find Caldwell, Roan. Then you'll let him go on alone. If he acts as if he is double-crossing us, pump him full of lead. Stay outside and wait for him." The Hat T boss turned an ice-cold cruel stare on Lamprey. "Don't think you can throw us down and get away with it, fellow. Even if you were to slip away from Roan it wouldn't help you any. Play us false, and you'll be buried inside of twenty-four hours. I'll see to that personally."

"I'm not going to throw down on you, Russ," Lamprey promised. "All I ask is you treat me decent."

"We'll get along fine, then. All right, Roan. Get going."

The two messengers walked out into the night. Jim eased himself gingerly down to the floor again. He had a

reprieve of an hour or perhaps two. It depended on how
long it took them to find Caldwell and get the letter.
After that somebody would take him out to the nearest
gulch and murder him. That would probably be Prentiss.

Chapter Thirty: PESKY TAKES CARE OF UNFINISHED BUSINESS

RUFE JELKS LOOKED AT HIS WATCH for the twelfth time in
half an hour. "Holy cats!" he cried. "What's keeping
Red?"

Pesky Kennedy rolled a cigarette and struck a match on
his thigh. "A girl," he suggested.

His companion brushed this aside impatiently. "He said
ten o'clock, and it's way past that. Twenty to eleven."

"What's eatin' you, fellow?" the squat cowpuncher
drawled. "When a guy is with a lady like Miss Eliot he
don't keep checking up on the minutes."

"I know. But Red is one of these punctual guys. I'm
worried. We had ought to have gone and made sure he
got back safe."

"Yeah! He'd let you do that, wouldn't he? Like he was
a kid who couldn't take care of himself."

Rufe paced the floor. "I wouldn't ride herd on that
son-of-a-gun for a million plunks a year. Right soon he is
gonna have me gray-headed." He added with annoyed energy, "Dad-gum the blamed galoot, I know he's all right.
He'll turn up with that doggoned grin on his face and
want to know what all the shootin' is about. Just the same,
I'm scared. He acts like he didn't know a bunch of Hat T
warriors were rarin' for a chance to pump lead into him."

"They been waiting quite a spell," Kennedy said, hitch-
ing a run-down heel into the rung of a tiptilted chair.
"With darned little results so far. One little pill in his
system, which ain't much in the corporate sagacity of a
gent like Red. I'll string along with the guy. He's sure

reckless, but he was born lucky."

A man walked into the hotel lobby and sauntered up to the desk. "Hear that shootin' awhile ago, Hob?" he asked the clerk.

"Why, yes, I did hear some guns barking," the clerk answered. "Anything special?"

"Some guys tried to rob the post office."

Rufe sat up and took notice. "What guys?" he asked.

The man grinned. "They left in a hurry and didn't have time to give their names. All but one of them. He stayed."

"Rubbed out?" Pesky wanted to know.

"Shot up considerable. It seems there were some soldiers roosting in the post office. Somebody must have spilled the beans, looks like."

"Did you hear who it was got shot?"

"Some Mexican. They took him to the hospital."

Jelks and Kennedy went into a huddle. It might be worth while finding out who the wounded man was. If Mosely had engineered the attempted robbery to get the Gandara letters this must be one of his men. Perhaps he might be induced to talk.

Rufe left instructions with the clerk. "When Mr. Silcott comes in tell him we'll be back right soon. We'll be obliged to you."

They went to the corral where they had left their mounts and saddled, then rode out to the fort.

"I reckon we better snoop around," Pesky suggested. "If we go asking too many questions they are liable to arrest us for investigation."

"That's right. Say, there's someone on the road ahead of us."

He turned out to be a drunken soldier. Apparently he knew nothing of what had occurred at the post office, but he told them how to find their way to the hospital. Their approach to it was from the rear. It seemed a good idea to tie the horses in a thicket of cedars. The hospital lights were perhaps a hundred yards ahead of them.

Kennedy was leading and pulled up abruptly. He had almost run into another horse tethered to a scrub cedar.

"Hello!" he exclaimed.

Rufe took his time before making any comment. He examined the horse, a big, round-bellied roan. His fingers found the brand on the shoulder and traced it.

"Run your hand over this brand, Pesky," he said.

Kennedy did so. The brand was a Hat T.

"Some other gent inspecting the hospital," Rufe said dryly. "I'm wondering why."

"To get a message to the wounded Mex," his companion hazarded.

"Sounds reasonable. We might drift along and take a hand."

They spoke in whispers, for they did not know how near the owner of the roan might be.

The crook-nosed man with rusty hair shook his head. "And maybe lose him in the darkness when he comes back for his horse, Rufe. I've got another notion. I'll take his horse and tie it up back there with ours. Then I'll stick around here till the fellow comes back. If you like, you can go dig up some info at the hospital. But don't stay too long."

"That's not such a bad idea," Jelks agreed. "One of us ought to run into him and maybe find out what he's up to."

"Keep yore eyes skinned and be sure he don't see you first, Rufe," warned Kennedy.

"Same to you, fellow," Jelks retorted. "If there's any fireworks, you set yours off first."

Rufe soft-footed through the darkness toward the rear of the hospital building. He was in a quandary. What he wanted was to find out who the wounded man was, and whether he had made a confession implicating others. But in the past five minutes a more immediate problem had arisen. He had to check up on this Hat T prowler and if possible frustrate whatever his purpose was in coming here. Moreover, he did not want to be caught and detained by any soldiers on guard duty. A hunch was prodding at him that the feud between the big ranch and Red Silcott was moving to a dramatic climax. Perhaps within the next few hours the issue would be decided one way or the other, and he would never forgive himself if he was not in at the finish.

Most of the hospital rooms were dark. It was a long, one-story adobe building and the windows, set deep into the walls, were low enough to give him a view inside. In one room a soldier lay on a bed reading a paper by the light of a coal-oil lamp. He followed the wall to the south end of the house. Peering round the corner, he saw a man on guard duty turn at the end of his beat and presently vanish in front of the hospital. Yet a moment, and Rufe's gaze found something else of interest, the figure of a man crouched close to the wall outside of a room from which a fan-shaped shaft of light spread into the night.

The man beneath the window was big and heavy-set. Jelks could tell that even while his body was huddled low to escape the attention of the sentry. As soon as the soldier had passed out of range the skulker rose cautiously until his eyes were high enough to see into the room. By the light coming out of the window Rufe recognized the ugly, flat-featured face as that of Jud Prentiss. The man was not more than fifteen feet from him.

Somebody inside the room was talking. He had a carrying voice, and the words reached Jelks.

"Better talk, my friend. To rob a post office is a government offense. You'll get off lighter if you tell us who was running this job."

Rufe edged a little closer. He could not make out the murmured answer, but the next remark explained it to him.

"Lying won't buy you a thing," the first speaker said sharply. "You understood English when the doctor asked you about your wound."

There was another low-voiced ripple of Spanish. It had the rising inflection of a question.

Evidently it was the doctor that replied. "I don't know yet. Too soon to say. You ought to get well if there are no complications. Better tell us what you know and get it off your mind."

The wounded man said in English, wearily, "Maybe I talk. I do not know."

What followed occurred so quickly that Jelks had not time to lift a hand to prevent it. The figure of Prentiss straightened. The light caught a long gleam of steel. In the stillness of the night a rifle roared.

Prentiss ducked down and was off, making for the brush with long, reaching strides. So completely was Rufe taken by surprise that the Hat T foreman had gone a dozen yards before Jelks had his gun out. Even then Rufe did not fire. He could hear running feet, excited voices, the stir of men waking to action. It was time to be off, if he did not want to be caught and charged with the crime. Swiftly he followed Prentiss.

The sound of that rifle startled Kennedy as much as it had his companion. That the Hat T spy had got Jelks was his first thought. Nor did the sight of a thick, ungainly figure crashing into the cedar grove change his opinion. He moved forward quickly, with catlike vigilance, .44 in hand.

Prentiss jerked to a halt at the place where he had left his horse. The stabbing eyes of the killer searched the darkness. Had he made a mistake as to the spot where he had tied his mount? With the rumor of the pursuit flowing in on him, fear came to the man. He was in a desperate hurry and had to get into the saddle at once. This was where he had left the animal. He was sure of that. Could it have broken away?

A harsh voice from the edge of the heavy foliage of a stunted cedar answered the unspoken question. "Lookin' for yore horse, Jud?" it asked.

The foreman whirled, shaken by the unexpected challenge.

"Who is it?" he demanded hoarsely.

"Pesky Kennedy. I told you that business between us wasn't finished."

The guns sounded almost at the same instant, but all the breaks were with Kennedy. He was in more shadowed darkness. He had been ready for the explosive moment, and a rifle is no weapon for quick work at close range.

The shock of the bullet swung Prentiss halfway round. He staggered a step or two. His knees weakened, and he plunged to the ground.

Cautiously Kennedy moved toward the still body. He pulled up, to face a running man.

"That you, Rufe?" he snarled.

"Yes. You all right?"

"Yeah—I thought he'd got you."

Jelks stooped over the body. "Dead as a stuck shote. Right spang through the heart, looks like."

"He's had it coming a long time," Kennedy said curtly. Already he was headed for the horses. "Come on, Rufe. We got no time to talk. Hell's gonna break loose when the U. S. Army gets started."

They swung to their saddles and galloped through the brush. Not until they were beyond any danger of pursuit did they slow down. Kennedy spoke first.

"Jud sure didn't live up to his rep tonight," he said. "Had a crack at you an' me both and scored two misses."

"He didn't shoot at me," Jelks corrected. "I doubt if he saw me at all."

Pesky pulled up, to stare at his companion. "Sounded like a rifle to me."

"Yes. He fired at someone in the hospital."

"At who?"

Jelks shook his head. "I don't know. The wounded Mexican was in the room, and two or three other men. They were trying to get him to tell who was back of this post-office holdup." He added slowly, "Jud couldn't of missed at that distance."

"No. But I don't get the idea. What good would it do him to bump off an army officer?"

Reluctantly Rufe put into words the fear in his heart. "Maybe it was Red."

Kennedy frowned at him, his mind puzzled. "What would Red be doing there?"

"Don't you see? He tipped Lieutenant Windom off they might try to hold up the post office. He might have been with the soldiers and then have gone out to the hospital to try to get a confession out of the Mexican. Who else would Jud want to kill?"

"Except the Mexican, if Mosely was afraid he might talk too much."

Jelks let that seep into his thoughts. It brought new hope to him. "That's right. It might have been the wounded man. He was weakening—was about ready to come through. Jud would shoot one of his own gang soon as not to save his own hide."

"The man he shot must of been the Mexican—or Red," Kennedy said.

"Let's get back to the hotel and see if Red has reported." Rufe suggested. "If he hasn't, I'm going to Windom's house."

The hotel clerk told them he had seen nothing of Silcott since they had left. He gave them directions to reach the Gandara house.

Jelks knocked several times on the door of the house built by the old Don. At last a feminine voice answered from a window above.

"Who is there?" it asked.

The young man gave their names. "Friends of Red Silcott—and of Miss Eliot," he added. "We want to talk with Lieutenant Windom."

"My husband isn't here," the woman replied. "He was called out on duty. Is there anything I can do for you?"

"We're worried about Silcott. He didn't come back to the hotel. Did he leave with your husband, ma'am?"

"No. He went before Lieutenant Windom. Some time near ten o'clock, I think."

"Did he say where he was going?"

"No, he didn't—not to me. Back to the hotel, I suppose."

"We're afraid he has been trapped by enemies, Mrs. Windom. Would you mind asking Miss Eliot if he mentioned going any other place? We hate to bother you at this hour, but the fact is we're mighty anxious about him."

"I'll ask her," Henrietta said, and vanished. Within half a minute she was back. "Anne has gone," she called down, plainly very much disturbed.

"Gone where?" Jelks asked.

"I don't know. She is not in her room. Perhaps she went downstairs for something. I'll see."

When Henrietta reappeared she was wearing some kind of dressing-gown. "Anne is not here," she said, her voice cold and hostile. "The only person in town who knows her well enough to take her out is Mr. Silcott. I don't understand it. Anne used to be so careful, so—"

She stopped, unwilling to criticize her friend before

these strangers. Back of her resentment was a sharp anxiety. It was not like Anne to do a thing like this.

"You're quite right, ma'am," Rufe replied quietly.
"Miss Eliot is the finest young lady I know. Something is
going on that I don't like. Some shenanigan. It's one of
Russ Mosely's damned tricks. Begging your pardon, Mrs.
Windom, for my language."

"How could he be responsible? She went into her room
an hour or more ago to retire for the night."

"Maybe she left a note," Kennedy suggested.

Henrietta went into the guest room and lit a lamp.
There was no note, but on the back of a chair hung a torn
necktie that looked familiar. She dropped it to the men
below.

"Isn't that the necktie Mr. Silcott was wearing tonight?
I found it in Anne's room."

The men examined the scarf.

"You're right, Mrs. Windom," Rufe agreed. "It's sure
enough his tie, and it looks like it has been through a
war."

"What was it doing in Anne's room?" her hostess demanded. "How did it get there?"

"All I'm sure of is that he didn't leave it there," his
friend answered staunchly. "Gimme a minute, ma'am,
and lemme try to think this out."

His thoughts raced furiously, trying to work out the
problem. The necktie had been the bait. He guessed that
much. But for what? Mosely was no fool. Plain horse
sense would warn him how disastrous a kidnaping must
be. This was something more subtle than that. Anne had
gone of her own free will. Why? What under heaven could
induce her to leave in the middle of the night with no
word to Mrs. Windom? Only one thing. An urgent fear
for the safety of the man she loved. If she was persuaded
his life was in imminent danger and that she could help

him, she would not hesitate a moment to go.

The necktie was Mosely's proof to Anne that Red Sil-cott was his prisoner. She had been made to believe that by going with him she could save Jim. The Hat T man had been tricking her, of course, but that was beside the point. She had walked into his trap, distrusting him, no doubt, dubious of the outcome, but not daring to miss any chance to help Silcott.

So far Rufe could follow the scheme. It had to be that way. Nothing else would fit the facts. But here his reason-ing bogged down. What did Mosely want with Anne? How could he use her—make her fit into the pattern that cir-cumstances had woven? He had not been moved by any sentimental or passionate urge. The man was too cold-blooded for that. Did he think she had the Gandara letters or at least could tell him where they were? Not unless he was the worst judge of character in the world, and nobody could say that of Russ Mosely. Any lunkhead cowboy would know that Red Silcott was not going to tell Anne anything that would bring her by any chance into the danger zone. He was that kind of guy, a man to ride the river with.

In four curt sentences Jelks laid before the others his analysis of the situation. Henrietta nodded her blond head, blue eyes big with excitement. What he said seemed to her a reasonable explanation, up to a certain point. She put her finger on the difficulty that had stumped Rufe.

"But what does he want with Anne?" she broke out. "He can't be so *crazy* about her as all that. He isn't just a reckless boy in love."

"I don't get it," Jelks admitted. "She fits in somewhere, though. That's a cinch."

Kennedy offered an explanation. "Thought you claimed to know that stiff-necked friend of yores, Rufe," he jeered. "Let's say Mosely has got him. Russ will enjoy that considerable, but far as getting the letters goes—no potatoes. For Red won't talk. He would be a fool to tell where they are, since he will be rubbed out soon as that devil lays his hands on them. So Russ pulls one of his fast, slick ones. His idea is that when Red knows Miss Eliot is his prisoner he will crash through with the info wanted. They will make a bargain. Red will give him the letters and Miss Eliot will be returned here right side up with care."

Again Henrietta's blond head assented vigorously. "You've got it!" she cried. "This man Mosely will get the letters, and then Anne and Mr. Silcott will be turned loose."

Neither of the men contradicted her prediction, though both of them knew it was not going to be that way. Miss Eliot would come back, and Red would never be seen alive again. The only chance of saving him was to find out where the Hat T hole-up was and to get there before the Gandara letters reached Mosely. It would be a race against time, with all the odds against them.

"We'd better get to Homer Caldwell right away," Rufe said to the other man. "Red left the package of letters with him, he said. First off, Mosely will collect them."

"That's right," Kennedy agreed.

They started at once to find him.

Chapter Thirty-One: LAMPREY CHOOSES HIS SIDE

OUTSIDE THE SIDEWINDER SALOON Roan Judson and Jesse Lamprey tied their horses to a hitch-rack.

"I'll do the talking," Roan said bluntly. "You keep yore trap shut."

The bartender filled the order for two whisky straights, and Judson poured his down in one gulp. He could drink any given quantity without any perceptible effect on his yellow, jaundiced face. Before he lifted the refill he dropped a question casually.

"We're looking for a guy named Homer Caldwell. Know where he lives? An old cowboy who runs a saddle shop."

"Sure I know," the bartender answered. "Cross the plaza and go north. Two blocks from the corner of the Governors' Palace. A one-room adobe house all by itself, 'with a picket fence round it. You can't miss the place. I reckon the old boy will be pounding his ear by now, though."

"I reckon he'll have to get up and turn over to us a saddle he's been making for me," Judson replied. "We're hittin' the trail tonight, me an' my friend here."

Lamprey hammered on the door of the cabin until a sleepy voice inside wanted to know who in tarnation was making all that fuss. Jess told him he had a letter for him from Red Silcott.

"All right. All right."

Jesse heard the oldtimer rolling out of bed and waited while a lamp was being lit. He hoped that Roan Judson, standing back of a cottonwood the other side of a ditch, would not grow impatient.

The cold, ruthless words of Russell Mosely came back to him. *If he acts as if he is double-crossing us, pump him full of lead.*

Caldwell had a .45 in his hand when he opened the door a few inches and looked out. "I'll take that letter, young fellow," he said.

Lamprey gave it to him. The door closed. Jess knew the old cowpuncher was reading the letter. Presently the door opened again.

"Come in," Caldwell invited, the piercing eyes in the lean, bony face fixed suspiciously on the messenger. "He says yore name is Lamprey. That right?"

"Yes." Jesse knew the voice in his chalky throat was dry. "You a friend of his?"

Lamprey nodded. "We're neighbors."

"Hmp! He's got neighbors none too friendly. Where was Red when he wrote this?"

"He was talking things over with his lawyer, Stratton. Something came up about the letter, so they decided they wanted to read it again."

"Fine. I'll take it to him." Caldwell reached for his trousers and started to pull them on.

"Red said you were to give the package to me," Jesse protested uneasily. "Didn't he write that in the letter?"

"Maybe he did, but I reckon I'll go along with you. The package ain't here, anyhow. I'll have to go get it." The old cowpuncher dragged on his boots and disposed of the revolver where he could get at it with the least delay. "All set. Let's go."

The two men passed within ten feet of the tree where Roan Judson was concealed. As they did so Lamprey gave information to the Hat T gunman.

"You gimme the letters, Mr. Caldwell," he said. "That's all you have to do. I'll get them to Red. He doesn't want you to come along."

"Oh, I reckon he won't care." The mind of the old man was filled with doubts. He did not like Lamprey's manner, his explanations, or any part of this sudden night call for the package. A child could have seen that the messenger was frightened. Why need he be, if this was on the level? "I was to give this to him personally, so I aim to do it."

"He won't like it. The matter is confidential."

"Hell, if he don't like it he can lump it. No kid like Red can tell me where to get off at. I was roping 'em in the brush country before he was born." Caldwell spoke casually, but his eyes and ears were busy.

They crossed the plaza and the saddler unlocked the

door of his shop.

He lit a lamp, then turned swiftly on the young man, eyes stabbing at him. "Who's the pilgrim with you on this?" he snapped.

"With *me?*" Jesse gasped.

"That's what I said. Think I'm a lunkhead? Think I don't know a guy followed us from my house and is waiting outside? You gave it away when you looked back. Come clean, fellow. What's the game?"

Lamprey was caught. He could not lie out of this. He could not run away from it. The jaws of the trap were closing on him. If he betrayed the Hat T outfit, they would get him for it later. If he let Silcott die, the friends of Red would know he was in the plot. It was characteristic of him that he followed the line of least resistance and yielded to the immediate pressure. No doubt another factor influenced him. He was weak, but not a villain. There was an urgent impulse in him to save Silcott if he could.

His face was ashen, his lips bloodless. "They've got Red up in the hills and are going to kill him," he murmured.

Caldwell asked the most important question first. "Where have they got him?"

"At the old Sandoval Ranch. They wanted these letters. He wouldn't talk and they beat him till he was senseless. Jud Prentiss did it. Orders from Russ Mosely. Then they caught my wife, Anne Eliot—and Red wrote this letter to you. It was Roan Judson followed us. They don't trust me." Lamprey's mouth trembled. "Roan is to kill me if I double-cross them."

Somebody knocked on the store door. Jesse leaned against a counter for support. "He's—there now." The words came from a throat dry as a limekiln.

Homer Caldwell padded to the door, the revolver ready for action.

"Who is there?" he asked, his voice harsh and cold.

"Rufe Jelks and Pesky Kennedy. For God's sake, let us in. The Hat T outfit have got Red."

The oldtimer knew the voice and flung open the door. He wasted no time. "Where are yore horses?" he demanded.

"Outside here," Rufe answered. "Listen, Homer. Russ—"

Caldwell's voice rode down the other. "You listen. They've got Red at the old Sandoval Ranch. Lamprey will take you there. Ride hell-for-leather if you want to find him alive." Abruptly he swung round on the messenger. "Got a gun?"

"No," quavered Lamprey. "They took mine from me."

Caldwell thrust his .45 at him. "Here. Take this—and use it. I'll be with you boys soon as I can slap a saddle on a bronc. But don't wait for me."

"Roan Judson is outside," Jesse reminded him.

There came the clatter of a horse's hoofs.

"No, sir!" the old cowboy cried, his voice slipping to an excited falsetto. "He's lit out for the hide-out. Fork yore mounts, boys."

Already Rufe was running for the street. "Where's yore bronc, Jess? We got to jump."

"In front of the Sidewinder!" Lamprey cried, at his heels.

They rode out of town on the gallop. Roan Judson was not far ahead of them, they knew, driving his horse savagely to make the best possible time to the old Sandoval place.

Chapter Thirty-Two: ANNE INVESTIGATES

RUSSELL MOSELY struck the Cerrillos Road and brought Anne to the lane which led to the old Gandara house.

"Have to leave you here," he said. "You haven't far to go, and nobody will bother you."

She slipped down from the saddle, a slim, tired little figure, and looked up at him pitifully. "If you'll save Jim Silcott from—from his enemies—I'll do anything in the world for you that I can."

Irritably he pushed her insistence from him. "I've told you half a dozen times I don't know where he is. Go home and sleep. He's all right, I expect. Bad pennies always turn up again."

He turned away abruptly and swung to the saddle. Without another word he rode into the darkness.

Anne did not at once go home. She walked down the road to the plaza, crossed it, and moved down the street leading to the Exchange Hotel. Not a soul was stirring in town. The road was deserted, and even the saloon lights seemed to have tempted no customers.

In the hotel lobby one lamp was lit. The night clerk was asleep, his lank body stretched over two chairs. Anne wakened him, to ask if Silcott had returned and gone to his room.

The man came drowsily to life. "No, ma'am, he hasn't showed up since six o'clock," he told her. "His friends were worrying about him considerable. I dunno why."

"What friends?" she asked.

"Those two cowpokes—Jelks and Kennedy." He was wondering what she was doing here. What right had any decent woman, young and good-looking, to be inquiring for a man at this time of night? He could see she did not belong down on the row. His guess was that she was a lady. Etched on her pale face was a desperate anxiety.

"Are they here now?" she inquired.

"No, ma'am. They went out looking for him. Quite a spell since."

"Did they say where they were going to look?"

"No, they didn't, not as far as I heard. There was some trouble at the post office, some fellows trying to rob it. They left right after that. Then they came back and asked was Silcott here yet. When I said he wasn't they beat it again."

"If they come in will you please tell them I want to see them?" Anne said. "I'm staying with the Windoms, at the old Gandara house."

"Yes, ma'am, I sure will."

When Henrietta saw her friend's face she had not the heart to pour out on her all the accumulated reproaches she had been saving. She listened to Anne's story and took her into her arms at once.

"You poor sweet," she comforted. "Maybe it's not as bad as you think."

"Then why did Mr. Mosely drag me over the hills? What did he want with me? I can't make sense of it."

"Mr. Silcott's two friends were here," Henrietta explained. "When they saw the necktie they figured it all out, that this Mosely was using it as a kind of bait to get you to go with him. They thought Red, as they call him, had been captured by the Hat T gang and that Mosely was taking you to him in order to make him talk. But I guess they were wrong, since you did not see Mr. Silcott or any of the enemy gang."

Anne thought swiftly, furiously, trying to fit into a pattern the happenings of the hill trip that had not seemed reasonable to her. Mosely's strange talk at the deserted cabin—her sense of its unreality—the unexpected tapping of the woodpecker and her guide's haste to be off—the apparent lack of purpose in the ride from that time. If she had the key to what it meant! Were Jim's friends right, that she had been taken to break his will and force him to surrender the letters? But he had not seen her any more than she had seen him. No, but he might have been in

the cabin, a prisoner, and heard the talk between her and
Mosely.

"Is there such a bird as a New Mexico night woodpecker?" she asked quickly.

"I don't know. I never heard of it. Why?"

The missing bits of the jig puzzle began to slip into
place. Jim must have done that tapping. He had been trying to let her know he was there. For some reason he
could not call to her. Perhaps he was gagged. She had
been taken to the deserted ranch to let her friend know
she was in the power of Mosely, but of course his enemies
had not let her see him so that she could not later testify
against them. It was one of Russell Mosely's smooth tricks
to make Jim turn over to him the Gandara letters. And
Jim would do it, on condition that they send her home
safe. After that, when they had the letters, his life would
not be worth a Mexican *peso*. There was no time to be
lost. She must get help to him at once.

Anne turned her fear-filled eyes on her hostess. "Where
is Raleigh?" she asked.

"I don't know exactly," Henrietta answered. "There
was some trouble and he was called away. A soldier came
to get him."

As if Anne's question had been his cue, Raleigh Windom walked into the house. "Hello!" he cried, surprised
to see them up. "Why aren't you girls in bed trying to get
some of that beauty sleep?"

"Listen, Raleigh!" his wife cried. "His enemies have
got Jim Silcott. She was up in the hills, with that *awful*
man Mosely. I mean Anne. And Jim's friends were here.
They think so too, on account of the necktie. Do something about it quick."

Windom held up a protesting hand. "Wait a minute,
honey. I don't understand any of this. Let Anne tell it,
please."

Anne told the story briefly, swiftly. Just back from the hospital, Lieutenant Windom told just as compactly the tale of his own past few hours.

"Mosely must have had a busy night," he said. "Jim advised me to guard the post office. With the Colonel's consent I did that. It was attacked. We drove off the out-laws and wounded one. He was taken to the hospital and the wound dressed. While we were trying to get from the man the names of his accomplices he was killed before our eyes, shot by a rifle through the window. The assassin had a horse stationed in the brush about a hundred yards from the hospital. Before he reached his horse he was killed, not by one of our men. Who shot him we don't know, though we heard horses galloping away. The mount of the dead killer carried the Hat T brand."

"One of Mosely's men," Anne said. "Sent to kill the wounded man before he confessed."

"Yes. It must be that way. But who killed the killer? Could it have been Jim Silcott, by any chance? If so, why would he run away afterward?" Windom snapped out another question, which covered the reason for telling his story. "Does any of this tie up with what you've been through, Anne?"

"I don't know!" she cried. "But we can't wait to knot up loose ends, Raleigh—not if we're going to save Jim. I think I can take you to the deserted ranch. Can you get some men to help you at once?"

Windom looked at his watch. "I'll move fast, Anne. You be ready here. I'll pick you up."

"Can I go too, Raleigh?" Henrietta asked. "If Anne is going, it would look better if—"

The young officer cut her off promptly. "You cannot. I'm taking Anne only because we have to use her as a guide." He turned and ran out of the house, calling over his shoulder, "Back soon."

Chapter Thirty-Three: YEAGER GIVES RED A BREAK

PACING THE FLOOR NERVOUSLY, Mosely showed more anxiety than his victim. Waiting was a nerve-racking business. Anything could go wrong so easily. Why had Jud Prentiss not returned? What was holding up the men he had sent with Silcott's note to Caldwell? A man of no loyalty himself, he put little dependence on the faithfulness of his employees. They would betray him if they were hard pressed or if there was enough money in it.

Even if all the breaks were resolved in his favor—the Gandara letters destroyed, Juan rubbed out before he had a chance to talk, Silcott buried in a gulch with a pile of stones over his unmarked grave—even then he would have to work fast and smoothly to dissipate the cloud of suspicion that must hang over him. There was Jesse Lamprey too, a weakling he dared not leave at large as a witness against him, and there was unrest among his own men. Well, he could fix all that up, give him time. First off, he had to meet the immediate difficulties confronting him.

Yeager said sourly, "Looks like this night will last forever."

The fat little man did not like the outlook. This was not his kind of villainy. He was a killer, and on occasion had picked off men from ambush. But that was out-in-the-open stuff. He did not hold with torture, with the cold-blooded murder of a game man trapped and hogtied. Moreover, suspicions kept sifting through his mind. If it came to a showdown, given a chance, Mosely would try to shift the blame of Silcott's death to the shoulders of his subordinates. There would be no sidestepping, Yeager resolved. The sight of Red, sick and physically broken but spirit still undaunted, got through his hide and pricked whatever touch of self-respect he had left. Silcott was doomed. He knew that. Mosely dared not leave him•alive now. But he made up his mind to have no part in the final tragedy. Russ could get Jud or Roan to finish the job for him.

Silcott lay in a corner, his eyes closed. He could hear the watch in his pocket ticking away the seconds of a life that could not have many more minutes to run. It had been a long time since Judson and Lamprey had ridden away with his note to Caldwell. Soon they must be back. Then—

Abruptly Mosely pulled up in his stride, head lifted to catch the faint drum of hoofs. What he heard was the clop-clop of a horse galloping toward them. That would be Prentiss, he guessed, with news of one danger wiped out. His gaze slewed round to Yeager, stopping on the way an instant to pick up Silcott, who had propped himself up on a forearm to listen better.

"Put out that light, Pete," he ordered.

Yeager opened the lantern and blew out the flame.

A rider's boots hit the ground as he dragged his mount to a halt. "Roan Judson," he announced hoarsely.

Mosely threw open the door.

"We gotta get outa here *prontito*," Judson snarled. "Hell's to pay, Silcott's friends have got Lamprey. Jelks and that double-crosser Kennedy. They'll get the whole story from him."

The Hat T boss saw the house of cards he had built falling about his head. "What were you doing?" he de-manded.

"Waiting outside like you told me to do," snapped the cowpuncher. "Was it my fault they walked in right at the wrong time?"

"All right. Saddle the other horses. Let's get going. Be with you in a minute." Mosely wheeled back into the house.

"We got damned little time," Judson called in after him. "They'll be here in three shakes of a cow's tail, likely a whole passel of them."

"Where do we go from here, boss?" Yeager asked.

"We get out, and take Silcott with us if we have time. Gag him, so he can't shout. They may crowd us." The voice of Mosely rasped like a file on iron. "If we have to stand 'em off before we get saddled, settle this bird's hash and come a-running to us."

"Nothing doing," Yeager flung back. "If you want him bumped off do it yoreself."

"You fool, we've got to get rid of him to protect ourselves."

"That's yore lookout. He don't mean a thing to me dead or alive." .

The two men glowered at each other in the darkness. Mosely had no time to subdue rebellion now. He gave way.

"All right, you lunkhead, I'll take care of him myself. Watch him till I get back."

Those in the cabin could hear the sound of his running feet as he followed Judson to the hollow where the horses were picketed.

Yeager laughed hardily, without mirth. "You've got the Czar of the Powder Horn scared stiff, Red," he said. "My guess is he's near the end of his crooked trail."

"Yes," agreed Silcott. "Maybe I won't beat him across the divide long."

"You son-of-a-gun!" The Hat T man could not keep the admiration out of his voice. "Don't anything faze you? He'll get you if it is the last thing he ever does."

"Unless he's too crowded for time," Jim said coolly. "You never can tell."

"By God, I give it to you, fellow." The cold eyes of the fat little man gleamed. "He's fixing to throw me down by putting the blame of this fool business on me. If he can. . . . By jumping Jupiter, I'll give you a break."

He crossed the room, fumbled with his fingers on the floor, and came back to the prisoner. "Here's a friend maybe you can use, Red."

Into Silcott's hand he thrust the revolver that had been taken from him a few hours earlier.

Yeager walked to the door and stood listening, his back to the man he had just armed. The night breeze carried a faint rumor of riders traveling up the gulch.

"Yore friends, I reckon," the outlaw went on coolly. "Well, tell 'em I was in a hurry and for them to make themselves at home."

He vanished from the doorway. Jim heard the sounds of his hasty departure.

Through Silcott's torn and aching body there beat the warm excitement of hope. The miracle had come to pass. He had a chance for his life. With a weapon in his hand he was no longer defenseless. Stiffly he pushed himself to his knees, got a foot on the floor, and raised himself painfully to a standing position. The walls at the corner braced his shoulders. He waited, ready for whatever might come.

In the hollow where the horses were picketed Judson was busy saddling a sorrel when Mosely joined him.

"Better shake a leg," he said. "We ain't got no time to lose."

"You don't know that." The voice of the Hat T boss was harsh and strident, belying the assurance of his words. He knew the margin of safety was close. "Lamprey may stand 'em off. They can't know anything. All he has to do is put up a good bluff."

"Hmp! You know damn well they'll get it all outa him. He hasn't got the guts of a louse."

Mosely slapped a saddle on a chestnut gelding and adjusted it to the blanket underneath. He reached under the belly of the horse for the cinch. Beneath his surface thinking ran the thought that all he had builded was crashing down. His scheming had come to nothing. The man lying in the cabin was the one who had frustrated all his hopes. From the first this reckless fool had bested him. The fellow had had the devil's own luck all the way through. A wild and bitter rage swept through Mosely. His enemies might drag him down, but this one would not live to laugh at him.

A man's feet pounded over the ground toward them. Yeager panted out a warning. "They're coming up the arroyo. Be here in four-five minutes. Maybe less."

Mosely gave orders, slapping out the words curtly. "Saddle your bronc, Pete, and wait here. I've got a job to do. Be back in no time at all. We'll cut across the hills and hit the road for home."

He finished cinching the chestnut, swung to the saddle, and rode to the house. Before he reached it he heard riders.

Someone said, "Spread out, boys. Don't bunch up so close." One of the men rode through the brush toward Mosely, who drew up his horse, wrist resting on the horn of the saddle with revolver ready for action.

The unknown rider jerked to a halt at sight of the Hat T man with an exclamation of alarm. He was in the moonlight, and on his face was stamped the panic that was sweeping him. Mosely knew him now. The man was Jess Lamprey.

"So you threw us down," Mosely said, his voice cold and cruel. "After I warned you."

Lamprey had Caldwell's .45 in his hand, but it never occurred to him to use it. "Don't, Russ, don't!" he cried out. "I'll explain."

The gun of Mosely, held steady in its place above the horn of the saddle, roared an answer. Jess caught at his belly with both hands and leaned forward over the neck of the horse. Slowly he slid to the ground, head first.

Mosely wheeled the chestnut and dashed for the house. He swung from the saddle and strode into the house.

"Where are you, Silcott?" he cried hoarsely, glaring around in the darkness. "No use hiding. You're bucked out and headed for hell."

Jim gave him one chance, though he knew he was a fool for doing it. The man, outlined in the moonlight, filled the doorway, a perfect target for his enemy waiting in the darkness.

"I'm here, Mosely, with a gun in my hand," Jim answered. "If you're wise—"

The Hat T man fired, blindly, in the direction of the voice. Before the echo of the shot had died Silcott flung his answer across the room. Mosely staggered, sent another bullet crashing into the wall, and a third through the roof. For Jim's second message had plowed into his heart. A moment he clung to the doorpost, his fingernails biting into the wood, then plunged forward to the floor.

Jim did not stir. He watched the prone figure, to protect himself against any sudden movement. But the body lay there, slack and still. It would never move again of its own volition.

Outside, a shout lifted.

"Are you all right, Red?"

Silcott recognized the voice of Jelks. "All right," he called, and knew that somebody was dismounting. Leaving the supporting wall, he moved forward to the door. He saw Rufe running forward, a .45 in his hand.

The face of his friend was one wide grin of delight. "Boy—boy, I thought they had got you this time. When I heard those shots inside—" Jelks caught him by the shoulder and started to pound him on the back.

"Don't!" yelled Silcott, and twisted away.

Rufe stared at him, looking into a face grown old and haggard. "What's the matter with you?" he asked. "You haven't been shot?"

"No. Whipped." He added in explanation, "Mosely had Jud Prentiss do it to make me talk."

Jelks ripped out a savage oath.

"Jud won't bother you any more. Pesky took care of that. As for Mosely—"

A man rode out of the brush and joined them. He was Kennedy. "They have done lit out, looks like," he said. "I heard them going lickety split through the brush. One of 'em killed Jess Lamprey."

"That shooting in the cabin, Red?" Jelks said by way of question.

"Pete Yeager gave me back my gun at the last minute," Jim told him wearily. "When Mosely came back to finish me I got him."

Rufe yipped out a yell of joy, and a moment later modified it. "I better make sure he's not playing possum. That fox is full of tricks."

"I think he's dead," Silcott said listlessly. "There's a lantern in there somewhere."

Kennedy found and lit the lantern. He stooped over the body on the floor and examined it.

With an expressionless face he looked up. "Mr. Mosely will never be deader," he said callously.

"He was sure asking for what he got," Rufe said. "This busts up the whole Hat T caboodle. With Jud and Russ both gone their warriors will be hunting cover from Mexico to Montana."

Silcott groped for a wall and slid down. He had fainted again.

"Look out for his back," Rufe said, raising the unconscious head on his arm. "They beat him up to make him talk."

The sight of Silcott's back appalled Jelks. There was no inch of it not discolored with black blood and criss-crossed by wheals and tattered flesh ripped out by the belt buckle.

"We've got to get a doctor for him," he said. "And we'll need a wagon to carry him to town. He can't ride."

Kennedy nodded. "I'll stay with him. You go get the doc and make arrangements for a wagon."

"I hate to leave you. If those birds come back—"

"They won't. The game is up, and they know it. My guess is that Pete and Roan are headed for the Raton Pass right now, or else for the Rio Grande."

Jelks rode fast. At the edge of town he drew off from the road to let half a dozen riders pass. He recognized Anne and called to her. Caldwell was one of the party. So was Lieutenant Windom.

The old Texan flung a question at Rufe. "Make it in time?"

"Yes."

"Then what in 'tarnation are you doing here?"

"There has been a fight. I came for a doctor."

"Is Jim hurt?" Anne asked in a low voice.

Jelks picked his words. "He's bunged up some, but I reckon he'll make the grade." He added, reluctantly, "Two men killed."

"Outlaws?" Windom wanted to know.

"One of them. Red got hold of a gun and fought it out with Mosely. He killed Russ." Rufe turned his eyes away from Anne. "The other was one of our rescue party—Jess Lamprey."

"He was killed?" Caldwell asked.

"By Mosely, as we were closing in on them."

Anne's big eyes stared at Rufe out of a startled face from which all the color had been washed.

Chapter Thirty-Four: A MILLION STARS SHINING ON THEM

JIM DID NOT SEE ANNE while he was in the hospital. He understood the reason why she did not come but sent by Henrietta a little cluster of roses.

"With her love," Mrs. Windom said.

He looked at her skeptically. "Weren't you ever taught to tell the truth?"

Her blue eyes danced. "Well, she meant it if she didn't say it."

Silcott wondered about that. He hoped so. Just now her mind was preoccupied with the memory of the man whose name she had taken. There had been no happiness for her in the marriage. It had been the silly mistake of a girl who had let her judgment be swayed too much by moonlight and romance. But he was dead, and the decent proprieties must be observed. Months must pass before she and Jim could show any interest in each other. Whatever thought and emotions they might have must be hidden in their hearts.

"Has she gone back to Blanco?" he asked.

"Yes," Henrietta replied. "With her husband's body. She and his brother Phil decided to bury him there. Phil is a nice boy."

"Yes. Anything new about the feud?"

"No. I don't think there is one any more. The Gandara letters will decide the case. So everybody says. And nobody wants to push the fight against the settlers now. Rufe says the Hat T hands will drift away and look for other jobs, at least all of them who have been mixed up in any of Mosely's meanness."

"I reckon so. A sister of Mosely lives at Colorado Springs, I believe. She will probably sell out. The Hat T will likely be broken up into smaller ranches."

His guess was a good one. There was quite an influx of new settlers in the Powder Horn. The political group which under the leadership of Russell Mosely dominated the county fell apart and new alignments were made. The most influential leader of the group in control was Silcott. He had been the first to challenge the dictatorship of the Hat T, and almost single-handed, except for the constant help of one young woman, he had broken the stranglehold of Mosely on the district. Since he wanted nothing for himself, his views held more weight with the people. The *Sentinel* supported strongly those standing for the abolition of graft and the return of power to the voters.

During those months, though Anne and Jim were working for the same cause, they saw very little of each other, and then always in the company of others. Sometimes she wondered if his interest in her had flickered out. Men were that way, she reminded herself. They took fancies to new girls until the novelty had worn off.

Meanwhile Anne was busy, as Rufe put it, "collecting brothers." She received proposals without the slightest warning. A good-looking cowboy would drop into the office, hang around for a while, remind her that they had met at a church social, and ask her to share his indigence. This was a man's country, and attractive young women were scarce. Anne had read of a shipload of girls being sent to Seattle in the early days with a view to matrimony, and it had seemed to her amusing. She understood it now. A live marriage broker ought to be able to do a good business in the West. There was a plethora of men eager to take on the duties of husband, but unfortunately for them Anne had decided exactly who she was going to marry—if she ever did.

It was in early Spring that Jim came into the office of the *Sentinel* waving a telegram jubilantly. Anne was busy, her sleeves rolled up to the elbows, for the paper was going to press in a few minutes.

"Message from Stratton just reached me," Silcott told her. "The case has been decided in our favor. You'll have to rip up the front page and get the good news on it."

Anne's eyes lit up. She gave him a firm, inkstained hand to shake. "Congratulations, Mr. Silcott."

"Mr. Silcott?" he queried. "Since when?"

"Since you have become a stranger to me," she said lightly.

"Oh, I don't like that," he protested, flushing. "I've been awfully busy, but I don't want to be a stranger."

Her cheeks took or a color to match his. "Fine. If you aren't a stranger you had better get to work. We have a lot to do and haven't much time. I'll push the blizzard story to an inside page and make a spread of this. Sit down at the desk and write the lead. Follow it up with a history of the whole fight from the beginning. I can give you two columns. Let yourself go. It will be the biggest story we have this year."

Grinning, Jim took off his coat, sat down, and reached for copy paper. His embarrassment had vanished. This was like old times.

"You sound like a hard-boiled editor," he said. "And I can remember when I did the bossing in this office."

They worked until late at night. After the forms were locked up they went together to an all-night Chinese restaurant and ate a delayed meal. Both of them were hungry, and they tucked away ham and eggs, biscuits, apple pie, and coffee.

He walked back with her to her boarding-house in the moonlight, and the comradeship that had been renewed as they worked together gave place to shyness. He had a great deal to say, but it was all dammed up in him. At the gate he found no words but a stiff "Good night."

She echoed the words and turned to go down the path to the house. Her loveliness knocked at his heart. He could not let her go like that.

"Wait!" he cried. "Let's walk up Round Top."

Anne made no answer in words but came back at once to join him. She did not look at him for fear he might see how much she loved him. Together they climbed the hill and looked down on the few late lights of the little town. Until they had reached the summit they had filled with commonplaces silences that threatened to grow too significant. Now again speech failed them. And suddenly the dam broke.

"Do you remember that first night you came here?" he asked.

"Yes," she said, and did not add what was in her mind, that life then had begun for her.

"I fell in love that night, though I did not know it at once," he continued. "I had never been in love before."

"You mean—with me, Jim?" Anne replied, and knew the answer—knew it by the drums of joy beating in her blood.

"Of course. It could not ever have been anybody but you."

"I've felt that so long about you," she murmured.

There were a million stars shining down on them.

"All of them out to celebrate with us," Jim told Anne ten minutes later.